SILVERHORN

Marri Champié

Kasva Press

St. Paul / Alfei Menashe

Kasva Press
Alfei Menashe, Israel
St. Paul, MN

www.kasvapress.com
info@kasvapress.com

Silverhorn

ISBN's:
978-1-948403-06-1 Trade Paperback
978-1-948403-09-2 Ebook

T 10 9 8 7 6 5 4 3 2 1

SILVERHORN

Dedication

For my son, Beau Value, the Golden Boy who filled our younger years with adventures, and who makes my life as a writer possible.

For how could the motion of a shadow in a field
Be a person?
Or the flash of an oriole-wing
Be a smile?
Or the turn of a leaf on a stream
Be a hand?
Or a bright breath of sun
Be lips?

from "Dream"
by Witter Bynner

Wide the water between root and twig
and great the argent magic.
Ancient the circle that tied us to the wild power,
to the primordial blade, to the silver-branched crown.
We forgot the Lia Fáil, forsook the Emerald Land
to worship the glittering mountain
on swift and mythic hooves.
The Wanderers named us Hart of the Wind
— Staghorn —
The Old Ones called us Sithé.
There are none to call us now but root and stone.

Ancient Chant

THE CANYON

The yellowpine bark was rough. Her breath came hard and her heart hammered. Below, Silverhorn Creek rushed over stairs of granite that cupped water into dark pools. Wind in its lofty top swayed the ponderosa's massive trunk against her gloved hand; a finger of air touched her cheek. It smelled of fall.

Any moment, the sun would clear the eastern ridgeline; lines of light fanned the pale sky. Her stomach growled. Across Silverhorn Canyon, the granite staggered into gray distance. She could never climb those crags, even if she found a way to cross the creek in its deeply-carved valley. She never had.

Willa shrugged the sling from her shoulder and sat on a stone above the trail, resting her rifle across her knees. She raised her binoculars and scanned the stone ledges. Nothing moved.

Suddenly, white flashed in a leggy pine. Her heart tripped. It was only a bird — a camp robber. She sighed. She saw nothing. She always saw nothing. Maybe the legend wasn't true. Maybe nothing lived in the Silverhorn Crags. Maybe the Silverhorn Stag was a myth, like gods and alien abductions and politicians who didn't lie.

Willa didn't believe that. She believed with stubborn insistence in the unbelievable. But why? Why should she believe in a legend — a very old legend? She believed it because Sara Blackhawk told her it was true. She believed it because Sara's husband Joseph Yellowgrass, almost a legend himself, had once spoken of the legend of the Silverhorn as if he had witnessed it. She believed it because something inside compelled her to believe it.

Silverhorn Crags was a fortress where people didn't go, because they couldn't. Other than crossing the uncrossable creek, the only way into the high country of the Silverhorn was to go hundreds of miles around through roadless wilderness to the east. No one did that. This made for mystery. People were tantalized by mystery. The Native Americans had legends about the Silverhorn, and Idahoans in New Britton had embellished the stories for a century or more. Occasionally someone came to town and tried to uncover the Silverhorn's secrets. They left eventually, defeated by the impossible granite.

Willa stood up, shouldered the rifle, and looked down. This spring, the snowmelt had been phenomenal — runoff rushed down Silverhorn Canyon twenty feet deep. Chocolate-colored water had climbed the canyon walls until the tops of trees rooted at the normal waterline were submerged. Boulders as big as a pickup truck had moved; the sound of them bouncing in the flood shuddered the canyon. The reservoir that held the water for the ranch stock had ruptured and the lower fields flooded, drowning much of the winter wheat.

Now, though, the water was low even for October. Summer had been hotter than usual, with not a hint of rain since May. For the first time in Willa's life, the headwaters of the Silverhorn held no leftover snowpack even in the highest peaks. Water in the Silverhorn would never be lower unless it stopped altogether. Tomorrow she would hike the west creek-bank, down in the canyon below the trail. Maybe she would find a way across the creek, a ford that had been hidden by the water until now.

Once every year she made the difficult journey up the west bank of the Silverhorn from its confluence with the Middlefork to where the creek fell from sheer granite, a hanging glacial valley cut eons ago. If she found a way to cross the creek below that point, she might be able to find some unseen path that climbed the granite of the east canyon wall.

Willa climbed another mile up the steep path. Maybe she'd get lucky and find one of the big bucks that lived in the canyon. Every couple decades some hunter shot a Silverhorn muley that wandered away from its home territory; the event inevitably reawakened sportsmen's interest in the area. Willa's dad had shot a Silverhorn buck when he was younger, before he lost his leg in Desert Storm. The trophy hung over the fireplace; it was a record for a non-typical buck killed with a bow. The Silverhorn deer were uncommonly large even for high-country mule deer, and had atypical racks with more than the four points of standard large muleys — her biologist friend Regi said they had unusual genetics.

Her stomach growled again. Sunlight lanced through the red leaves of the huckleberry bushes and the yellow aspens; the glare made her eyes water. She turned to go back. Out of the corner of her eye she caught a glimpse of movement: the grey coat of a deer flashed out of the brush and crashed away uphill. It never stopped to turn, so she couldn't tell if it was a buck or a doe. She glanced down. Sunlight reflected off the granite and water. In an elbow of the creek, flood boulders were stacked high. Across them lay the trunk of a fallen tree, uprooted from the far creek-side; the broken end of it almost touched the west bank.

Willa stopped breathing. Something hot shot through her — as if she'd swallowed an ember from a campfire. Slowly she let her eyes roam upward, appraising the sheer rock on the opposite canyon-side. Her eyes stopped at a glowing clump of aspens. Light flashed from something brilliant.

Wet leaves, she thought. The gleam off a forked branch blinded her. When she closed her eyes to cut the glare, a ghost image swam black and green against her eyelids. It looked like a branched crown above two luminous eyes. When she blinked, nothing was there.

Her dad had taught her still-hunting, and she was almost as good as he had been. She stood unmoving for another ten minutes but still saw nothing. When she finally turned down the path, she had to hurry. She didn't want to miss her father's doctor appointment.

Tomorrow, she thought. *Tomorrow I will cross the Silverhorn.*

A strange dread came over her suddenly. She heard a distant cry; it sounded like a cougar. She glanced behind her. The sunlit path was empty. She shivered and began to trot.

Another thought settled on her then: *Tomorrow my life will change.*

Man stands face to face with the irrational.

He feels within him the longing for happiness and for reason.

The absurd is born of the confrontation between human
need and the unreasonable silence of the world.

Albert Camus

At The Café

Sunny the Labrador retriever jumped into the back of the pickup. He'd sleep all the way to town and all the way home, without moving much more than to get up and wag his tail when they came back to the truck.

Willa fastened her seatbelt and started the engine. Her dad sighed and leaned back.

"How was hunting?" he asked.

"Nice. Saw a deer."

"Buck?"

"Don't know. I'll check again tomorrow. I didn't want to be late."

"I appreciate that. What will you do while you wait?"

"I'm meeting Regi at The Café. Then I'll do some grocery shopping."

"I'm sorry to take so much of your day."

"Dad. Don't say that. You know it's no big deal. This is important."

The new prosthetic leg would take time to fit, and extra time for her dad to learn to use it. There also were some recent developments related to Gulf War Syndrome and some innovative treatments Dr.

Lossman planned to try for her dad's lingering fibromyalgia and sleeplessness. The doctor wanted to run a few new tests.

"About last night —"

"Don't worry about it," she answered brusquely.

"I can't help it."

"I know, Dad. It doesn't matter — I really don't mind. But your blood test today is important and you shouldn't have alcohol in your blood."

"I didn't mean what I said."

"I know that," she said, and smiled at him. "I love you."

"I don't deserve it."

"Yes, you do."

"You're good to your old man," he laughed. His face was seamed from squinting into the sun, but his jaw was still strong, and his blue eyes were focused today.

"Well, Captain MacLeod, you're my only guy, so I guess I have to be," she said.

"What about that genius guitarist — Ramon or something?"

"Rincon. His name is Rincon, Dad, like the surf spot in Santa Barbara. Rincon Young. He's just…just another guy. They're all the same except they aren't all good guitarists."

"When's your next gig?" he asked.

He was studying her, and she wondered if she looked odd, or if something was out of place. She touched her spiky white hair self-consciously; it felt normal. It was even paler than her dad's hair, and just as short. Her straight, firm jaw was like his too; she recognized her own reflection when he tipped his head and looked as stubborn as she felt. She was wearing black. She always wore black, so there was nothing unusual there. The moonstone earrings her friend had made for her were longer than her hair. She always wore them — they made her feel as beautiful as they were. The tiny diamond on the side of her nose caught a beam of sunlight. Her dad's attention was distracted by the flare and his eyes finally dropped.

"Friday — at the Mississippi Studio in Portland, and then Saturday at the Showbox in Seattle. Then we'll do some recording here in the ranch studio — some new stuff. The band'll be staying in the bunkhouse until the show at Boise State before Thanksgiving."

"Good money?"

"It'll do. I can afford groceries."

Her dad sighed.

"What?" she asked.

"I wish you would finish college."

"I wish you would quit drinking," she shot back.

He was silent for a few seconds.

"Regi Ann has a good job and a husband," he said finally.

"So?" she said, impatient. "I have a job."

"Singing in a band doesn't last forever."

"I'm a writer, not a singer," she said. "And I don't need a degree or a husband for that."

"You need a man," he said bluntly.

"I have you."

"Young women need more than their dad — their lame, drunk old dad."

"You're my hero."

"Some hero!" he scoffed. "Besides, a vibrant, beautiful woman in the prime of her life needs a man for physical reasons. She needs sexual fulfillment, not a hero. A young woman can't have sex with her dad."

"Why not?" she asked, knowing how he would react.

"Willa Reagan MacLeod, that isn't even funny!" His expression was shocked and angry.

"You think that never happens?"

"Not in a normal world. You shouldn't talk like that, even in jest. If someone heard you say something like that…they don't understand your odd way of thinking. Jeez, you need a mother." He ran his hand over his face.

"Make up your mind — do I need a man, or a mother?"

"You have a sick, sick sense of humor. Where did you get that from?" He met her eyes and she smiled wickedly. "Not from me, you didn't!" he protested.

"Okay, I'm sorry. I didn't mean to shock you. I'll sleep with Rincon if it makes you feel better."

"Shit." He leaned his head back and closed his eyes.

He was silent the rest of the way to town. She helped him get out of the truck, but he refused to lean on her and used his cane to walk into the doctor's office. She kissed him on his cheek; his eyes were still bloodshot from last night.

"After the tests, you need to eat. I'll bring something by, or send it over from The Café."

"Don't worry about it," he said gruffly.

"I won't," she said.

Regi was waiting for her at The Café. She'd already ordered coffee for them both, and was eating a piece of Sara Blackhawk's famous huckleberry pie. Regi's brown hair was pulled into a braid and she was in uniform; the name bar said R. A. Zumwalt, Idaho Department of Fish and Game. Because of her initials, Willa often called her Raz. Willa slid into the booth facing her friend.

"How's your dad?" Regi asked.

"Worried that I need a college degree, like you, and a job and a husband — no, no, no, wait, I take that back — a man to have sex with."

"Your dad said that?"

"Yeah."

"Boy, that must be tough for him to talk about. What did you tell him?"

"That I'd sleep with him."

Regi stared at Willa and put down her fork.

"Don't do that," she said.

"Do what?"

"Say outrageous things to change the focus of a conversation away from something important."

"What's outrageous about a father wanting to have sex with his daughter? Or a daughter wanting to have sex with her father? Don't you think it's normal?"

"Why would I think that?"

"Because — if a man loves his wife, and the daughter is like his wife, wouldn't he feel that way?"

"I wouldn't know. I'm not a man," Regi said curtly, "and I'm not like my mom."

Willa looked at her directly.

"But you married your dad."

"What — ?" Regi sputtered.

"They look exactly alike — right down to the little goatee thingy. They even sound alike."

"They are absolutely not alike," Regi said hotly.

Sara Blackhawk approached their table, set a piece of pie in front of Willa, and slid into the booth next to Regi.

"She's right, you know," Sara said.

"Who is?" Willa and Regi said together.

"You," she turned to look at Regi, "married a man who looks like your father — though his personality is quite passive by comparison. And you," she turned back to Willa, "twist conversations to hide who you really are. And yes, men do have issues with daughters, as daughters do with wanting a father image. Willa's right — it's normal."

"No, it is not," Regi insisted.

Willa met Sara's eyes. Neither woman replied.

Regi sighed. "I could have been friends with Norma Jean Daughtry; she was nice to me, you know. But no — my best friend is a rock singer with very odd ideas who spends her free time chasing a ridiculous legend. I don't suppose you found it yet."

"Tomorrow," Willa said.

"Yeah, yeah. I'll get some more coffee." Regi got up to fetch the pot from the warmer.

Sara was studying Willa.

"Did you find something?" She had raised Willa — when Willa's mother vanished, Sara had moved out to the ranch to help out, and she still came out to the place two days a week. She knew what Willa was thinking, what she didn't say.

Willa lowered her gaze to her hands.

"No. Just a way across the creek."

"I see."

Willa looked up again. "Is it really true, Sara?"

"Is what really true?" Regi asked, coming back with the coffeepot. Sara's black-haired daughter Brooke came right behind her and took the pot when Regi finished pouring.

"Do you need anything else?" Brooke asked.

"Another piece of pie and some sage sausage," Willa answered. "You?"

Regi shook her head.

"And a lunch for my dad at the clinic, please. He likes BLT's and the apple cake."

"I'll have Jesse run it over," Brooke said.

"Is what really true?" Regi repeated.

"The Silverhorn legend. It is a legend," Sara replied carefully. "Many legends are based in fact."

"Baloney. Legends are just superstition," Regi countered.

"I looked up 'Lia Fáil' and 'Sithé'," Willa said. "They're Celtic. Pre-Irish. Why would the Shoshone have Celtic names in their chant?"

"It wasn't their chant. Just because they repeated it doesn't mean it originated with them. It was a chant of the Hart of the Wind."

"What was the heart of the wind?" Regi asked, puzzled.

"They were the Ancient People: a clan sometimes called Sithé, who lived here before the wandering people crossed the land-bridge from Asia."

"Were they mongoloid types, like Native Americans?"

"They were European."

"Whoa, Sara!" Regi looked alarmed. "Don't let your tribal folks hear you say that. It might change some of the rules over grandfather rights. I don't think they would like that very much."

"I tell them all the time. I can't be an anthropologist and tribal archaeologist and not be honest with the facts. There's evidence of genetics that aren't tribe-related in various places among the Pacific archaeological sites. Some appear to be Polynesian, others Micronesian. I don't think we've even found the most ancient human habitation sites. People migrated more during the last Ice Age than most folks today realize — there is evidence of European DNA in Asian groups east of the Gobi. Which way were they going? How did they migrate from that point? Vikings came to the Americas long before it was "discovered" in the 1400s, most likely to hunt and fish. Possibly to conquer or settle. It's very possible that non-Asian, European groups migrated to the Americas during the last Ice Age, or even earlier. It's likely, even — far more likely, to my mind, than that they didn't. After all, they were already intermixing. They were mobile. Why would only one DNA group end up in lower western America, when in Asia there are blended populations, and Vikings are known to have visited eastern America?"

"I suppose the tribal council is one hundred percent behind this theory of yours?" Regi said wryly.

Sara clucked disgustedly. "Very funny. The council isn't focused on prehistoric Ice Age migrations and populations like they are on pre-Columbian history. The fact remains that the last Ice Age made it both possible and necessary for people to move around. They came here from east and west and who knows where else."

"And what does this have to do with the legend?" Willa asked.

"Only that history isn't what we're told it is — by anyone. Various legends suggest that there was a group of white people already living in the Pacific Northwest when the Siberian mongoloid people migrated over the land-bridge. Some of the old pictographs are distinctly Celtic-like," Sara said. "I believe the Silverhorn legend is older than Native American — "

"Baloney," Regi interjected.

" — And probably older than Celtic," Sara continued.

"Really?" Willa asked. 'What's older?"

"Solutrian? Magdalenian?" Sara suggested.

"Nonsense." Regi glowered. "How do you know all this?

"There is evidence that isn't talked about in traditional circles."

"Whatever that means. You just encourage her, Sara."

"Better she should get a man, eh, Regi?"

"Men are good for a few interesting things," Regi said wryly.

"Indeed," Sara agreed.

"Okay, so I'll sleep with Rincon if that'll make you all happy," Willa said acidly.

"Does he make you happy, Willa?" Sara asked.

She laughed. "He's good for a few 'interesting things' — but he would never make me happy, so I don't ask him to."

The bell hanging over the door jingled and three men in camou-flage entered The Café. One had short gray hair; the others were younger. All three looked fit.

"How's the food, ladies?" the taller of the two younger men asked as they passed the table. Static made his long hair stick to his camo cap as he removed it. Willa watched him take in Regi's uniform and then smile at them, almost bashfully.

Willa frowned. She wanted to tell them it was terrible.

"Great," Regi said. "Try the pie. You boys hunting?"

"Yeah." He stopped at the table while his companions found a seat. "My dad and I have two regular-hunt deer tags, and my friend has a late-hunt draw tag for the muzzleloader buck hunt, so we can hunt for a while. We heard there were some big bucks in these mountains."

"Occasionally someone takes a nice buck out of here," she replied. "Nothing all that exceptional."

"What about a place called the Silverhorn? We heard tell there were some record deer in there."

"You can't hunt the Silverhorn," Regi said carefully, glancing at Willa.

"Why not?" His voice was even, friendly.

"The only access is through private land."

"Well, we'll have to get permission then," he said agreeably. He had a nice smile and even teeth.

"No one ever gets permission."

"That doesn't sound friendly."

"It's nothing to do with 'friendly', it's just the way it is. Try the apple pie. The apples come off the trees out back. Pink when they cook."

"Thank you…" he squinted at her name tag, "R. A. Zumwalt. Jake Collins." He offered his hand, which she took. "Nice meeting you ladies. We'll probably see you around."

"I'm sure of that, Mr. Collins," Regi replied.

He glanced at Willa again before turning away.

Regi stood up.

"I have to get back to work." She kissed Willa's cheek. "See you tomorrow?"

"No. I'm busy tomorrow," Willa said.

Regi tapped her cellphone. "Call me, then," she said as she left.

"So," Sara said. "Tell me again why you are hunting the Silverhorn."

"I'm looking for a legend. It's not the same as hunting like those guys are doing," Willa answered, a bit defensively. "I want to know if it's real."

"You can't be so sure you know what a bit of legendary poetry really means," Sara said slowly.

"So you say." Willa recited part of the legend: "'Touch the crown of horns and know the world.'"

"You hunt with a gun what you want with your heart. Looking for a legend is fine — but why do you think you need to kill it?"

"'The blood of the Silverhorn gives life,'" Willa continued.

"The legend doesn't say you have to shoot it to get that life," Sara reminded her, as she had done many times before.

"How else do you get blood from a deer?" Willa argued, as she had done many times before.

"Words have many meanings."

"I'm a songwriter, a poet. You don't have to tell me that."

"Then why do I have to tell you that?"

"I'm going to look, is all."

"So you say." Sara stood up. "I'll be out to the ranch tomorrow."

"I'll be gone."

"I know."

He was a wise man who invented beer.

Plato

WHEN STRANGERS CALL

Her dad was worn out. Jeb, the ranch hand, already had the chores done when they got home, so the ex-Ranger captain cracked open a beer. The new prosthesis had rubbed a raw spot, and he took it off. Willa barbecued steaks, sautéed the last of the garden zucchini, and made a salad. Her dad pushed his steak around on his plate. He knew Willa wouldn't get him another beer, so he clambered tiredly to his one good leg to get it himself.

"Maybe you should get two or three while you're there, so you don't have to get up again," she said peevishly.

"Don't start, Willa. You don't have to be here to watch me destroy my life — I could do it much better alone. Less guilt. Don't you have a man to go find, or a deer to shoot, or something?"

Tears burned her eyes. She dashed them away so he wouldn't see how vulnerable she felt. She was too old to cry.

He opened the beer and subsided into his chair.

"God, Willa. I'm sorry. There's nothing better than having you here. Please. Don't make it so hard." Submissively, he ate his steak.

"You're right," she agreed. She got up and fetched a beer for herself. "I may as well salute the muse. I'm getting nothing done sober, not even setting a good example for you. To whoever it was who first brewed beer." She raised the bottle.

Sunny got up from beside her dad's chair and barked twice. Jeb came in the kitchen door. "There's three hunters here to see you," he said, looking back and forth between them, not sure whom to tell.

"Tell them to go away," she muttered.

"Willa, honey, that isn't polite. Show them to the porch, Jeb. We'll come out in a minute."

"They were at The Café," she said. "They want to hunt the Silverhorn."

"No reason to be rude."

"They can't hunt the Silverhorn."

"I didn't say they could. But we will be polite."

"They won't like it," she frowned.

"They never do," he agreed. "But smile anyway." He took his cane and struggled to his feet.

The three hunters sat on the porch, admiring the sunset. Jeb leaned on the porch rail, his brow pulled into a scowl. The visitors stood up when Willa and her father and Sunny came out. The younger man, Jake Collins, who had stopped at their table at The Café, did a double-take when he saw Willa.

Jake performed the introductions: Jake Collins, his father Ryan Collins, and his friend Brian Nokes, all from Boise. The old man looked formidable; he was probably military. He and his son seemed well-intentioned and honorable. They were intruders, though.

"Ronan MacLeod," her father said, giving them his hand. "This is my daughter, Willa."

Jake stared at her. "Yeah, we met at The Café. Sort of." Sunny wagged his tail when Jake petted his head.

"Can I get you fellas a beer?" Ronan asked.

"Dad," she hissed. Then she remembered what he said and smiled at them.

"That would be nice, thank you," Jake told her dad.

Resignedly, she brought out a six-pack of Alaskan Amber and passed the bottles around.

"I'm sorry if I sounded rude," she said. "We were in the middle of dinner."

"What do you do, Collins?" her dad asked the older man.

"I have a consulting firm. Most of our business is military contracts and a few agency contracts. We have some commercial accounts that aren't real big."

"What do you consult about, if it's any of my business?" he said.

"Equipment, mostly. Experimental stuff that's being tested. Water purification, contaminated soil cleanup, safe minesweeping, power generation and battery systems. More of the same. Interesting work. Saves lives. My son is an engineer, so he does some of the hands-on development. I have the military know-how. It makes for a good team. What with the conflicts in the Middle East and Africa and the disasters in Indonesia, we've been pretty busy."

"This year, the economy has given us a little breathing space on the commercial end," the younger man added. "So we scheduled some time to hunt, do some hiking, fishing, see the country."

"It's good country to see," Ronan MacLeod agreed. "When you've been away from it, like when I was in the Middle East, it's all you think about when you look around at that treeless, waterless wasteland."

"You lose your leg in the war, sir?" Ryan Collins asked.

"Gulf War. Landmine. Rolled our Humvee over."

"I was Air Force, myself," the man said. "Pilot. Retired after 'Nam."

"Army," her dad said. "Ranger."

"You military too, Miss MacLeod?" Brian Nokes asked. He was smallish, with brown eyes and soft features. There was something about him Willa didn't like — beyond the fact that she disliked the three of them on general principle.

"I'm a rock singer," she said, laughing at the absurdity of the idea of her being in the military.

All three of the hunters stared at her.

"For real?" Jake asked. "Anything we've heard of?"

"Blackwater," she said.

"As in 'Night is When the Stars Die'?"

"You've heard it?"

"That's a good song."

"Thank you. I wrote it." She was pleased. Still, she wanted them to leave. She shuffled her feet.

"You play the twelve-string, then?" he asked. "That's you with the Guild in the cover photo."

"Yeah. I'm not much of a musician, really. I write the songs. The band does the magic with them."

"You have one fine lead guitarist," Jake said. "He reminds me of some of the old seventies and eighties guitarists — Beck, or Vaughan."

"Yeah, he's hot," she agreed. "Chloe's the real musician, though. She can play sax, violin, keyboards, piano, flute. She's amazing. I even heard her pick the accordion once."

"I'll have to pay more attention. I used to play guitar — that's why I noticed your guy on lead. Still have my old Stratocaster."

"You any good with it?" she asked.

"Ehh, average. Nothing like your guy."

"You still play?" she asked, interested despite not wanting to be.

"Oh, the guys get together occasionally for barbecues and stuff. I don't have the time, really."

"We're going to be doing some recording here at the ranch in about two weeks," she said slowly. "You should come out and sit in if you're around."

"I'd love to come listen," he said.

"Can you work a sound board?" she asked.

"I can learn," he said.

"I could use you, maybe. Depends on the band." She felt like kicking herself for even asking him.

"We'll be around."

Jeb leaned against the porch post and eyed Brian Nokes, who fidgeted with his beer but didn't drink it. "You a musician too, Nokes?" he asked. "Or a consultant?"

"Neither," Nokes answered, a little too quickly. "Law enforcement."

"Ahhh. No economic downturn for that," Jeb said and spat off the porch.

"Would you like another beer?" Ronan asked as Jake put down his empty bottle.

"No, sir," the elder Collins said. "We won't keep you. Maybe another time. We wanted to ask permission to cross your ranch to access Silverhorn Canyon."

"We don't let anyone hunt here," Willa said.

Ronan nodded his agreement when Collins looked to him for a second opinion.

"We just want access; we won't hunt on your property." His tone chilled noticeably.

"That has never worked out very well for us, Mr. Collins. So we have made it a policy to not give anyone access." Just then, her father reminded her of the picture of him on the mantle: he drew himself up and looked very much the Ranger captain.

The older man tried not to let his disappointment show.

Willa picked up the bottles. "You'll have to excuse us. Dinner is getting cold. Thanks for dropping by."

"Sure. Sure. We'll be going. Tell the missus we're sorry to have kept you from dinner." Collins Senior shook her dad's hand again.

"It's just Willa and me now," Ronan said.

"I see. You sure you won't let us have access to Silverhorn Canyon?" Collins asked.

"Sorry, sir," her dad said. "Ranch policy. Try the Aspen Breaks to the east of New Britton. There're some nice bucks in there."

"We'll do that."

Dinner was cold. She ate hers anyway.

"I didn't know you had a hit," her dad said.

"Yeah. Top ten last week."

"Maybe you don't need a degree. Have I heard it?"

> *"Driving the edge of darkness beneath a lonely sky.*
> *The empty road is narrow and I'm trying not to cry.*
> *Tonight the fallin' stars are blazin' arcs across the sky;*
> *You know I never realized that night is when they die."*

"I don't think I've heard that one."

"I'll give you a copy tomorrow."

He started to get up.

"I'll get it," she told him. She brought two more bottles. She opened his. "I just can't carry you when you fall down."

"That's what Jeb is for."

"You can't keep blaming yourself for whatever happened to her," she said suddenly.

"Your mother was fragile and moody — I knew that."

"It still wasn't your fault. You weren't even here."

"Anyway, she's not the reason I drink. I don't need a reason other than to kill the pain. So ... *are* you sleeping with Ramon?"

"Rincon."

"Well?"

"Do you want me to be or not?"

"I don't know."

"We don't sleep — I never stay that long. He does drugs."

"What kind of drugs?"

"Booze. Pot. Coke. He binges."

"Do you?"

"No. I don't need that. He's a problem for the band."

"Do you love him?"

She laughed. "Not even remotely. As a guitarist, he might be hard to replace."

"Good. A young woman does need a man now and then."

"I'm still looking."

We are princes below the stone.
We are the Hart of the Wind.
We diminished, became few.
We fled for fear the magic would fail.
I am the last Sithé.
I called when the leaves fell.
I watched from the shadows.
I am alone.

CROSSING THE SILVERHORN

Frost settled at dawn. Willa shut off the four-wheeler under the big fir at the trailhead and let her eyes adjust to the sudden darkness. She put the key in her pocket, shouldered her rifle, and started up the trail. Her footfalls made no sound. Silverhorn Creek fell noisily over the rocks, but the trail was silent. Nothing moved. The soundlessness felt like waiting.

An hour later, she stopped above the elbow in the creek. Her breath came hard and white — the air didn't move at all, which kept the cold from digging in. Her fingers and toes were painfully chilled, though. The gray light was just enough now for her to pick her way down the steep slope to the creek.

Silverhorn Creek, named for the tall, shining peak at the canyon's headwaters, was deeper than any of the other creeks that fed the Middlefork. The basement granite of its bed had been cut by eons of glacial ice. Time had only smoothed a little of the sheerness away on the near side of the canyon, where sun and weather had more leverage. The other side — the east bank — was cloaked in shadow.

Willa lost her footing on the crumbled granite and slid partway down the slope on her butt. A bush stopped her, and she stayed a moment to catch her breath before getting back on her feet. Cautiously, she negotiated the last hundred yards down to the bank. So dark and deep was the water, she could see nothing in it other than inkiness. One August she'd tried to swim across one of the creek's deceptively still pools, and hypothermia had set in almost immediately. Regi had been with her that day; if she'd been alone, she would have died in the Silverhorn.

There was enough light to see clearly now. Water swirled darkly around the boulders piled in the elbow. A single stone rested like an island in the black water near the west bank. It was blocky, and larger than a pickup truck. It amazed her that the flood water had moved such a huge thing. She could get to it if she jumped. There was a narrow skirt of filigreed ice around the boulder's edge. If the top was wet, it would be slick. She put the sling over her head so it crossed her chest bandolier-style, the rifle secure against her back. She took a deep breath. Then another. Then another — and jumped. One foot slipped, and her heart tripped, but the other foot landed solidly and she caught her balance by reaching a hand up to a tree fallen against the boulder.

The bottom of the broken end of the fallen snag was chest high; just a few inches of it overhung the rock where she stood. Her legs and arms were trembling. Willa closed her eyes and breathed deeply. A limb-spar stuck out on the right side at about eye height. She tested it; it felt solid. She pulled on it. It held. There was another limb, higher and to the right, just out of reach. She pulled on the points of the snag's broken end. The wood wasn't rotten. She put weight on it. The cracking sound made her heart race faster, but the sharp end held.

With fear leaking saliva into her mouth, she grabbed the limb near her with both hands and pulled herself up, slowly, until her foot found purchase on the end of the snag. She let go with her left hand and took hold of the higher limb. She tested it; it didn't budge. Inch by inch she pulled herself higher onto the snag. She had her right knee on the first limb, her arm around the second limb, and both feet on the end of the snag when something beneath one foot gave way. She grabbed for a third branch on the top of the snag and just dangled there, letting the thunder of her heart subside until she could again hear the roar of the water beneath her, and her arms and legs stopped trembling.

When she could breathe again, she crawled onto the top of the snag, hugged it, and laid her head against it.

What did happen to Mom? she wondered suddenly. Sara said her mother had gotten the phone call from the Army chaplain explaining that Captain Ronan MacLeod was seriously injured and was being airlifted to Germany. Then her mom put on her coat, left Willa with Sara, and said she was going for a walk. She was never found. Sara told the searchers she had looked out the kitchen window and seen her on the trail to the upper meadow, headed in the direction of Silverhorn Canyon.

The creek surged below Willa. Had her mother thrown herself into the deep water? That's what people thought, but they never found her body. People said her mother was strange — that the maternal side of Willa's family was given to odd behavior and periods of madness. Willa's grandmother had a fatal heart attack at thirty-three — she was on Librium most of her life. Her great-grandmother talked to ghosts and ultimately committed suicide. Her great-great-great-grand-mother, whose middle name Willa bore, also committed suicide. Willa admitted of herself that she was driven, intense, and tended to be a little "poetic"; but for the most part she felt like a normal young woman — as normal as one could be, all things considered.

She chuckled. If Regi saw her lying here on this snag, fifteen feet above the rushing water, would she agree that Willa was normal? Maybe she should ask Regi. Carefully she eased her cellphone from its cargo pocket. One bar showed. It was 7:45; Regi would be up and rushing to get ready for work. Willa held down the third speed-dial button. It took a long time to ring.

Regi answered immediately.

"I thought you were hunting," Regi said. It sounded as though she was driving.

"I am," Willa answered.

"You usually turn your phone off."

"Yeah." Willa let the silence hang a moment. "Those guys came out last night."

"The deer hunters from The Café?"

"Yeah. They took it fairly well when Dad said they couldn't hunt here."

"The long-haired guy's sort of a stud," Regi said.

She would think that, Willa thought.

"Do you think my mother killed herself?" Willa asked.

"What — ? Damn it, Willa, why do you do that?"

"Do what?"

"Change the subject. Unsettle me when you talk."

"Shhhhh, don't yell, the deer'll hear you," Willa said. "Do you think she did?"

"No!" Regi shouted — then, more quietly, "I don't think so. I don't know…" She paused. Willa heard the gears shift. "There must be something deep down inside me that really is disturbed."

"Why do you say that?" Willa asked.

"Because I love you. You — of all the people I could be friends with. And you say unsettling things and ask me questions that keep me awake at night. You know Kenne does look like my dad? I never noticed before. I couldn't let him touch me last night. I may never be able to again."

"Oh, yes you will," Willa said wickedly.

"God damn it," Regi said.

"Raz," Willa said, serious now. "Would you say I was normal?" Because Regi was annoyed already, Willa expected her to blurt out an answer immediately — but instead, she gave the question her usual studied regard. Willa heard the creek rushing beneath her while she waited for Regi's verdict.

"What's that I hear?" Regi asked suddenly.

"Silverhorn Creek."

"Where the hell are you?"

"On a snag hanging over the creek."

"You are fucking crazy!" Regi shouted. "You're gonna get killed in that damn creek."

"Am I?"

"Crazy? No. Normal? With your weird white hair that just grows that color, and a diamond in your nose? Hell, no. How did you even get born in this town? Gonna get yourself killed in the Silverhorn? I hope the hell not. I don't want to have to explain it to your dad. I don't want you to be normal, just so you know. Who else would make my life interesting? I'm hanging up now."

The phone went dead.

Willa put the phone away, pushed herself up, and sat on the snag horseback-style. Two branches stuck straight up. She'd have to stand up on the snag to shinny around them. She scooted along astraddle until she reached the first obstacle. She tested the branch. Solid. For a moment she wondered why the tree had even fallen — then she remembered the power of the spring flood. Warily, she stood up and eased around the branch, then crawled on hands and knees to the next one. She tested it — when it broke off, she almost lost her balance. It left a short stub, too long to crawl over and too short to hold on to. She studied the remaining distance — twenty feet, she guessed. She looked down. There was a jumble of boulders below her — the closest ones on the top of the heap were dry.

Willa stood up again. She didn't look down. With her eyes on the east side, she stepped around the broken branch and walked the remaining distance. The snag had no root end; the tree must have broken off upstream and floated down until it caught on the large boulders piled in the curve of the creek. She stepped off the tree and down a cascade of stones to stand on the water-smooth granite of the east bank.

The creek bed was solid stone, cut across by the water so the shore edge was wide and flat. And icy. She walked with care. A little upstream, a tiny trickle of water came down a seam opened in the wall — a cleft wide enough for her to fit in. Her feet slipped a little on gravel and bits of granite, but her hands found purchase in depressions on either side of the slot. It almost seemed that there were steps carved out for her.

Sunlight drifted down the west slope, but she was in shadow as she forced her way up, her legs aching from the climb. What did rock climbers call such a formation — a chute? A chimney? She was sweating despite the cold.

She finally pulled herself onto a ledge and just lay there, breathing hard. She closed her eyes and let the muscles in her arms and legs recover and the sweat stop trickling between her shoulder blades. She drifted into a doze.

When she woke, she sat up and glanced down at the creek, now far below. The thunder of it was a steady rumble in the stone. Willa put her knit hat in a cargo pocket and ran her hands through her short platinum hair to dry the sweat. She could smell the mousse she used to spike it. *That'll scare off the deer*, she thought.

She heard something whisper her name: *Willa*.

It must be the creek chatter, she decided.

On the upstream side, the ledge she was on climbed farther than she could see. Downstream, it disappeared into a brilliant grove of aspen and yellow tamarack trees. She stood up and fitted the rifle sling back onto her shoulder. A little dizzy with the height, she walked into the grove. Above, granite dissolved into boulders and soil, out of which grew hundreds of yellow-clad trees — a cathedral of golden light. Beneath her feet the granite was covered with aspen leaves and golden tamarack needles. Even the air was lambent with golden radiance. She paused, transfixed with the magic of her surroundings. The air moved suddenly, a gust hit her, and she heard what sounded like the ringing of tiny bells. She took out her cellphone and took a picture, and wondered, as always, how to make it take a video.

When she looked at the tiny screen to see if her photo had captured the ethereal quality of the light, there was a figure in the center of the picture. Her head snapped up.

The buck stood about fifty feet away, watching her. He was twice the size of any buck she had ever seen — almost the size of an elk. She let out a breath she hadn't known she was holding. Above the buck's head was a magnificent circle of antlers that gleamed like pure gold in the strange light. Even his eyes reflected gold from the trees.

Willa eased the rifle from her shoulder. The buck gazed at her calmly. She bolted in a cartridge; the sound of the magazine was so loud she expected him to flee. His gaze never left her. She raised the rifle and looked through the scope. It was on ten-power, and the buck's face was all she could see. She looked into eyes the same color as her own — blue as a summer sky.

"Oh my god," she breathed, lowering the rifle. Neither of them moved. Her hands trembled so badly that she put the safety on and slung the rifle back over her shoulder. Leaves swirled around her, and again she heard bells ringing. The stag walked forward until she could almost reach out and touch him; she realized his horns were silver, so polished that they mirrored the golden light. With each step he took, gold leaves swirled into the air like coins. There was no fear in the gaze which never left her face. She wondered if there was fear in hers, or just the wonder she felt throbbing in every beat of her blood.

The stag lowered his head. *He will kill me now,* Willa thought. But it didn't matter. An antler-tip touched her gloved hand. The stag's head rose, and the spreading, heavy antlers faded and began to dissolve as though the molecules that composed them were diffusing into the air. Willa was transfixed, and she blinked to clear her vision, thinking she must be hallucinating. The heart shape of the stag's grey and white face wavered as if it were under rippling water or seen through foggy panes of old glass. The outlines of the stag's huge grey body softened, and the animal stretched and grew taller, fading for a moment to something wraithlike and insubstantial — and then a man, clothed in mist, stood where the stag had been moments before.

Though Willa was tall, he was at least a head taller; she couldn't tell just how much more, because the ghostly shadow of antlers shaped a luminous crown above his brow. He was clad in gray leather with a silver belt. A silver and deer-horn amulet rested on his chest, hanging on a heavy chain. His pewter hair was braided and woven with tiny bells that chimed faintly.

"I could have killed you," she whispered, surprised that her voice still worked.

When he spoke, it was like the aeolian laughter she heard in the forest on dry afternoons — a voice just beyond hearing, words just at the edge of understanding. The words were not English. But she understood.

"I called you," he said. "A long time ago."

She studied his face. The jaw and cheekbones were strong; his high forehead was darkly seamed by sun and weather. His eyes were fanned by laugh lines, but when she looked into them they seemed sad beyond measure. He reached forward then and touched her face, the tips of his fingers brushing her cheek.

When she awoke, she was lying on the ledge at the top of the granite chimney.

She sat up, realizing that she had fallen asleep and must have been dreaming. The rifle lay on the ledge beside her hand. Her head was cold. She looked for her knit cap, and found it in one of her cargo pockets. She stood up, brushed leaves from her vest and hair, and put her cap on — the braided ends on the flaps swung against her face like fingers. She picked up the rifle and checked the magazine. There was a shell in the chamber; she lifted the bolt and ejected it so it wouldn't fire accidentally if she fell.

She walked into the aspen grove.

The sun should have been up in the canyon by now, but the sky had turned grey. Yellow leaves and tamarack needles lined the ledge, but everything was shadowed and dark. She walked to where she had dreamed she saw the deer. There was a cleft in the wall of granite a few feet away — it looked like it might be a cave. Willa eased into the opening.

Space widened around her. She fished in her pockets, found her headlamp, and turned it on. She was in a cave, maybe ten feet wide and thirty feet deep. Willa followed the wall until it turned and disappeared. She fixed the light to her head, worried she would disturb a bear or a large cat — she remembered the cougar scream she'd heard yesterday. Willa touched the rifle for reassurance. Had any human ever set foot in this place before her?

She walked a short way and heard water. Her headlamp glinted off something shiny. She turned so the light defined the space for her. It was another chamber, bigger than the first one; crystals glinted in the walls and ceiling, big ones the size of her forearm. Water dripped into a small pool. Leaves had blown in and piled deeply into one corner;

it looked as though something had bedded there. She explored the chamber as well as her light allowed. She walked over to the pile of leaves. There was no musky smell of coyote or stink of bear.

Above the leaves was a hollow space — a vug — lined with crystals. It had filled up with leaves. She brushed them out, and something small fell onto the leaves below. She picked it up; it was a little carving of a stag, made from a single quartz crystal so clear that it caught the light from her headlamp and scattered rainbowed stars onto the cave walls. She reached into the opening again and pulled out a candle stuck into a blackened metal holder adorned with interlaced leaves and birds. When she reached in a third time, her fingers touched something soft and she pulled it out. It was a rectangular package wrapped in chamois and tied with a leather thong. It looked very old. She reached in one last time and felt around — the last item in the cavity was another chamois-wrapped package, this one tubular.

Willa untied the strings of the last package. Inside a wooden tube was a metal writing instrument with a quill tip, along with a vial with something dark inside that had dried up long ago — some sort of ink. When she laid the chamois flat on the floor to re-roll the items into it, she saw that its smooth inner surface was decorated with pictographs. She retied the strings, careful not to damage the fragile leather.

Next, she unwrapped the other package. Inside the chamois was a small book made of something softer and thicker than paper. She opened it. The first page was highly decorated with scrolling and interlaced symbols. *Almost Celtic looking,* she thought. Carefully, she closed and re-wrapped it.

She held the items with awe and dread. If she took them, would it be stealing — or was the owner centuries dead? How long had it been since anyone was here? There were no other human things in the chamber, and the leaves in the hole had clearly been undisturbed for a long time. But she had dreamed of a man — or something man-like — and these might be things he cared about. She felt around in her leg pockets. In the first one, she carried nothing of value but her hunting license, the four-wheeler key, her cellphone, a government-issue spiral note pad, and a pencil. She had two folding knives and extra ammo in another pocket. She found dried nectarines and a granola bar and her sunglasses in her vest. In the bottom of another small pocket was a totem she'd forgotten she had with her: a cougar carved from turquoise. The Santa Fe carver had told her it was for luck in hunting. It had a tiny stone tied to its back — coral or something red — and black inset eyes. She felt her ears; she had on her usual earrings, made for her by her artist friend in Arizona. They were quarter moons hung with little stars cut from silver and set with small opals, sapphires, and moonstones. She took them off. She untied her pink bandana from her neck, smoothed it open, and centered the cougar totem and the earrings on the cloth. She added the small stainless-steel knife, the nectarines, and the granola bar, and tied the bandana into a small bundle. She had nothing else but the tiny diamond stud in her nose, but that was so small she didn't think it was worth leaving.

She put the chamois-wrapped tube with the pen and vial back into the vug, along with the candle and its holder. Then she placed the bandana-wrapped packet into the opening. She took out her notepad and pencil and printed: "I will return the stag and the book if you ask me to. Willa." She stuck the note under her offering. With great care, Willa wrapped the stag carving in her cap and put it, along with the book, in her largest pocket.

When Willa emerged from the cave, the sun had come out again. Eerie gold lambency suffused the grove, as it had in her dream. She put on her sunglasses. Next to the toe of her boot, a small gleam caught her eye. She picked it up. It was a tiny bell.

Reality is a sliding door.

Ralph Waldo Emerson

The Unexpected Things You Hear

There was a slight breeze, and the frost had burned off the west canyon trail. She was sweating now from her nerve-wracking trip back across the creek on the deadfall tree. Warmth and rising moisture diffused the speckled sunlight cast through the last falling leaves. Willa took off her vest, then pulled her sweatshirt off over her head, tied it around her waist, and zipped the vest back on. Her cellphone said it was 11:40 AM. She was hungry — she wished she had kept the nectarines.

Out of the corner of her eye, she caught movement, and froze; then she heard footfalls. Willa slipped into the shadows under a large fir tree and leaned tightly against its trunk.

Dressed in his camos, Brian Nokes was alone as he eased up the trail. He carried a rifle and a backpack. To all appearances, he looked to be hunting. He passed Willa's position under the tree without seeing her. She could have reached out and touched him.

Something was not right about the man — she sensed a furtiveness in him. She stepped out onto the trail behind him.

"You are trespassing," she said. Her voice came out overly loud in the quiet forest.

His hand went to his hip as he turned; the only thing he carried there was a cellphone. His hand dropped and he shifted his feet for balance.

"This is National Forest," he said evenly.

"*This* is private land. National Forest is across the creek." She kept her voice as low and even as her anger would allow. "If I remember correctly, my father told you very clearly that we do not give anyone access to the canyon." His reflective glasses hid his eyes so she couldn't read his expression. She was glad for her own sunglasses — Nokes would not see how angry she was.

"That seemed pretty arbitrary," he said slowly. "Landowners should give the public access to public land."

"'Arbitrary' doesn't matter. We don't have any obligation to give the public access. This is private land and you are trespassing." She hadn't felt this angry since Rincon came drunk to practice soon after he joined the band. Rincon had not made that mistake again.

"I will escort you off our property," she told him firmly, and stepped aside so Nokes could precede her down the trail. He resisted — it was a palpable thing. Wordless, she waited, a half smile disguising the grit of her teeth. She was taller than he was. She stood very straight on the uphill side of the trail. When he gave in, the set of his shoulders shouted his resentment.

They walked for a mile in complete silence.

She took out her cellphone and sent a text to her dad: "Send Jeb to trailhead to escort trespasser off ASAP." She took a picture of Nokes for good measure.

The rifle over his shoulder was a nice one — a Browning with a fancy wood stock.

"I thought you had a late-hunt muzzleloader tag," Willa said casually.

Nokes didn't answer right away.

"No," he finally replied. "That's Jake's tag."

"Oh," Willa said. "I must have misunderstood. That's good, 'cause you wouldn't want to shoot something illegally, on private land, when the local Fish and Game officer already knows you're in the area." She knew Nokes was lying — he was trying hard to sound casual, but his heart was racing and he was breathing too fast.

"Yeah." He didn't turn around. "You friends with that Fish and Game chick?"

"Umm-humm," Willa said. "Best friends, all my life. That's a nice gun, though," she added. "The Browning semi-auto, right? Pretty big gun for deer. You like it?"

"Yeah, it's the 7-mm mag. I don't know how I like it yet — it's new. Hope I do. It cost a lot."

"Brownings do," Willa said, although privately she was thinking that it was the sort of gun one bought only to impress others. She was not impressed.

They were less than a mile now from the trailhead. She hoped Jeb would be there.

"What do you shoot — for deer, that is?" Nokes asked. Was he trying to be polite now?

"This is an ought-six. Winchester model 70. It was my grandfather's gun. Pre-'64. Nothing fancy. It's all I need."

"You need guns a lot?"

"I don't need a lot of anything."

Somehow, Willa knew Nokes was seething — not just about getting caught, but about her being a woman, and worse, a woman in command of the moment. And also about something else — something that ate at him. She could read his thoughts from the set of his head, the stiffness of his shoulders, his silence. He wanted to hurt her; the thought came through as if he shouted it. She shook her head to dislodge the unpleasant buzzing he caused. The trailhead was just around the next bend. She sighed in relief: her dad and Jeb were sitting in the pickup at the trailhead.

The two men got out when they spotted Willa and Nokes coming down the trail.

"I'll take the rifle, son," Jeb told Nokes, "until we get off the ranch."

Stiffly, Nokes faced Jeb and her dad. He obviously wanted to refuse, but he eased the rifle from his shoulder and handed it over. Jeb unloaded it and placed it in the pickup's front seat.

Her dad put his arm over Willa's shoulder.

"You okay?" he asked quietly.

"Yeah. But this guy's trouble. I think I'll give Regi a buzz," she said under her breath.

She pressed Regi's speed-dial button again.

"Twice in one morning on a hunting day," Regi answered. "This has to be a record."

"It's after twelve," Willa said. "You busy?"

"What's up?"

"Caught Nokes on the trail. Now he says he has a regular deer tag. Maybe you should check him out? Jeb and Dad are driving him off the property."

"I'll see what I can do. How did your little adventure go?"

"I don't know," Willa said.

"What does that mean?"

"I think I saw him."

"Saw who?"

"The Silverhorn Stag."

"What do you mean *think*?"

"I'm not sure it wasn't a dream."

"What? Were you sleeping out there?"

"I don't know. It was weird."

"You smoking that funny stuff your drummer has?"

"Come on Regi — you know me better than that. I'm sending you a photo I took of him with my phone."

"Sounds like a long story that I need to hear in person. I'll talk to Nokes. See you later?"

"I gotta leave tomorrow. Back Monday night."

"Send the photo, I'll look at it. Tuesday, then?"

"Yeah."

Sunny greeted her at the barn when she put the four-wheeler up. When Willa got to the house, Sara had bread rising and something else cooking that made the house smell wonderful. Her helper was cleaning. Sara always brought help with her — sometimes a family member, sometimes an intern she was sponsoring. Sara's laptop was open on the kitchen table and she was staring at it morosely.

"What's cooking?" Willa asked, unloading the rifle before she put it in the corner to take to the gun safe later.

"Dinner. Did you eat?" Sara asked. They both heard Willa's stomach growl. Willa grinned.

"Sit," Sara commanded and set a plate down. What looked like hot quiche and pan-fried potatoes made Willa's stomach growl again. "Fruit or salad?" Sara asked. "There's some melon."

"Oh, melon, please!" Willa said, removing her excess gear before she sat. She took a bite of everything before pausing.

"Ummmmm.... What are you working on?" Willa asked, her mouth full.

"Contract proposal for the coming year. General operating costs. Money for computers for the office and for the museum. The proposals have to be in by November tenth." Sara sounded disgusted.

"Why are *you* doing it?"

"The agency assistant who was working on it got married all of a sudden and moved to Nevada. She didn't finish the job first."

"She probably worried about that a lot before she took off."

Sara gave her a black look and resumed typing. Willa gave her friend a smug little smile and drew the knit cap from her pocket. Without unrolling it, she set it on the table with a little flourish.

Sara stopped typing. "What did you find?"

Sara had always seemed to be able to read Willa's mind. Now, though, Willa found herself tuning in to Sara's thoughts — all her senses were heightened, and she heard the sudden pounding of Sara's heart and felt the tense stillness of her holding her breath. Sara's simmering anticipation was a sensory assault.

"Breathe," Willa told the woman she loved as a mother. Sara's plump, dark face relaxed a little and her amber eyes rose from the cap on the table to Willa's face.

"You're expecting something. What are you waiting for?" Willa asked curiously. Sara's reaction was instant — shock, fear, excitement, wonder.

"You found him," Sara breathed in awe.

"I found something, certainly." Willa unknotted the cap's long braided ties and unfolded its ear flaps, then reverently took out the stag carving and set it on the table. The irregularities in the crystal caught the light and splayed rainbows around the kitchen. The crystal stag was leaping, his legs folded against his body, his head thrown back so his horns connected to his shoulders and formed a whorled pattern. His body was incised with intricate designs that added to the scattering of the light.

Sara turned the stag in her hands. "This is amazing. Where did you find it?"

"In a cave on the Silverhorn's east side."

Sara was probing the carving with some sort of emotional energy that Willa could actually feel; it grated the exposed skin of her arms and face like rough cloth.

"It isn't Native American — well, not tribal, anyway," Sara said.

"No, it looks more Celtic to me."

"Could be modern."

"Not likely, given where I found it."

"Was that all you found?"

"There were a few other things."

"Aaaand...?"

"A tarnished candleholder, with a candle in it — silver maybe. It had animal interlace designs."

"You know what animal interlace is?"

"I studied art, remember?"

"Not for very long," Sara said with a touch of her motherly sarcasm. She hadn't been happy when Willa dropped out of the university.

"Long enough to remember the history part. I've got Janson's

History of Art — I look stuff up all the time. We studied animal interlace."

"Hmph. Was there anything else?"

"A metal quill pen holder and a little jar, probably for ink, rolled up in a wooden tube and wrapped in chamois."

"Did you bring them?"

"No."

"Why?"

"Because I didn't have enough stuff to leave in exchange."

"What did you leave?"

Willa reached for her earlobe.

"My earrings."

"The earrings your friend Kit Carson made? They're your favorites."

"And my small Leatherman knife. A turquoise cougar totem. My lunch."

"Why on earth would you do that? You expecting someone to miss this thing?"

"It seemed fair."

Sara studied Willa's face. She stroked the carving with her thumb, hefted it, and set it back between them on the table. "There's more that you aren't telling me."

Sara was making a visible effort to be calm, but her pulse was thrumming wildly. Willa drew out the chamois-wrapped book and laid it carefully next to the stag.

Sara didn't move. She just looked at it. "What is it?" she asked finally.

"An anthropologist's dream come true."

Sara's eagerness stroked Willa's skin, raising the hair on her arms. Still, Sara didn't move.

"Go ahead," Willa said. "Open it."

With the care of someone practiced in handling venerable and ancient objects, Sara untied the leather laces, and then unfolded the chamois so the book lay in the center of the skin. The bright overhead light made the pictographs painted on the skin appear almost alive: scenes with groups of people and deer painted in browns and black and gray, with a dash of red here and there. "The wrapping is Native American," she commented. "But the book isn't."

"You should take it and have a long look at it while I'm away this weekend."

Sara nodded, eager. She finally touched it. "It's old. Hibernian, perhaps."

The book's heavy bone cover had an enameled medallion in its center, surrounded by a carved design of interlaced thorns or horns and an edge of black metal. Willa touched it, remembering the horns above the stag-man's head.

What do you see? Sara wondered, seeing Willa's gesture. Willa didn't realize Sara hadn't spoken the question aloud.

"I don't know. I had a dream —"

Sara's raw emotion bombarded Willa's senses. She shook her head to clear it. She distinctly heard Sara say, — *he touched her!*

"In the dream. In the dream, he touched me with his antler," Willa responded, confused. "Is that important? . . . Why am I hearing you in my head, Sara?"

You're reading my thoughts because he touched you.

An icy chill shivered between Willa's shoulder blades and down her spine. Her hands went to her mouth as if to keep words from tumbling out on their own. She almost couldn't catch her breath.

Tell me.

When she could breathe again, Willa described everything that had happened from the moment she left the trail on the west side of Silverhorn Canyon. She said the words slowly, not just to inform Sara, but to replay the events in her mind's eye and try to decide if her experience had been real, or just a dream triggered by her nerve-wracking crossing of the Silverhorn.

When she stopped speaking, she placed the tiny silver bell on the table. It glimmered there like a drop of pure light. Her hands trembled.

Sunny went to the door of the mud room and wagged his tail slowly. A vehicle door slammed and the sound of Willa's dad on the porch broke the reverie. Carefully but quickly, Sara re-wrapped the book and placed it in her bag. When Ronan came into the kitchen, Willa had the carved stag in her hand.

"Well. I think we set that Nokes fellow straight. Regi came around while we were dropping him at his rig. She gave him the third degree. I doubt he'll try that again." Her dad was pleased with himself. "He doesn't much like you, though, sweetheart."

"I don't care," Willa said. "He doesn't have to. He just has to leave me alone. I don't like him much either."

"Now honey, you're pretty hard on folks sometimes." She sensed the pride he took in his assessment of her.

"There's something not right about that guy," she said. She moved her hand. The quartz stag flashed.

"What's that?" he asked, curious.

"Something I found." She showed it to him.

"Where'd you find something that pretty?"

"In Silverhorn Canyon."

"Really?" he asked. Willa sensed fear stirring in him. Then he saw the tiny bell still lying on the table. He touched it with his finger — and his sudden anguish hit her so hard she gasped. She covered the bell with her hand.

"What's wrong, Dad?" she asked. She hadn't seen that naked helplessness in his eyes since he told her about coming home from the hospital without a leg, unable to go and search for his missing wife.

He shook his head, unable to speak around the fear rushing through him. *Don't leave me, Willa,* he pleaded. But his mouth didn't move.

As Wanderers, we crossed the ocean on ice and dry land.
It was a time of glaciers and we followed the herds.
We were starving, we were frozen.
The Old Ones welcomed us, took us in,
fed us, protected us, told us stories of the Hart of the Wind.
We remembered their stories.
We kept the stories in our hearts, and protected the Sithé until
they passed from the land.
We still keep the watch.

THE STORY
KEEPER

His brown, steady fingers fed the tiny fire just enough dry fuel that it wouldn't smoke. Light from the flame reflected in his hazel eyes, and glinted from a place inside him so ancient he seemed to peer inward into dreams instead of outward from memory. Often, for Joseph Yellowgrass, memory became dream and dream became memory, inseparable, impossible to distinguish one from the other anymore.

Do dreams glimpse into the past and peek into the future at the same time? he wondered.

Could his vision span across the wheel of time to reveal whether his dedication to the watch was futile? Or was his diligence still vital to the thread of a story that had almost vanished from time's weave? When he tried to see into that distance in waking time, all he did was remember the past. And the past was infinitely sad.

In the forgotten Bitterroot tongue his name had been Young Mountain Lion Who Walks The Tall Winter Grass. His family and friends called him Yellowgrass; and now he barely remembered how his name looked and sounded in the ancient language. He had watched many of the Old Ones leave the sanctuary mountain, entire family lines plucked from the weave, some to the finality of death, some to vanish forever, and one family to guard the access to the Silverhorn. He was there for the death of his friend Æeod Mac Vin from a Clan arrow — holding him in his arms as his friend bled out — and had leaned close to hear Æeod's final whisper: "Keep the watch, my friend. Watch over my sons."

Time passed, and Yellowgrass watched helplessly as Æeod's eldest son, Kellwyc, was felled by a trapper's bullet. By then, as far as Yellowgrass knew, he was the last Story Keeper.

Joseph Yellowgrass hunted the high, inaccessible meadows and mountains of the Silverhorn Crags alone for a long, long time, and he watched the Silverhorn until almost everything he had known was lost. Those were the decades upon decades of anguish, when he searched his soul for a reason to keep anything — the stories, his promise to Æeod, the fruitless watch over the mountain.

Then he met a young Clanswoman with strange, beautiful eyes so deep that looking into them was like staring into his own soul, whose hair fell through his hands like cold, black dreams. She too was groping blindly for answers that were unfamiliar to her because her blood — unlike his, which had been crossed with the

Old Ones — was pure Clan. Her name was Sara Blackhawk. She became his soulmate, his anchor in this swiftly changing world, and the strength he needed to keep the faith. She, too, became a Story Keeper, even though it wasn't in her blood. Of all the things that surprised him, she was the most unexpected. She gave him a reason to live, and a new voice of hope when all his hope seemed lost. She was the one thing he would never be able to cleave from his spirit. He might have forgotten the name he was born to, but Sara Blackhawk gave meaning to his new one.

Joseph put more small pieces of wood on the fire. It didn't smoke, but threw off simmering warmth that kept his hands from freezing. He was careful and concealed. In all the years he'd watched, no one had never seen him, or stumbled across his campfire on a dark night, or come face to face with Yellowgrass unexpectedly on one of the thin, high trails of the Silverhorn Crags. There were many ghosts who haunted the mountain — Yellowgrass was just another shadow that vanished into the rocks or faded into the trees.

Joseph Yellowgrass favored this high overlook in the crags when the need to be especially vigilant compelled him to spend more time at his watch. The ledge was almost inaccessible to anyone who walked on two legs, and Yellowgrass used a hidden path up to the sheltered niche of granite. From its vantage, he could gaze down the entire length of Silverhorn Creek and out across the pastures of the MacLeod Ranch.

A playful dervish of air caught at his fire and swirled tiny embers above his head.

He'd climbed to his watch every day since Sara told him that Willa MacLeod had found a way to cross the creek. He'd watched her cross the water, and in that moment he felt time shift and move strangely. He knew that his life had changed — that all of their lives were forever changed. And he felt a shadow of darkness slip into the canyon that day.

He pulled the cape of mountain lion skins around his shoulders to keep the wind from chilling his back. He was an old man. He'd almost given up on dreams. If not for Sara, he might have — but how does a Story Keeper stop being a keeper of the stories? Could he just go down the mountain and fade into the new world, as if the Hawk Clan had never existed? When he mused on that idea, he knew that leaving his watch — or leaving the world by choice — were not options for him.

Joseph Yellowgrass raised his wise, age-seamed face to the wide sky. Tiny flecks of snow touched the hard, high planes of his cheekbones. He was handsome still, and his skin, while weathered, was supple — nothing like the brittle, dry parchment he had touched on the faces of generation after generation of tribesmen before they faded and let themselves die. He began a song.

Wide the water between root and twig
And great the argent magic...

The slow, mournful chant drifted down the Silverhorn as nothing more audible than the errant voice of wind in the rocks.

He spends his nights with the fans,
He uses away the days;
He doesn't hear the sands
Slippin,' slippin,' slippin' away
'Cause he's killin' time, killin' time
Thought he had the time
To keep killin' time.

WM

WAITIN'

The driver dropped Willa's bags at the Airport Sheraton before taking her to Mississippi Studios. The studio had offered Blackwater the theater for a morning practice session; it had been two weeks since the band had been together and she wanted to get everyone warmed up and in sync.

Sticks, Neil, and Chloe were already there. Willa paused in the shadow of the theater door and watched them for a few minutes. Chloe was a gift, and earned her keep many times over — Willa appreciated her all over again as she watched the three of them set up and tune up their instruments. Chloe played keyboards, piano, electric hip-harp, and alto sax, and was positively heart-twisting on the violin on a couple of numbers. On occasion, she also managed a great imitation of the old 1970s Taj Mahal Band's stork-legged flute player to bring the house down with the older crowds. She was tiny, her skin the color of rich, dark mahogany, her eyes brilliant green, and her wildly kinky hair the tan of soft-cured deerskin.

Neil, the bass player, was proficient enough on keyboard or piano to fill in when Chloe was busy on another instrument. Willa had once heard him play a steel guitar achingly enough to rip the soul right out of someone's heart.

Yeah, mine, Willa thought with a chuckle.

Neil had a nice singing voice and kept the band organized — he doubled as their agent, arranged all their appearances, and handled the finances. He was dashingly dangerous-looking with the *café au lait* skin of his mixed Louisiana heritage, his glittering black eyes, and long straight black hair tied at the nape of his neck.

He actually looks like an old-timey card shark, Willa laughed to herself.

Sticks had been with her the longest. His singing was off-key half the time, but as a drummer he was an animal — and he could belt out the hard, loud pieces in his raspy voice and somehow sound sexy. He could lock with Neil something ridiculous. He was Willa's height, with smoldering, dark eyes that turned down at the outside corners, and he seemed to set women on fire — which Willa found curious and amusing, since Sticks had a thing for her even if he didn't let stand in the way of flirting with all the groupies. For all that he might seem like a typical wasted rock drummer, in the end, Sticks was both her staunchest defender and her conscience when it came to Rincon.

Doug Jones — Jonesy — who played rhythm guitar and sang back-ups and harmonies arrived with his guitars, and Willa went on in with him to the theater. Jonesy was the normal guy: short brown hair, hazel eyes, no drama, happy all the time, from a musical family in California.

Willa herself played the acoustic-electric six- or twelve-string guitar, some piano, and harmonica. Mostly she sang lead. She wrote all the songs, sometimes with help from Chloe and Jonesy. It was her band, and she called the shots. She set her two guitars down and opened the first case.

"Hey, Willa, let me do that," Chloe said, taking the big 12-string from Willa's hand. Chloe could tune it when no one else could.

"Where's Rincon?" Willa asked.

"Not here yet," Neil growled.

Of course he was late. Rincon's crying electric guitar was off the hook, in a mournful, unforgettable way that reminded Willa of Eric Clapton. Someone with his kind of talent was bound to come with drawbacks, and Rincon was definitely trouble for Blackwater; but he was a melodic monster. He had a voice when he wanted to use it, but he didn't sing much — unless Willa wrote a song just for him, like "Waitin'". His falsetto worked perfectly on that one. And he was a pretty boy, something Willa had always had a weakness for.

They got set up and warmed up, hoping Rincon wouldn't be too late to practice. The people cleaning the place stopped to listen when Willa sang the band's new song that was currently climbing the charts — "Night is When the Stars Die". She played the twelve-string on this one and Chloe worked out on the woeful sax, with Neil handling keyboards. Audiences always loved a slow, sad ballad.

Willa liked the feel of their music today. The energy from everyone was positive, and she sensed that the band members still liked playing "Night is When the Stars Die" best of all their songs. She was pleased about that, since "Night" was her own favorite and featured her deep, bluesy voice.

They practiced a whole set without Rincon, with Chloe filling in for his guitar solos on violin and sax. Willa decided that they didn't sound too bad, even without their hot lead guitarist — Chloe was confident and clever at improvising.

Sticks had been smoking pot — he smelled of it. It took the edge off his hyper personality, and he was dependable, stoned or otherwise. His rhythm was sharp and unfaltering; Willa liked how crisp he sounded today.

Neil was running extra rhythms on the bass that sounded decent, but she knew by his frown what he was thinking: He was concerned that Rincon's tardiness was just another symptom of the lead guitarist's unreliability and disrespect for the band. Willa could tell that his anger at Rincon stemmed from worry for the band's reputation.

Jonesy, as easy to get along with as ever, simply enjoyed the music, and gave off no sense of anything other than contentment over how good they sounded.

They were in the middle of a song when Rincon finally strolled in. It didn't take any special intuition to know that he was high on something: his beautiful green eyes were bloodshot, his words were slurred, and his insolence annoyed everyone and raised Willa's hackles. In the past, Willa had quietly put up with Rincon's crap. Artists were notoriously sensitive, sometimes off-putting, sometimes even crazy; when they came in a pretty package they often got away with some pretty awful behavior. She was done with that.

Willa heard his thought: *Do these dumb fucks think they can do this without me?*

She stopped the song. "We can do this without you," she told him, "but it sounds pretty good when you join us."

She'd startled him. *Better keep the boss happy*, he thought, loud and clear.

After practice, while the band stowed their equipment, she took him aside.

"No booze, no drugs. Not today, and not tomorrow in Emerald City. Understand? What you do in your free time, I don't care."

Rincon instantly dropped the smug, willful attitude, and replaced the infuriating look of defiance on his face with an equally infuriating sultry smile.

"Anything the lady wants, the lady gets," he said, slipping his arm around her waist. He smelled of cedar — soap or something. His animal magnetism made her suck in her breath sharply; she grew uncomfortably warm. She didn't like what his body language and his arrogant thoughts were saying. She slid out of his embrace.

"No booze. No drugs. No Willa," she told him, trying not to sound breathless.

He read her don't-mess-with-me expression and countered it with a soft laugh that made her knees go a little weak. His teeth were white and even in his perfect face, and his green eyes said he knew she was wearing no underwear beneath her jeans. He licked his lips.

"Okay, little lady — whatever the boss wants."

He let the rest of the band do all the grunt work, though — everything except for putting his own guitar in its case.

That night, Blackwater followed the warm-up band; it was a nice change from the days when *they* were the warm-up band. They rolled through a long set of their hard rock songs, broke it up with a group of softer, slower songs to give themselves a breather, and then got the adrenaline flowing again with three of their earlier hits. For the show's finale, they segued into the slow intro to Rincon's solo song "Waitin'". He was hot, and brought the audience to its feet with his guitar solo locked with Chloe on the flute. Willa saved "Night is When the Stars Die" for the encore. She sang the verses in her throaty alto voice, playing the rhythmic runs on the big, sweet Guild 12-string:

> *Tires are hummin' down the homeward highway*
> *Stayin' right between the yellow lines.*
> *The old 460 big block's runnin' smoothly*
> *On this silver Thunderbird of mine.*
> *But I got a tight grip on the wheel and I'm prayin'*
> *That nothin' on this outfit comes apart,*
> *The sign says don't stop here on the shoulder*
> *'Cause there's no passin' lane for broken hearts.*
>
> *Driving the edge of darkness beneath a lonely sky.*
> *The empty road is narrow and I'm trying not to cry.*
> *Tonight the fallin' stars are blazin' arcs across the sky;*
> *You know I never realized that night is when they die.*
>
> *You know, there ain't no junkyard nowhere for used lovers*
> *And they say they just don't make replacement parts;*
> *These days the fellas say they don't take trade-ins*
> *On abandoned, beat up, broke down big ol' hearts.*
> *There's a guy who runs a station down the highway,*
> *Fixes anything at all if you pay his fee*
> *But he never, ever does repairs on credit*
> *And he never ever gives a warranty.*

So I'm driving this cold highway tryin' not to fall apart
Tryin' to make it home with all the pieces of my heart.
The fallin' stars are blazin' in arcs across the sky;
You know I never realized that night is when they die.

When Chloe came in for her sax solo, most of the audience lit their lighters. Tears burned down Willa's cheek — her voice got husky and broke on the final verse. The audience loved it. The band repeated the chorus. Rincon and Chloe did the mournful riff at the end, and then Willa finished the last bars with just the twelve-string and harmonica as the music faded. There was a moment of breathless silence before the audience erupted. Blackwater took their bows — Willa folded her palms together and thanked the crowd for coming, and the group left the stage. It was a rush, riding the emotions of such an enthusiastic audience in a small, intimate venue. Words failed her.

Mississippi Studio's manager was gushing; "You guys were otherworldly! Like a cross between the Eagles, Queen, and Van Morrison — all that nice vocal harmony and instrumentals. But MacLeod's got the big, deep smoky-voice bluesy thing goin' on," he said. "That was hot, man. Hot! We need to book you back."

Willa left him to Neil so she could pack up her own guitars and help with the mics and the rest of their stuff; she didn't have to be told that they had earned their keep that night. She just wanted to get the band out of there and go eat something — her stomach felt hollow.

Mississippi's sound guys and the kids from the warm-up band helped them pack up. She gave them her business card, and tucked their lead guitarist's name away in her guitar case. Chloe and Neil would leave tonight with the van, to get all Blackwater's gear to

Seattle for tomorrow's gig at the Showbox. If the band got much busier, she'd have to invest in larger, more accommodating transport — something like a small bus, or maybe even a full-size one.

They passed on the Pix Patisserie and settled on Thai Ginger for something to eat. After that, Willa kissed Chloe and Neil goodbye — she could tell that they were tired but content, and both of them had no problem sleeping while the hired driver took the wheel. They would get their vacation tomorrow night; the group had a couple of rooms and a suite reserved at the W Hotel. Monday would give them all a fun break at the Pike Place Market. Unlike Portland, everything in Seattle was within walking distance of the Showbox and the W.

She felt only a little guilty about putting Jonesy together with Sticks and Rincon in the hotel suite tonight — he'd make certain they didn't get hammered, and get them up in the morning so they didn't miss the plane.

Later, when Rincon came knocking and she didn't answer her door, it took him a long time to get the point. "Come on, baby. Let me in, Willa, I need you," he murmured. She leaned against the door and thought about how it felt when he kissed her. He knew she was there. He whispered, "Come on, baby, I'm waitin'," inches away from her ear. Finally, though, he gave up. If he had kept trying a minute longer, she would have opened the door.

Unsettled, she got out the carved crystal stag and placed it on the hotel bed. It caught the light and dashed rainbow beads on the walls and windows. Had she been dreaming the other day in Silverhorn Canyon, or did she really see the Silverhorn Stag morph into a man with lonely eyes and strong, angular features? The tiny splashes of light moved as if they were dancing in a breeze. The drapes billowed. The lights circled, flowed together, and coalesced above the stag carving. The image of the Silverhorn man appeared in the swirling lights, his sad blue eyes fixed on her.

"Willa MacLeod." His voice was made of wind and soft bells.

"Who are you?" she asked, certain she was dreaming.

"Coér Mac Vyn. Corwyn, Wind's Heart. I called you. Many lifetimes ago." When he smiled, she heard the bells continue their quiet chiming.

She awakened face-down on top of the covers, the crystal stag beneath her hand. She glanced over at the clock; it wasn't quite five A.M. She crawled under the covers and went back to sleep.

She made the flight, just barely. Jonesy said nothing. Sticks was relieved and amused. And Rincon refused to look at her. Her stomach growled — she'd gulped the cup of coffee she grabbed in the hotel lobby. She took the window seat. The Horizon Air flight lasted fifty minutes; as usual, they served Starbucks coffee along with some nice cookies, and her stomach settled a little. She didn't speak to the others, but spent the flight composing new material.

Next to her, Rincon edged closer to peer at her notepad. She had some paired lines written down, and was scribbling musical notes underneath them, and chords along the margin. He studied her work for a spell.

"What's with this cross-over country ballad stuff?" he finally asked.

"People like it," she replied, her mind elsewhere.

"I'm a rock musician." He sounded truculent.

She stopped writing and studied him.

"You know the difference between a rock song and a country song, Rincon?"

"What's that?"

"Very little. Just the beat, actually — switch it from 4-4 to 2-4 or 3-4 and it becomes country. Then you change the way you accent the words and notes a little, and you replace the guitar riffs with a violin, which, incidentally, you call a fiddle. That's about it — except you leave out the sax and add a steel guitar. Or maybe a banjo if you really want to get down-home." She grinned suddenly. "You think you could play a steel guitar, Rincon? How're your banjo skills?"

"Fuck that," he grumbled. "You goin' country?"

"I could play a steel guitar. That mournful sound — I like it. You'd be the only one of us who couldn't make the jump. But no, I don't plan on going country. More blues, more country-rock maybe. Not straight-up country."

"What about you?" he asked. "You and your spiky white hair and black leather pants, not to mention your bad-girl lyrics. You aren't very 'down-home', woman." He tousled her short hair, pulled her close, kissed her a little too long. She felt the twist in her gut; the slow creep of heat spread from there.

"Hey, swap out the spiky heels with my Frye boots and I'm there. The song themes stay pretty much the same. But you know me — I like being edgy, and I don't like overdoing the twang. But I sort of like it all, you know . . . I once ran into a local Idaho cowboy singer who made a rap song out of 'The Strawberry Roan'. It was cool."

"What in the fuck is a Strawberry Roan?" he asked. "An ice cream flavor, or a bad date?"

"A mean, pink-colored horse that no one could ever ride — strawberry roan is a coat color of a horse."

"Why would anyone sing about that?"

"People sing about everything. It's a story song about someone who considers himself the very best at what he does, and about the thing that finally defeats him."

> *"I turns over twice, and comes back to earth*
> *and takes to cussin' the day of my birth.*
> *I guess there're some ponies I'm not able to ride,*
> *There're some of 'em left, they haven't all died."*

"It's about humility," she concluded.

"You tryin' to tell me something, MacLeod?" He looked at her suspiciously.

"Boy, did you go way off with that one," she laughed. "You must be feeling guilty."

"Screw that, woman. You gonna make me share a room with the boys again tonight?"

"No, Rincon. You don't have to. You live in Emerald City, so you can go home and not be bothered with us after the gig. That way you don't have to stay clean or sober one minute longer than necessary."

"Dude. You're so on my ass. Why're your panties in a twist? Except," he leaned closer, "you go commando, so that isn't what's in a twist. You need to chillax, woman. Maybe you need a different kind of twistin'."

"Maybe I'm just taking my life more seriously these days."

"That's what drugs are for," he whispered against her ear. "And me. You know you want me."

"What do I want you for, Rincon?"

He didn't say it out loud, but she heard his answer anyway. It made her blush.

The Showbox concert went even better than the one at the Mississippi — Willa decided it was because Rincon was sober and behaving. He smiled a lot — he knew they were hot that night. He did an incredible job with both the vocals and the guitar work on "Waitin'" — better than she'd ever heard.

I been waitin', waitin' for that little thing you do, sugar
Waitin' all day long.
I hear your footsteps outside my door
I hear you breathe my name
I been waitin', waitin' for that thing you do to me.
Come on baby, don't keep me waitin' no more.
Hey hey, come on.

Take me with you sugar
Make me burn with fire
Keep me burnin' baby,
Take me higher.

I been thinkin', thinkin' of the way you do me sugar
Thinkin' all day long.
Now I need you so bad it's like pain
What I got for you is like fire
'Cause I been thinkin', thinkin' of the way you do me
Come on baby, baby come do that to me again.
Hey come on, come on.

Take me with you sugar

Make me burn with fire
Keep me burnin' baby,
Take me higher.

He really threaded the ending, moving in close and singing it to her. The audience went wild.

'Cause I been waitin', waitin', bring it to me sugar,
Don't keep me waitin'
I hear your footsteps baby, crossin' the floor
And when you touch me baby
I ain't waitin', waitin', I ain't waitin' no no baby
Ain't waitin' for the waitin' no more.
Hey hey, come on come on
Waitin', baby, yeah yeah
Waitin' no more
Yeah yeah yeah.

The show ended like the last one, with "Night" as the encore; the applause followed them as they left the stage. They packed up their equipment and walked to a nearby Irish pub, where a group of fans coaxed them into joining their table.

Rincon sat next to Willa and bought her a beer. Chloe sat on her other side and bought her another one. Willa relaxed and leaned against Rincon; briefly, he put an arm around her and kissed her neck, setting off a tingle in her back and thighs.

"I been waitin', baby," he whispered into her ear.

Willa shivered, but with an effort she forced her attention away from Rincon and started talking with Chloe about the song she'd begun writing on the flight to Seattle. The two of them leaned their heads together, while Neil and Sticks did their best to run interference with some overzealous fans who seemed to think the women were just being coy.

There was nothing at all coy about the women zeroing in on Blackwater's lead guitarist. By the time the rest of the band left to walk to the W, Rincon had his own little mob of groupies hanging on both arms.

"I'll catch up with you," he called out as the others stood up to leave. Arm in arm and laughing, Willa and Chloe, Jonesy, Sticks, and Neil staggered back to the W and went up to Willa's room — Neil had booked her the WOW Suite — for a nightcap. The suite had a bank of floor-to-ceiling windows with an incredible view of Seattle; the lit-up Space Needle looked like something out of The War of the Worlds. Soon, Chloe and Neil slipped away to their room.

"We goin' country?" Sticks asked, taking out a joint.

"Nah," Willa answered, pouring herself a second cognac.

"Rincon thinks we are." He tried to pass her the joint but she waved him off.

"Rincon thinks a lot of things," she muttered.

"Rincon doesn't think often enough," Jonesy commented.

"I do have some new material I'm working on," she said. "Kind of mellow, bluesy stuff — we'll slow-rock it. It'll be great for the sax, violin, and even the guitar — just don't tell Rincon. We'll work on it when you guys come to the ranch."

"You done with Rincon?" Sticks asked.

"Can't be done with something that never got started."

"Weren't you guys kinda tight?" Sticks refilled his glass.

"Nah. I was just taking my dad's advice."

"What advice was that?" Jonesy asked.

"That I needed a man to have sex with. The job's still open."

"You inviting us to stay, woman? That'd be sweet." Sticks put on an exaggeratedly eager expression.

"Absolutely not," she laughed. She kissed him to soothe the sting of rejection, even though he had fully expected and intended it.

"Dude, you are such a cruel woman," Sticks said, running his hand over his mouth. "Beautiful women shouldn't be so mean."

"Yeah, yeah, yeah. Get used to it."

"She knows Rincon'll show up later," Jonesy said.

"Dude, she'll give him the mitten and he'll come to our room and whine all night," Sticks grumbled. "Babysitting Rincon isn't our gig. Maybe you should let him in, Willa."

She thought she might. But Rincon never showed up.

I've kept the faith,

waited at the gate of the mountain

until the reason for waiting is obscure

and I can't remember it any more.

Perhaps it was all for nothing —

except that I still hear the bells.

RM, personal journal

THE THINGS
FEARED

His leg pained him. Actually, everything pained him, but today the leg hurt as though it was still there, mangled and shredded by the landmine and the Humvee. Phantom limb pain, the doctors called it. Days when the leg hurt, his confusion was worse and the dizziness made him feel detached. Right now, he couldn't remember what day it was or whether Willa was supposed to be home. Jeb was out looking for strays in the high pasture — he'd left after breakfast. Ronan should have asked him where Willa was. He hadn't asked, because then Jeb would know he was having one of his bad days and would have postponed his work to baby-sit him.

Captain MacLeod decided to check Willa's room. Maybe she was writing. She did that — holed up at her desk when the muse took her. She had a personal relationship with that muse; she wasn't your average ranch girl by any measure. Painfully, he made his way to his daughter's wing of the house.

When had they built this house? he wondered. It wasn't the old house he grew up in. When he came home from the hospital the last time, it was just here. How long had that been? Three, four years? Before Willa began singing with her new band. Willa sold her maternal grandmother's land near town to get the money to build this house. There was a new high school on her grandmother's property now.

"We don't need the land," she'd said. "The town needs a new school."

"Why do we need a new house?" he asked.

"No stairs for you to struggle up or fall down."

He didn't go to her part of the house often. He was grateful that she stayed here, and gave Willa space so she wouldn't feel strangled or resent being stuck around him. And she did want to be here — the place drew her.

That's what frightened him. The place drew Megan too — Willa's mother. Where was she, anyway? Why couldn't he remember where Megan was? Or if she was coming back?

Willa never locked the door to her wing or the doors of her rooms; that told him she didn't mind if he went there. She did lock the safe in her closet, though — she locked the guns in there, and, he supposed, whatever else she didn't want him to see. Jeb had another safe in the bunkhouse for the ranch guns. Neither one of them was going to let him find an easy way to kill himself. He only thought about that on the days when the pain was like it was today.

Willa wasn't in her bedroom or her office. He limped back to the writing desk in her bedroom — an old secretary of her great-grand-mother's that she'd stripped and refinished. It was open, and a wooden box rested on the desk pad. He eased wearily into her chair. On the desk was a photo of him and Megan with Willa when she was a toddler. He was in the old Willys jeep and Willa was on his lap; Megan stood beside them. The big deer he'd shot was across the jeep's hood, and his compound bow was propped against it. Willa's hair was as pale as his, her eyes the same distant blue. His daughter looked nothing like Megan. Even then, Willa had the same strong jaw, the same long limbs he had. He and Willa were laughing — the same big mouth. Megan was a smallish woman, beautiful in a soft, quiet way, with brown hair, hazel eyes, and freckles. Her mouth was quirked in a tiny smile. Megan had a habit of watching them in that amused, quiet way while he and his daughter approached each day with boisterous enthusiasm.

Also on the desk was a portrait of him in full dress uniform. His dog tags hung over the picture. Next to it, a framed shadow box displayed his medals: the Medal of Honor, the Distinguished Service Cross, the Southwest Asia Service Medal, and the National Defense Service Medal. He brushed his hand across them and felt old.

In a silver frame was a picture of Willa and Regi at Regi's wedding, with their heads together and grinning — two exotic birds in silk and ribbons. He regretted that there was no photo of Willa with some handsome young man looking a little foolish and unjustifiably brave. He hoped she would find him soon, someone who deserved her and would make her happy.

He opened the box that was sitting on the desk. The tiny silver bell he had seen before had been placed on top of the ribbon-tied letters he'd written to Willa and her mother from Saudi Arabia and Kuwait, and, later, from the hospital. Why did they keep them? They didn't say anything that would alarm a wife or a little girl; no deep musings from a soldier who feared for his life every day. He picked up the bell and it chimed softly. It made him afraid, but he couldn't remember why. Beneath the packet of letters was an envelope with Megan's careful handwriting on it: "Sara — give these to Willa someday. Meg."

He opened the envelope. Inside were two more tiny silver bells, just like the first one.

He started to cry. Sunny got off Willa's bed and bumped his leg, worried.

Why do you fear yourself? a voice whispered.

The voice seemed to come from inside him and all around him. The venetian blinds swayed. He put everything back in the box and shut the lid, but he could still hear bells ringing. He reached for his cane and struggled to his feet.

In his own study, Willa had placed his oversized recliner so that he had a view of the mountains and the big TV screen at the same time. He wrote for a while as he worked on a bottle of Crown Royal — today wasn't a beer day. The whiskey didn't help either, so he swallowed a few pain pills. He scrolled through the channels, and finally settled on a college football game. He took a few more pain pills. When the whisky bottle proved to be empty, he got up to get another.

The floor came up and hit him, hard. He lay there, unable to remember where he was. *Megan. Where was Megan? No, Willa. He needed to call Willa.* He tried to reach the telephone on the end table, but couldn't manage it. Sunny nosed him and whined.

"Sunny. Phone!" He vaguely remembered that Willa had taught Sunny that — to bring the phone.

Sunny whined again after he dropped the phone on Ronan's arm. Ronan tried to use it but couldn't remember which numbers to push. Something about 1... Willa had told him to use the 1 button. He tried holding down the 1. He closed his eyes and the world spun away. Distantly he heard a voice. Willa's voice? Maybe it was Megan? He couldn't remember what to say.

"Megan?"

He heard bells ringing and the wind whistling softly through his study.

What do you fear, Ronan MacLeod? the wind whispered.

Something worse than death, his thought answered.

The band met up at Cutters Crabhouse for brunch. They shifted their seats around so everyone could enjoy the spectacular harbor view, and when Rincon showed up Willa found herself squeezed between him and Sticks. Chloe, Neil, and Sticks sipped mimosas while they waited for the food to arrive. Rincon asked for a coke, which he surreptitiously spiked with something from a flask he carried; Willa decided not to make a point of it, since he'd remained on good behavior while the band needed him sober. She and Jonesy decided to stick with coffee, which was up to Seattle's high standards; they finished a full pot between them, and they'd started on their second one by the time the food came.

Just after she took her second bite of salmon cake with hollandaise sauce, her phone played "Home on the Range".

"Don't answer it, MacLeod," Rincon said in her ear as she pulled the phone from her pocket.

"Who's 'Home on the Range'?" Sticks asked, trying to read the display. "Says 'Home'."

"Must be her father," Rincon said. "Let the dude leave a message."

Her dad never called when she was away from home. She answered the call.

"Hello — Dad?" There was only silence. "Jeb? Sara? Hello?" She heard Sunny whine.

"Megan?" a voice whispered.

"Dad. Dad, it's me, Willa. Dad. Answer me. Dad!" She turned to Rincon. "Move. Move. Let me out!"

Rincon jumped up, startled at her intensity.

"Dad?" Still no answer. Willa thought for a second, and turned back to her bandmates.

"Give me a phone." She looked at Sticks, whose phone was on the table. She snapped her fingers at him. "Phone. *Phone. Now!*" He handed it over. She keyed Jeb's number. No answer. She tried again with Regi's number. Regi answered after the first ring.

"Hey girl. Aren't you in Seattle?"

"Raz — go to the ranch. Go right now. Call me when you find my dad."

"Okay, sweetie. What gives?"

"Dad called me. There's something wrong. He won't say anything. Maybe he can't. Will you go?"

"I'm going as we speak. Do you want to stay on the line 'til I get there?"

"No. He's still on my phone."

"Has he been drinking?"

73

"Probably. He didn't say anything but Mom's name. He never calls me when I'm gone. And I can hear Sunny whining."

"Where's Jeb?"

"He didn't answer. Probably rounding up cattle."

"I'm on my way. I'll call you."

"Thanks!"

"Sit down, MacLeod," Rincon said. "Finish your breakfast. Or is it lunch by now?"

She glared at him for a few heartbeats. Then she handed Sticks his phone. "Thanks, Sticks. I gotta go. Neil, can you take care of the bill?"

Chloe wrapped Willa's salmon cakes in a napkin and handed them to her. "You might get hungry, hon," she said.

"Where're you going, MacLeod?" Rincon asked. "Runnin' 'cause Daddy called? Maybe I better come with you for a little skin on skin before you go. That's what you need, woman."

"You..." she gave him a look he had never seen before. "You don't see anything but yourself—and even that's just skin deep."

"Dude," he said. "Chill, woman, chill."

There was fire in her eyes. They all saw it. "Go fuck your own skin, Rincon. And no drugs or booze when you get to the ranch, if you want to keep your job."

She left them with their mouths hanging open. Sticks got up from the table and followed her out of the restaurant. He had to jog to keep up.

She tried to get a response on her phone again. "Dad? Dad, are you there?" The line had gone dead, so she ended the call. She called the ranch number again, and got a busy signal.

"What's the deal, Willa?" Sticks was out of breath.

"I asked my dad to call me if something ever went wrong and he needed help. He's never called me before when I'm with you guys. Remember? I always call *him*. He never calls me. I heard the dog whining. I taught Sunny to bring my dad the phone if he couldn't get it himself." She slowed to a fast walk so they could both catch their breath. "Maybe it's nothing. Maybe he's just passed-out drunk. How long's it been?"

Sticks checked his phone. "Eight minutes?"

"Too soon for Regi to get there." She tried the ranch again. Busy. She started jogging again. They crossed First at the light.

"What're you gonna do?"

"Regi'll call me. I'll be at the W by then. I might have to go home.... Guess I sort of gave Rincon a piece of my mind."

"Well, woman," Sticks gasped, struggling to keep up. She slowed to a walk again. "I'd say it's clear he ain't the guy you're taking home tonight. But if you ask me, he only cares because you don't want him. If you wanted him, the dude wouldn't give a crap."

"That's pretty much what I figured. I just don't work like that — not anymore. How long is it now?"

"Eighteen minutes."

They turned into the lobby of the W.

In the elevator, she tapped her foot impatiently. "It takes twenty minutes to drive to the ranch from The Café. That's if you have your foot in it and don't slow down for the turns or the dirt road. Regi's a little closer. But she has to put her shoes on, get her truck out...."

They reached the WOW suite and Willa fumbled for the key card.

"Twenty-one minutes," Sticks said, as she slipped the card into its slot.

"Home on the Range" played three notes before she could answer.

"Is Dad okay?"

"He's breathing, but unresponsive. The ambulance is on its way. I think he overdosed on pain meds, but I'm not sure. He fell and hit his head, near as I can tell."

Willa started to cry. Sticks held the door open and guided her in.

"Don't cry, sweetie," Regi said. "I'll take care of him. I'll call you when the paramedics get here."

"I'm on my way home," Willa answered in a small voice, and ended the call.

Sticks poured her a small glass of cognac and water, then put her guitars on the bed.

"We've gotta get you a couple more guitars for home so that you don't have to fly with these," he commented. "It's too damn much trouble to keep dragging these ones back and forth with you. They need to stay with the rest of the equipment." He got a wet towel for her face. Willa took a deep breath.

"I wanted to do that, but didn't want to take it out of band money," she whispered.

"Dude, I think the band has the coin now. I'll pow-wow with Neil. Rincon, we can axe, even though he can shred. You got the stuff, babe. Here," he put her suitcase on the bed. "Pack. I'll get on the handle with the concierge and get your flight changed."

"I'll make sure everyone shows up next weekend," Sticks assured her as he put her guitars into the trunk of the hotel limousine. Willa was in black leather pants and wore a long black leather coat. She had her dark glasses on so that no one would see her weeping. Sticks thought she looked dangerous; everyone in the lobby and on the street turned to get a second look. He took her arm and kissed her. She could feel what that did to him, so she kissed him back. She gave him a tight smile.

"You're my guy, Sticks," she said. "Thanks."

Chloe and Neil came running up as she was about to get into the limo.

"Sorry," she said, hugging them. "You guys stay and have fun. See you next weekend. Bring your long johns and coats, and your roughing-it clothes."

Rincon was with Jonesy, halfway down the block. He saw Willa kiss Sticks, hug the others, and get into the limousine, looking deadly interesting.

He glanced at Jonesy. He couldn't read the expression there. He seldom could; Jonesy didn't react much.

"Man. There goes one hot bitch — best I ever had. I never run for any woman, but maybe this time —"

Jonesy turned and looked him full in the face. This time Rincon could read his expression clearly: Jonesy thought he was an idiot.

"Man, you're an idiot," Jonesy said, just in case Rincon hadn't gotten the message.

"Hey, dude. What's up with that?"

"Willa's one wicked fine woman, but you never, not for a minute, 'had' her. You were lucky she liked your pretty face for a little while, that's all. She doesn't need you. Maybe it would've taken her longer to figure it out if you hadn't been such an asshole. You might want to spin on who signs your paycheck and why we even get a paycheck — then show up to the ranch with a little better attitude and no drugs. Her dad's an ex-army Ranger."

"Wow. When the man spills, it's a big one."

"Listen, dickhead. You got chops. But this band isn't about you and your guitar — it's about Willa's songs. Get your shit together, man. You know she was talking to the warm-up band's lead guitarist at the Mississippi."

"Dude — that guy can't shred for shit .... She goin' country on us? I won't play that country crap."

"You know she doesn't like country."

"What about that Strawberry Roan crap she was going on about?"

"You're an idiot."

Dogs and philosophers do the greatest good and
get the fewest rewards.

Diogenes

AN OLD STORY

Willa went straight from Boise Airport to St. Luke's Hospital. Apparently visiting hours were anytime at all when the patient was your father, you're wearing black leather from neck to toe, you're taller than almost anyone there, and you're angry. She arrived just as her dad was being bundled up to be transferred to the VA Hospital; he was stabilized for the moment, and the administrators seemed eager to wash their hands of a potential deadbeat case. When Willa growled at them and showed her insurance card, they rolled him back upstairs to a private room.

Once the orderlies and nurses finished hooking him back up, all but the floor nurse left the room. The nurse muttered something under her breath as Willa pulled a chair close.

The case doctor found Willa with her head on her father's hand, weeping.

The doctor cleared his throat softly. Willa glanced up, and the fierceness in her gaze obviously startled him, because he took a double take.

"If you aren't his daughter, then Mr. MacLeod has a female doppelganger," the doctor said with a self-conscious laugh.

"Daughter. Willa MacLeod," she said, standing up so she could look him straight in the eyes. They were the same height. "Is he all right now?"

"For now. It seems he overdosed on his pain meds, combined with alcohol."

"Crown Royal," she said helplessly. When the doctor smiled in amusement, she returned a grin. He was going to be honest. She liked him.

"I'm Jamie McInally. I'm the internal medicine resident. I've requested Mr. MacLeod's records from the VA."

"He's a captain, Dr. McInally. Captain Ronan MacLeod. He earned a Medal of Honor. Dr. Lossman in New Britton just took some tests last week. My dad has some serious Gulf War symptoms — fibromyalgia and sleeplessness. Pain all the time. Some days are worse. Dr. Lossman mentioned some new treatment…."

"I'll consult with Dr. Lossman."

"Thank you."

"Is the drinking a problem?" the doctor asked carefully.

"Yes and no."

"Meaning?"

"He never drank before he lost his leg and my mother disappeared — before this constant pain. I would rather have him alive and drinking than the alternative."

"Perhaps there's a better alternative. Maybe I could help with that. I'll review his history and then do some research, take some tests — you know the drill."

"I nag him about it — but that's all. I'm afraid of losing him, so I suppose I'm enabling him. He nags me about my love life, and I nag him about his drinking. We're pathetic, I guess."

"Do you have a degree in psychology to qualify you for this self-analysis? I rather doubt the 'pathetic' part, Ms. MacLeod. Don't beat yourself up. Sometimes people do what is necessary to survive. You said your mother disappeared. Is she in the picture now? Did she ever come back?"

"No." Willa shrugged. "No, my mother is gone. It was a long time ago. It's a mystery that haunts my father, is all — really, it still haunts us all. Some people think she killed herself. And call me Willa, please. I would like to think we do better than that — survive, I mean. Maybe we don't...."

"Why does he nag you about your love life?"

"Because I don't have one."

"Do you drink, Willa?"

"Occasionally — mostly just to be social. I'm not much into it; I like a clear mind."

"So what do you do to survive?" The question sounded curious, rather than prying.

"I write. It turns out that the Muse is particularly fond of a spirit offering — alcohol is part of the ritual to appease and encourage her. My Muse spends half her time stone cold sober and probably mad at me as a result. That means either I'm a lousy writer, or else my Muse is very forgiving and helps me out anyway out of charity."

The doctor kept his appraising look. "What do you write, Ms. MacLeod?"

"Willa," she reminded him. "I'm a poet and a songwriter."

"Are you published?"

"I sing with a rock band. Blackwater."

"Hey! I've heard them. I like the new song — something about stars dying. I'm not much of a rocker, more of a Jason Isbell, Amos

Lee, John Gorka country-folk kind of guy. I hadn't really listened to Blackwater before they started playing that song a lot on the radio. I like it."

"I write all our stuff."

"I guess your Muse is forgiving, then."

"Thanks." She flashed him her big smile. But then she frowned: "Will my dad wake up soon?"

"We put him under mild sedation. We took x-rays, and he doesn't have a concussion from the fall. I think he just passed out from the meds and booze — I have him on a saline drip to help clear that stuff out of his system. He should wake up soon. The nurse will monitor him and notify me if he doesn't. Were you with him when this happened?"

"No, no, no.... We had a gig in Seattle. We stayed an extra day, just to mess around. I caught a flight when I got the call."

"Ahh. He was alone, then?"

"Yes and no."

"Meaning?"

"Jeb, the hired hand, was out with the cattle. Sunny was with my dad."

"Sunny being...?"

"Our Labrador retriever. He brought Dad the phone. I have my number programmed in for speed-dial on number one."

"Maybe, Willa, it would be a good idea to get your dad one of the new GPS 911 alerts. It might be easier than teaching Sunny to make a phone call."

She nodded, then rummaged in the pack she'd dropped on the floor and handed him a CD. The cover showed constellations super-imposed over black water, with a meteor streak across the middle;

when the light hit the picture from the right angle, Blackwater was spelled out across the water. In small white script across the bottom was the CD's title, *Waitin'*.

"Here," she said. "Maybe you'll find something else you like. When do you think Dad can go home?"

"First let's see if anything else is wrong. I'll run some tests tomorrow. Depending on how he seems when he wakes up and what the tests show, we'll make a decision then. When he does go home — assuming that we find no complications of course — he shouldn't be left alone."

"That's not a problem."

"I have to ask you this . . . . In these cases, it's required that I make an assessment of a patient's mental health to be certain they aren't a danger to themselves. Do you have any reason to believe your father tried to commit suicide?"

She stared at the doctor, dumbfounded.

"I thought you said he took too many pain meds," she said finally.

"That's true. But I have to decide if it was accidental or intentional."

She looked over at her dad as if to read his sleeping face.

"I think he just wants the pain to go away. He wouldn't leave me intentionally." She felt suddenly unsure. "He gets lost and wants to not feel it. I'm sure he took the pills intentionally — but not to kill himself. He did it to kill the pain."

"I guess I would call that accidental," the doctor said gently. He waved the CD at her. "I have a feeling I'm going to like this."

"Thanks. I hope you do."

83

Captain Ronan MacLeod was diagnosed with an inflammation in the knee joint, which gradually subsided with aggressive antibiotics. Dr. McInally also started him on new pain medication — an N-type calcium channel blocker. He was released from the hospital after two days.

"I'm sorry Willa," were his first words as they drove out of the hospital parking lot.

"Damn it, Dad, will you stop apologizing to me — please?"

"You had to cut your trip short."

"I can shop online," she growled.

"But your time with your friends — the band I mean. With Ramon — "

"Rincon. That didn't work out so well."

"That's too bad."

"No. Actually, it's a really good thing." She gave him her biggest grin.

Uh-oh, she heard him think, and waited.

"Okay. I'll bite. Why is it a good thing?"

"Because I felt really awful cheating on you."

"Shit. Why did I ask?" He leaned his head against the headrest. "Whose wheels are these, by the way? Nice ride."

"Yeah. Cadillac Escalade. I liked it so much, I bought it. It has the little step thingy that comes out so you can get in easily. I just picked it up from the dealer this morning."

"I didn't know you wanted a new car." He ran his hand appreciatively over the leather seat.

"The seat heats up. I didn't know I wanted one either. I needed to do something to keep myself busy while you were getting all those tests, and I was too distracted to write much."

"So it's my fault. This is a little middle-class and stodgy for you, isn't it? Hope you got a good deal."

"Stodgy? That's a great word — no one ever uses it. I love this thing, are you crazy? And, Dad — with the gas prices now, they're giving these things away. I got it for less than half what they quoted me last year — half what the truck cost three years ago. They gave me a good trade-in for the Jeep, and I paid cash for the difference, so they threw in an extended warranty and lifetime oil changes. And I really do like it."

"I see. You wanted a new car instead of a guy. Sometimes you think like a man." Her dad tried to smile, but mostly just managed to look tired.

"Well, let's see how my new guy drives, shall we?"

Two hours later, when they pulled off the highway onto the ranch road, she stopped the car and gave her dad a wicked little wink.

"So if this is my guy substitute, it needs a name. I christen it — him — Ramon! Want to try him?"

"Nah, sweetheart. Another time. You're doing great."

Jeb and Sara were waiting for them when they pulled into the ranch driveway. After showing off "Ramon the Escalade", Willa led them all in for lunch.

"I thought I'd stay in the guest house over the garage for a while," Sara said casually.

She met Willa's gaze with a "don't-you-argue-with-me" look that Willa was more than familiar with.

"Won't that be hard for you, with the restaurant and your Council stuff?" Willa asked.

She heard Sara's *don't test me, Willa*, though Sara didn't say that part out loud. "Brooke and Jesse have the restaurant under control most of the time. I'll go there to get the baking done in the afternoons. I can do the Council work by internet, and drop in at the office when I have to. Everyone's onboard with that." The even fiercer "don't argue" gleam in her eye told Willa she had better stop the discussion.

"Okay," Willa agreed. "That'll be nice."

"Besides, you have the band coming," Sara added. "You might need some help." Willa sensed that Sara had more on her mind than the band.

"Yeah. They'll want to eat, I suppose. But if you're cooking, I'll make them work harder for it. Sticks loves your chicken and biscuits and apple pie. I'll get my money's worth out of him."

"He eats because he's a stoner," Jeb commented. Willa heard him say "punk", but not aloud.

"Makes him a groove machine, Jeb," she laughed.

"Whatever that means," Jeb said grumpily.

"That means, Mister Purebred Super Cowboy Who Can Round Up Cattle In His Sleep, that he can really play the drums well. He's harmless, and a good friend." She grinned because she loved to argue with the ranch hand. She sensed that he enjoyed it too, although he would never admit it.

"That green-eyed pretty boy ain't so harmless," Jeb growled. "An' he don't like pie neither."

"Yeah, yeah. How would *you* know what a pretty boy looks like?"

"I know what trouble looks like," he answered. Willa didn't have to read his very black thoughts to know he didn't like Rincon.

"He won't be trouble this time."

"Hmph."

"And if he is, I'll let you take him to the barn," she said casually.

Jeb looked up at her sharply. "Seriously?"

"Yep."

"Okay, then. I'm holdin' you to that." He gave off a distinct sense of triumph.

"Just don't hurt his fingers."

"Okay then." He put on his hat. "I got work t'do," he said, and stomped out the door. His big cowboy smile didn't worry her a bit.

Sara came to Willa's office with the journal from the Silverhorn cave. That's what they were calling it, even though Sara was fairly certain the older parts of the manuscript were over two thousand years old; she'd traced the old Celtic script back that far, and had brushed up on her ancient language skills in order to translate.

"The first part is what you would probably classify as poetry," Sara said. "Sort of an epic poem, like Beowulf. It tells the story of a man called Æód Mac Nessa, a Sithé of great magic who fought in the Wars of the Totem Clans. Sithé numbers were dwindling. Æód Mac Nessa realizes that the supremacy of the Sithé is ending, so he makes a pact with the Hawk Clan. They make a great journey with the Sithé to a new home they call the Refuge, and later the Hawk Clan comes to be known as the Story Keepers."

She opened the book carefully to the front page.

"This is Æód Mac Nessa," Sara said. The ancient drawing in colored inks showed a man with an antler crown, wielding a sword.

"The second part of the journal is like a family tree — a list of the Mac Nessa descendants. And there are some final entries that I'm not sure I understand — something about a leaving." She showed Willa the page, but didn't touch it. The writing changed dramatically as the list descended. "But first and foremost, this is just a beautiful and very old manuscript."

"The American Book of Kells," Willa commented, turning back to the ornate first page.

"What do you know about the Book of Kells?"

Willa sensed that Sara was baiting her, so she sidestepped her question. "More like the Book of Bells. Look. He has bells around his antlers." Willa felt connected somehow to the book, thinking of her vision.

"You have a very valuable piece of history and art here. I would put it in the safe, Willa."

"More importantly, Sara, this confirms the legend! The picture looks like the man in my dream. Look, he even has the same amulet around his neck. Do you suppose he does some kind of reincarnation thing?"

"I think there are — or were — many of these people."

"Maybe I should return the book," Willa said.

"It's your call, Willa. Although I'm not sure anyone will care."

"He will care. The Silverhorn Stag. I know he's real. He calls my name."

Sara looked up, startled. She studied Willa's face intently before she asked, "Why you and no one else?"

"That's a good question. I hope to answer it."

"I don't think you should, Willa. I think you should leave it alone."

"Sara!" Willa was shocked. "What's with the big about-face?"

"I sense this is more dangerous than just researching a legend."

Sara was not telling her the whole story; Willa felt her hiding something. "I'll think about it," she replied. "I'm not quitting. You know I won't. I can't."

"...I know," Sara said. "I wish you only happiness, Willa MacLeod. Because I love you like a daughter."

Willa put her arms around Sara and held her tightly.

"I won't get hurt. I promise."

"I wish you could make that a promise you could keep, girl," Sara said. "Now I am going for a walk."

What Sara didn't say out loud would have filled a page in the journal.

> Without change, something sleeps inside us,
> and seldom awakens. The sleeper must awaken.
>
> Frank Herbert

SILVERHORN'S
MAGIC

It had snowed in the night, but the snow was melting fast. Willa parked the four-wheeler under the fir tree. This time, she took no gun into Silverhorn Canyon. When she reached the point on the trail directly above the flood bridge over the creek elbow, she paused to survey the crossing again. Snow lay in the shadows, and the opposite side of the canyon was white with it. There was quite a bit more water in the creek than the last time she'd crossed — it splashed over the top of the large boulder on the near side of the crossing. A small niggle of fear threaded her breathing. The crossing would be more difficult this time. More frightening.

The book felt heavy in her cargo pocket, almost too much to carry. She clutched the stag carving in her coat pocket to remind herself that her experience last time had been more than a dream. She gathered her courage.

A gust of air touched her face. She heard bells. Movement in the corner of her eye made her turn and look up the trail. The silver flash of his horns moving through the trees was what she saw first. The silver buck came down the trail at a swift trot, and as he moved through the shadows his form blurred and changed until he stood before her on the trail: a man half a head taller than she, dressed in leather and grey fur. His coat looked to be made of wolf pelts, and his boots were made from skins with the fur side in, cross-tied up to his knees.

"You came to see me." He spoke in a strange, rough-edged language, but she understood him. The bells in his braided hair gleamed softly and chimed as he turned his head. Her breath snagged — he was wearing her moonstone earrings.

"Corwyn," she breathed, her heart beating wildly.

He smiled. His white teeth were even, and his eyes crinkled at the edges with laugh lines. "I am Coér Mac Vyn. Corwyn."

"Heart of the Wind," she muttered. "I thought you were just something I had dreamed."

"You are Willa MacLeod," he said softly.

"How do you know?"

"Your mother told me about you."

"What...?" she whispered.

He studied her. "We have things to speak of, Willa MacLeod. Is that why you came?"

"I don't know why I came."

"You didn't bring your rifle." His blue eyes were sharp and pale.

"I'm not hunting."

"Is that why you didn't bring it?" he asked, that half smile playing on his thin lips. He didn't appear as ancient as before, when she'd dreamed that she raised her gun and looked at him though the scope.

"Yes. No." She shifted her gaze to the creek.

"You were afraid to cross."

"A little. The water is higher."

"I will take you." The silver horns curled up out of his head, and then the rest of him shifted. The Silverhorn Stag blew hot on her hands. He knelt for her to get onto his back.

Grasp my horns tightly.

As she took the lower antler branches in her fists, he leaped to his feet and shot away up the trail. She caught her breath at their breakneck speed. When he turned and leapt down the slope toward the creek, she almost cried out in alarm. She dared not let go, lest she fall off and break something. The creek was narrower here. She closed her eyes to shut out the fear. She felt him leap the water, heard it rushing beneath them, and felt him land solidly. She opened her eyes. He bounded downstream, and up the chimney in the granite. She felt the bunch of his muscles as he climbed. When he finally stopped, they were on the shelf far above the water. The aspens stood white and naked of leaves now; inches of snow blanketed the ground. Both deer and human footprints marked the path.

She slipped from Corwyn's back, but held to one antler because her legs felt wobbly. He waited. She took a shuddering breath and let go. Instantly, the man stood beside her, his silver-branched crown disappearing slowly as the edges of his shape grew sharp.

He led the way into the rock chamber.

"Is this your — uh — place?" she asked. It was just as she had seen it before; the leaves were undisturbed. But the pink bandana was gone from the vug in the granite. She drew the book from her pocket and brought out the crystal carving. "Are these yours? I took them." She made as though to hand them back to him. The crystal stag lay on her gloved palm. He took her hand, closed her fingers over the carving.

"Keep them. They were left here for you. This is not my room. These things belonged to one of your ancestors — a long-ago grand-mother, I believe."

"A MacLeod?" she asked, feeling something inevitable settle on her.

"The Mac Clæúd kin left us long before your revered great-great-great-grandmother did. They have lived where you live now for many centuries. They mingled their Sithé blood with human and forgot how to change. They guard the path to the Silverhorn."

"Reagan Magnes, then," Willa said. "She was my great-great-great-grandmother. She showed up in town with a baby daughter. Married the town blacksmith. It was over a hundred years ago."

"Rìgan Mac Nessa."

"They said she was crazy," Willa said.

"What is 'crazy'?"

"Insane. Mad. Given to fits." She wasn't sure how to explain.

"No. A hunter killed her mate, Kiervyn Mac Nessa. She never got over that. She left here in order to save her daughter from the same fate. She believed the time of our people was over."

"Was she right?" Willa asked.

"I don't know," he replied, studying her face.

"In the end, she committed suicide."

"What is that?"

"She killed herself."

He grunted as if someone had kicked him.

"My mother and my grandmother..." Willa began. "The women in my family were considered — unstable. Sometimes insane, some-times close to it. My mother took drugs for depression."

"It is hard to be a Sithé amongst people who do not change, who do not know the Hart of the Wind. How are you considered, Willa MacLeod — crazy too?"

"I'm not much like my mother. More like my father."

"A MacLeod," he said. "Mac Clæúd was a strong clan. Loyal, but practical."

"How do you know?"

"It was always so. It was said that they always did what they had to do. The Hawk Clan, the Story Keepers, drifted away when the newcomers began to arrive; the Story Keepers no longer believed the songs of their fathers. We had to preserve what we had left."

"Who are the Story Keepers?" she asked.

"One of the Totem Clans. The Totem Clans are the brown-skinned people who came over the crossing in the north and settled here. It was long after my ancestors migrated from the east. The Totem Clans were not Sithé, but they lived peacefully with us for a time. Later, when they warred among themselves, their strife grew to include hatred for us. The Hawk Clan was the only one who stood by us."

"That was a long time ago."

"Many tens of hundreds of years."

She let her breath out slowly.

"Sara Blackhawk believes in the legends of your people," Willa said, suddenly realizing this was true.

"She is a Story Keeper."

"Yes, she is that. So is her husband, Joseph Yellowgrass," Willa agreed.

She realized she was still holding the book and the carving.

"If these are not yours, why do you wear the earrings?"

He grinned suddenly. "You left them as a gift. Is that not what the writing on the page meant?"

"Because I felt bad about taking the book and the carving. I felt I should leave something in exchange."

"You did not know that the things you found here were yours already. So — the earrings were not a gift? Do you wish them back?"

"No. They are a gift. I'm glad you like them."

"They have great spirit to them."

"A friend made them. He's a fine artist."

"Yes, he is. And the knife? I have never seen anything quite so small and clever in a knife. Is it a gift, too?"

She thought she might give him anything he asked for. She nodded.

"I liked the oat cakes in the package too. Thank you." He drew out the pink bandana from inside his shirt.

"This belongs to you — I think it was to keep the gifts safe, yes?"

She took it from his hand, and put it in her cargo pocket.

"What about my mother? When did my mother tell you about me?"

"When she came here to die."

She slapped herself in the face. "Maybe I'm still dreaming," Willa said, angry suddenly. "Maybe I will wake up now."

"You are not crazy and you are not dreaming, Willa MacLeod," he said softly. His eyes had darkened and they gleamed slightly. "Come with me. I will show you."

Corwyn lit a lamp. He led her into the mountain and upward. They walked and climbed up corridors through the granite for what seemed like a very long time. It grew cold and she zipped her jacket, pulling up the hood. Corwyn drew his fur hood over his own head. Finally, he stopped in a large chamber and lit more lamps.

It was a catacomb. There were niches in the granite walls, and in these niches lay the dead — many hundreds of them. He led and she followed. The further they walked, the less ancient the bodies seemed, the furs and beading that adorned them more intact. Corwyn stopped at a niche. The fur spread over this body was almost as new as the coat he wore. Silver gleamed in the soft light; strips of beading adorned the body.

It was her mother. The pale face was the same as the picture on her desk, hollow and shrunken with death, but remarkably preserved. Corwyn drew back the fur that covered Megan MacLeod. Her mother was in Levis and a plaid shirt under a jean jacket. The slashes on both her wrists were still visible.

"She killed herself?" Willa asked.

"No."

She faced him. "You killed her?" She was trying to understand.

"No. No. I would never do that. She didn't understand. It was an accident. She thought she was making a sacrifice." Corwyn put a hand on Willa's shoulder and squeezed.

"Your mother came here the day she heard your father was wounded. She knew only the bare bones of the magic. She knew that blood brings strength, power, life. She wished to give a blood payment for your father, to save him." He re-covered the body with the fur and drew Willa across the vast chamber. There was a stone ledge where many objects had been placed — things that appeared to Willa to be valuable — crystal bowls, silver, carvings, beading, and filled baskets.

"This is where we keep the tokens of our magic. She came here. I was not present. I am the only one left now, and I was not here." His distress was evident. "She took a knife." He reached out and picked up a very ornate knife from the ledge. "This one." He put it back.

"Then she cut her wrists and let the blood fall into a crystal bowl."

Willa saw that one of the bowls was dark inside.

"Why?" she asked.

"She believed that she had to make the sacrifice for your father to live. The blood of every descendant of the Sithé is drawn to the power of blood. But she didn't understand the way the magic works. I didn't find her in time."

"She was dead?"

"No. But I couldn't save her — it was too late. We talked a little. She told me of you. I told her of us, the Sithé. I tried to save her."

"Why didn't you bring her home to us?"

"How would I have explained that? She wanted to stay here, among her people. She asked me to tell you someday."

"My father almost went crazy when she vanished."

"Insanity is apparently a hazard for the Sithé and their descendants in the new world."

"Is that why you called me here? To tell me about her?"

He didn't answer right away. She realized that he had placed her mother here, honored her with fur and beads.

"Let us go where it is warmer," he suggested and she followed without argument. "It is better to come here in the summer, when it is only a little cold."

They went back downward. It seemed they walked for an hour, through a confusing labyrinth of corridors and caverns. Finally, he led her into a room where a low fire burned. He took off his coat. The heavy amulet around his neck swung as he leaned over to place fresh wood on the fire.

"This is my room," he said. "It's said that the Hart of the Wind once lived in a great city with many towers and rooms, a place where the magic was strong. This small place is all I have ever known. It is the refuge where the Sithé fled after the war with the Totem Clans. We were a great and powerful people who practiced magic and lived in a mystical city. Now, we have dwindled to one — one diminished old cave-dweller."

"Do you believe that story?" she asked.

"Yes." He lit lamps. There were two pinewood chairs and a table with writing instruments and an inkwell. She sat down. At the center of the table was the cougar totem she had wrapped in her bandana; it served as a paperweight for her note.

"Why didn't you go and look for the legendary city?"

"Where? Why?"

"I don't know. Curiosity?"

"I would be killed. As my brother was."

She felt a sudden sharp dread.

"Did my father kill your brother?" she asked, thinking of the Silverhorn buck hanging over the ranch fireplace.

"My brother died before your ancestor Rìgan took her daughter and left us. There were still enough of us to be a clan then. Your father's grandfather was not yet born."

"There is a great big deer mounted on the wall at the ranch. My father killed it here in Silverhorn Canyon. It was a record — a high-scoring deer for size."

"One of the lesser children."

"What does that mean?"

"The Hart of the Wind have paired with humans who have no magic. The children of those pairings sometimes have magic, like the Sithé, and sometimes they are only human. But once, long ago, one of our kin took his animal form and never changed back to a human.

It was said that he was not a normal man anyway, and everyone just thought he forgot how to change back to human form. He stayed in his other form and lived with the herds of deer in the Silverhorn Crags until he died. His deer descendants are bigger, stronger, and faster than ordinary deer, but they have no magic. They are only deer, not Sithé. When a hunter kills a Sithé, the Sithé dies a man, not a deer."

"That's an odd story," she said.

"It is a sad story," he said.

"My father needs to know what happened to my mother," she said.

"Will you tell him?"

"I don't know. He is sick right now. I just brought him home from the hospital."

"What is a hospital?"

"A place of healing. A place where there are doctors — healers."

"What happened?"

She told him about the war, about her father's leg, the lingering miasma they called Gulf War Syndrome.

"He drinks to kill the pain."

"Drinks spirits? For what pain? The one in his leg, the one in his head, or the one in his heart?"

"All three," she said sadly.

"And what do you do to kill the pain?" It was so like the question Dr. McInally had asked that she laughed. "I write songs. I play music."

"Where do you do this — at your home?"

"I travel with a group of musicians who play with me. Some of them sing. We travel all over the country and . . . ." She smiled slowly. "I make good money doing it too."

"A troubadour, then," he said.

"Yes. Something like that. I sing the pain for others to cry. But this pain is different. I need to tell my father what happened to my mother. He knows nothing of the Sithé."

"Are you certain he knows nothing?" He watched Willa work through the puzzle of her life. His eyes fell on the diamond in the side of her nose.

"No," she finally replied.

"And what do *you* know?"

"What you've told me. What I sense. What's in the book I took — or some of it."

He put more wood on the fire. "I have water. Or tea from the mint plant if you wish."

"Water," she said. He scooped some from a basin, set a small silver cup by her hand, and sat down.

She took three granola bars, a packet of jerky, and some dried pears from a pocket. She placed them on the table. His eyes brightened when he saw the granola bars.

"I have very little to trade," he said.

She was dumbfounded. "They are a gift," she whispered, studying him as he had studied her. He was lean, but not starving. She smelled a pleasant aroma of something he had cooked, or perhaps was cooking now. There were weapons on the wall — sword, bow, arrows, crossbow, spear, even a muzzleloader, and a carbine — all beautiful pieces, old and well cared for. He was no pauper. She shook her head. "A gift. It's just food."

"I will give you a gift then — in exchange."

"I don't need a gift," she said. "Is my father Sithé?"

"Your father carries the blood of the Mac Clæúds. His blood is mixed with those who don't have magic in them. But the blood is still strong — they were a strong clan."

"Was my mother Sithé?"

"A Mac Nessa. A little of the magic, a lot of the sight. Your mother was strong with the sight."

"What is 'sight'?"

"The inner eye. The vision that sees into the dark places — the spirit world, the inside of a man. The eye that looks on the power of the world that lies beneath the material surface. That is sight."

"Like yin and yang, sort of. Or some kind of yoga thing."

"What is that?" he asked.

"Beliefs from cultures halfway around the world from here. From the place the Totem Clans maybe came from originally."

"Those are not terms familiar to me. The Totem Clans did not teach this thing — yin-yang-yoga — to the Sithé."

She chuckled.

"Those traditions came long after the land bridge was covered with water. I think, when your ancestors came here, and then when the brown people you call Totem Clans came, the world was colder. Groups of people got hungry and traveled further for food. They could cross to this continent over the ice. It was a time when cultures and tribes got scattered away from their original homes. More formal beliefs — religions, philosophies — came later, to explain things that could not be explained."

He gazed at her thoughtfully. "You have thought about many things in your short life, Willa MacLeod. You are wise for such a young woman. Perhaps you also have the sight of the Mac Nessa."

"I'm not so young," she said defensively.

"How old is 'not young'?"

"Wow! That's a hell of a question. I'm twenty-six."

"And how would you think of me? Old? Or not so old?" He was laughing. The laugh lines broke the ancientness of his features and she thought he could almost be her father's age, or even younger.

She blushed to be caught in her own trap — he knew she thought he was old. She hesitated.

"I am more than ten times your not-so-young," Corwyn said gently.

That couldn't be true. She dropped her eyes so he wouldn't read her disbelief — tried to keep it from her thoughts in case he could read them.

"I have been hearing people speak when they aren't speaking. Hearing their thoughts, knowing their feelings," she told him quickly. "Ever since you touched me with your antler that day when I thought I was dreaming. Did you give me some sort of magic then?"

"I only awakened a small part of the magic you already have inside. I touched it awake so that you might see me truly and understand my words."

"The magic I have inside...." she whispered.

"It is probably very strong."

"I've never done anything magical. Well, other than write songs — which is a magic of sorts, I guess, but not really what we're talking about."

"You heard me call you. You searched for me here in the Silverhorn for years. You desired something from me. You did not kill me when you had the opportunity."

She stared at him. "It wasn't a dream. Your eyes were blue...."

"What did you desire, Willa MacLeod?" he asked.

"Blood," she said quietly.

"Why?"

"Legend says the blood of the Silverhorn Stag imparts power and life." She thought about what she was saying, and said the next with a touch of wonder: "And the touch of his antler gives insight."

"The legend is a little miss-said. To those who carry the Sithé blood, the blood of a full Sithé imparts power over the human nature. It is a thing carried in the blood — like a disease that runs in families. We must pass it to our offspring with our blood."

"They aren't born with it?" she asked, confused.

"Yes and no."

"I don't understand."

"A child is born with all the ingredients for being a Sithé. But the transfer of blood must pass the final spark. In ancient times, this was done as a rite of passage. There was an ancient term for Sithé who had not yet received the rite of passage: *Né Eùid Favayanna Sithénna*. That translates, roughly, as fawn-man or fawn-woman." He let her digest this for a moment. "Blood cries out to blood, kin to kin. You were compelled to seek this rite of passage from me because there is already magic in you," he said carefully. "What did you come here for, Willa MacLeod?"

She breathed out, dumbfounded. "Blood. Blood is the catalyst."

"Catalyst?"

"Like yeast to leaven bread. Or, like you said — a spark that lights a fire."

Corwyn nodded slowly. "I will give you this gift, if you want it, Né Eùissa Favayanna Sithénna. Fawn-woman."

Her heart was hammering irrationally. Her hands trembled.

"Do you wish it?" he asked.

The pulse jumped in her throat. "Is it a vampire thing?" she asked, feeling unreasonably frightened.

"What is a vampire? It frightens you, I can tell."

"An undead guy who sucks a person's blood. Then the person who gets sucked turns into a vampire and they have to suck more people's blood to survive."

He laughed. "A *Ba-gétharra sithéevæ*. We have legends of those, too. So did the Totem Clans."

He turned his palm up on the table. There was a scar across it, like a forked antler.

"This is much simpler. No one dies, and we can both continue eating your oat cakes. It is a gift that gives in both directions," Corwyn said.

"What does that mean?"

"It will help you to cross the creek when the water is high, and do many other things. In return, I will know more of you."

She tried to read his expression, to see any deceit in him.

"You came to me, Willa MacLeod," Corwyn reminded her.

She turned her palm up on the table. The tiny diamond in her nose flashed in the lamplight.

"Yes," she said. The pulse in her throat leapt like a deer.

"It is nothing to fear," he assured her. He took the amulet from his neck. When he pulled it apart, he held a miniature dagger with a handle of deer horn that had fit neatly into an ornamented sheath. Corwyn drew the blade across his palm. The blood welled quickly and flowed onto the table.

"Fell omens and demon-gods," he muttered, closing his fist quickly.

"What?" Willa asked, frightened.

"I am nervous," he admitted. "I have only given the gift once before now, in all the years since I received it from my father. I cut myself too deeply."

She relaxed.

"Perhaps you should handle the blade," Corwyn said with chagrin.

"No," she said, and pushed her hand, no longer trembling, closer to him.

Carefully he made a cut across her palm. It burned like fire but made only a thin red line.

"That was better," he muttered, with obvious relief.

He took her hand in his own bloody one, and closed them together palm to palm. He held her hand tightly within his — blood seeped from between their fingers. She couldn't take her eyes from the quarter-sized gem of their blood that glistened on the table. She felt strange. The light wavered oddly. She glanced up at Corwyn. Tears ran down his face.

"Oh my god," she said. "Are you hurt?" She tried to pull away, but he held her there.

"No," he answered softly. "I have just been alone for a long time. Wait."

Suddenly Willa felt sleepy. She yawned. Corwyn let go of her hand then, and stood up. He put on his coat. He clutched his hand tightly in a fist. She stood up too, feeling oddly woozy. In the lamplight, the stark red of his blood dripped from his fist onto the floor, splashing into a brilliant flower. She reached into her pocket and pulled out her bandana.

"Let me see that," she said. When he unfolded his fist, she wrapped the bandana tightly around the wound. She staggered against him, dizzy. Corwyn steadied her.

"I have to take you back now," he said urgently. "Or you will have to stay here for many days."

"They would call out the troops. That might not be a good thing."

The antlers appeared first, like a silver crown circling his brow. The brush of air touched her, and the bells chimed softly. Corwyn's image wavered and became softer, the edges blurred . . . and the Silverhorn Stag stood beside her.

Can you hold on? he asked.

She climbed onto his strong back and wrapped her arms around his neck. It all seemed a strange dream. In just a few strides, he took them quickly from the warmth and soft glow of the lamps and firelight to the brilliance of the day outside. *Not the way we came*, she thought.

Not the way we came, he agreed. They plunged downward. The cold bit like daggers and she was exhilarated. She heard the water, a distant voice that came and went. Everything moved dreamlike, became shadows and light. The long fur of Corwyn's neck was musky against her face, and the bells rang wildly.

They stopped. She looked around; they were beside the four-wheeler beneath the fir tree at the trailhead. Corwyn changed so quickly that when he stood beside her as a man, her arms were still around his neck. He held her so she wouldn't fall.

Irrationally, believing for a moment that she was dreaming after all, she pulled his head to hers and kissed him. She felt his surprise, felt him stiffen and try to draw away, but she locked her fingers and resisted, tasting his mouth with hers, tasting him until his resistance melted and he returned her kiss with his own fierce hunger. The fire in him echoed her own. The wolf fur of his coat brushed her face. Her blood sang. She would never let him go, never wake from this incredible dream. She wanted him — his scent and his taste flooded her reeling senses.

Corwyn finally drew away, holding her at arm's length.

"You must go back now," he said firmly.

"No, no, no!" she objected. Every fiber in her was alive, glowing with heat, and she wanted him with every molecule.

"It is the passage. Young women usually receive the rite from their mother or one of the sisterhood," he whispered against her ear. "Then when the fever takes them, they are not so much like a young buck in rut." He chuckled.

"Lusty, you mean?" Her intensity dissolved. She was so dizzy now, and the meadow was a blur of color.

"The fever will pass," he said. He put her on the four-wheeler.

"How do you make this thing go?" he asked. She turned the key and pressed the green button. It tried to start.

"I have to hold the gas lever, I think," Willa said, confused. "I don't remember where."

He repeated what she had done and moved his hands over the various levers and buttons until the engine caught and revved. He pressed her hands to the handlebars.

"You can do this. You must go home right now. Sara Blackhawk will know what to do."

"Corwyn," she pleaded. "Don't leave me."

"I will not leave you, Willa MacLeod," he promised. "I have been alone too long."

I remained true to the hope Morrīgan gave us
when we cast our fate upon the water.

WHEN THE MUSIC CHANGED

If not for Sara Blackhawk's firm insistence that the fever would pass, Ronan MacLeod would have called the paramedics. When Willa staggered in through the kitchen door, she was so hot that Sara put her to bed and draped her with ice compresses. She gave Willa feverfew tea and kept everyone out of Willa's room.

The band arrived to find Willa sick in bed and a firm cook-house-keeper-nurse guarding her door. Sara fed the band well and kept them away from her charge.

Ronan MacLeod didn't argue; he trusted Sara to make the right call with his daughter. Sara allowed him to sit with Willa for a little while on Saturday.

On Saturday night Regi came by the ranch with her husband, and, with Jeb as an extra guide and chaperone, ushered Willa's bandmates into town. A local band was playing at the Red-Eye Saloon. When everyone heard that the group sitting with Regi, Kenne, and Jeb were members of Blackwater, the party at the Red-Eye got wild. The local country band coaxed Chloe, Neil, and Jonesy onto the stage to play with them. A group of cowgirls brought their sights to bear on Sticks and Rincon, and it wasn't long before the two musicians were learning to swing-dance — reluctantly at first, then enthusiastically.

By Sunday morning, Willa was fever-talking and the band was sleeping off their hangovers in the bunkhouse — all of them, that is, except for Rincon, who didn't make it back to the ranch until late Sunday afternoon. Ronan was sitting with Willa, whose temperature had finally subsided a little, when he heard car doors slam and girls laughing.

Ronan got up painfully and went to look out the window.

"Who's that, Dad?" Willa asked hoarsely. Her eyes were still fever-bright.

"Some girls that Rincon picked up at the bar last night, I reckon — or maybe I should say they picked him up."

She heard the gruff disgust in her father's voice; apparently being around Rincon for a day or two was enough for him to learn to thoroughly dislike the guy. She sensed that her dad's pain had lessened and that he was feeling better. He wasn't hung over.

"They're just now bringing him back," he added.

"Good," she sighed. "He's staying busy."

Her dad laughed. "I'll say."

"You remembered his name," she said.

"Yeah. Always did. How are you feeling?"

"Strange. Awful. How long have I been out of it?"

"Since Thursday night."

"What day is it?"

"Sunday," Ronan replied.

"Where's Corwyn?" she asked, already feeling drowsy again.

"Who's Corwyn?" he asked in return. Willa felt his sudden fear — it reminded her of when he saw the bell she had brought home from the Silverhorn.

"The Heart of the Wind," she mumbled, and went back to sleep.

When Sara came in, Willa was sound asleep.

"Who's Corwyn?" Ronan asked.

"Corwyn who?" Sara replied.

"Willa woke up and asked about him. I just wondered if you knew him."

"Don't know a Corwyn," she said carefully.

On Monday, Regi came and sat with Willa. Willa asked for coffee, and, relieved, Sara brought in a pot for them to share. "Do you think she has some pie, too?" Willa asked — just as the door swung open and Sara returned, carrying a tray with three pieces of huckleberry pie.

When Willa picked up her fork, the line across her palm showed vivid red. Quickly, she closed her hand.

"You cut yourself on something," Sara said. "We worried it was infected, but the cut healed overnight."

"She must have picked up the flu or something at the hospital," Regi said.

"Didn't seem like flu...." Sara said.

Willa got the distinct impression Sara was deliberately hiding her thoughts. *How does she do that?* Willa wondered, following the woman with her eyes.

"The idea you might have something contagious kept the band members from bugging you, though," Regi winked at Willa.

Willa's eyes dropped to her plate. Regi choked on her pie.

"You know what this fever is," Regi accused.

Willa wouldn't look up.

"What? Is it some secret?" Regi scolded. "You almost die and we don't get filled in?"

"I didn't 'almost die'!"

"106 is a pretty scary temperature."

"Maybe she doesn't want to explain," Sara said.

Slowly, Willa's gaze met Sara's. *Story Keeper eyes*, she thought. She felt Sara Blackhawk go very still inside. *She sees into a person.*

"Who is the heart of the wind?" Sara Blackhawk asked her.

"Corwyn," Willa answered softly, hearing bells.

Regi gaped, and Sara took a slow breath.

Willa felt the pull of her friends' need for an explanation.

"The Silverhorn Stag," she whispered. "Hart of the Wind." She heard Sara's inward sigh.

"Baloney," Regi said. The sense of waiting evaporated.

"Okay," Willa replied.

"It's nonsense."

Willa didn't utter a word. She resisted the urge to look at her hand.

"Sara, tell her that it's nonsense!"

Sara flashed Regi a strange look.

"There isn't really such a thing," Regi continued.

No one spoke.

"Sara. It's only a legend! Isn't it?"

Willa felt Regi's fear for her. "You told me once that the blood samples of deer taken in the Silverhorn were different from any other deer population in the United States — some allele, or gene tag, or something, that made them unusual."

"There's an unusual allele among the deer in Willits, California too," Regi said slowly. "Makes them all white. The gene in the Silverhorn deer isn't a color gene like that — it's something much stranger. I'm not a genetics expert, I'm a habitat specialist — but I took the required genetics classes, and I've read the test data. The Silverhorn genes look like they were hybridized from some other species."

"So are mine," Willa said.

Regi laughed. "No way. You're just weird. No way it's genetic."

Willa said nothing. She opened her hand. The scar was a livid line.

"What is that?" Regi asked. Willa knew that Regi was thinking about all the weird things Willa had always done, and starting to wonder if her strangeness really was genetic.

Sara took Willa's hand and examined the wound.

"It's a razor cut," Sara said. Willa sensed jubilation growing behind the woman's placid brown face and dark eyes, along with a horde of deeply-held secrets. Sara didn't let go of Willa's hand; she ran her fingers over the guitar-string calluses on Willa's fingertips.

"It was a knife, actually," Willa corrected. "A ceremonial knife made for exactly that purpose. It was a good cut — not too deep."

"Why would you cut yourself?" Regi asked.

"I didn't. I would have botched it, I'm sure. Corwyn was careful with me, because he'd cut his own hand too deeply. It is the way one becomes blood-kin to the Sithé — the people legend calls the Silverhorn Stag. It's his blood that gave me the fever. I barely made it home — I don't remember anything after the knife cut, really." That wasn't exactly true, but she wasn't going to tell them that she had kissed a three-hundred-year-old man.

"I need to get up," she said. "I need to see the band. Have they been practicing, or just milling around in confusion?"

"A little of both, when they aren't eating or being entertained by someone. Even that pretty boy Rincon seems to be on good behavior — for him." Regi wanted to change the subject back — Willa felt her groping for leverage. "I ran into Jake Collins. He asked about you."

"How's their hunting going?"

"His dad got a huge deer over east in the Aspen Breaks. It'll be a record — Mr. Collins was pretty happy about that. And even though the regular season closed, they stayed on to help Jake's friend Nokes when the muzzleloader season opens in three weeks. They're all staying at King's motel. They eat at The Café every day and spend the days hiking — checking out the country."

"Nokes is a liar. I don't trust that guy. He better stay off this property."

"I told Jake we won't tolerate his friend's shenanigans. I told Nokes the same thing, but he wasn't listening. I don't think he has much respect for women. He's a cop, you know — but it's hard to imagine that he's a very good one. Let's hope he listens to his friend."

"Why are they friends, anyway?" Willa swung her feet around to the floor. Her head still felt woozy.

"Who knows? Maybe they grew up together, like us. Where are you going?"

"I'm getting up. I told you. Besides, I have to go vote tomorrow."

"What?" Sara asked her. "You didn't vote by mail?"

"Nah. I was too busy to send the card back. I have to take my dad anyway. He feels very strongly about voting in person."

"We're gonna have a Democrat for president, you know," Regi commented.

"I'm sure you're right. But the Republican will take Idaho — they always do." She turned at the bathroom door, remembering something.

Sara looked up as if she heard Willa's sudden dismay.

"My mother —" Willa began. "I have to tell my father that I know where she is . . . ."

"Where she is?" Sara asked. "Is she alive?"

". . . Where she's buried."

"Where is she buried?" Regi asked.

"In the catacombs way up in the mountain."

"There're catacombs in the mountain?" Regi asked with surprise.

Willa felt like she should cry, or feel something other than detachment, but there was too much distance between her and the vague memories of a dark-haired, laughing woman. The stone-cold face sleeping in granite on the mountain held no strong connection for her, just a distant sense of tragic loss. There were no tears for that sort of sorrow — just poetry.

"Now's probably not a good time. It's waited many years," Sara said. "It will wait a little longer."

"I want to know," Regi insisted.

"Later," Sara said firmly.

Willa walked into the studio and the music came to a ragged stop. They sounded pretty good — she wished they'd kept on playing.

"It's the hot chick!" Sticks joked.

"Not anymore," she said, grinning.

"Willa!" Chloe exclaimed. "Are you better?" She and Neil shied a little away from her.

"I'm fine. It wasn't anything catchy. I got a cut on my hand and it gave me a fever." She held up the hand to show them.

"Shit, girl," Rincon said, taking her hand and kissing the palm. "You gonna be able to play?"

"No problem. But I hardly do most of that, anyway. I can sing just fine." She drew her hand away, annoyed that he'd touched the scar.

"Good thing you didn't cut the tendon," Neil commented.

She sat down at the piano.

"I'm sorry I made you get behind here. I've been working on a couple of things." She played a few bars of music. "Here's a little something that I started thinking about last night. I only have one chorus, no verses yet. But I'll have it in a day or two. If any of you have any ideas, that would be great." She sang a few bars of a song — it had a bright bluesy rhythm.

> *It don't matter if the beat is slow*
> *And it don't have to be rock 'n' roll*
> *'Cause the pain is gone*
> *And I'm movin' on*
> *I got a brand new song*
> *I wanna sing that Southern soul.*

"That's all I have so far. I want it to be about music, and I would like the verses to move to blues in the beat and the lyrics. I'm sorry I don't have more yet. I woke up with this part in my head early this morning. I've been a little out of it for the last few days."

"I like it," Chloe said. "I may have some ideas. I'll work on them too."

"What else have you got, MacLeod?" Sticks asked.

"Something we can slow-rock. I'll play it." She played G-G7. "It's called 'Try a Little Smile'." She sang the song for them.

Baby I see you're hurtin',
That depression rides you hard.
Time to try a little smile —
Your hands and heart feel empty
And trouble's drawn your card.
Yeah it's time to try a smile.

If you can't see it, just wait a little while
You know, things on the outside don't always look so grand.
If you can manage, just try a little smile
You never know when it'll touch the inside of the man.

You know, every day don't send rain
And every day don't shine.
Still, baby's gotta smile —
Cause when you're done with your pain
You just might help with mine.
Now ya gotta try a smile.

If you can't see it, give it a little time
Sometimes the answers are hidden beneath the pain
If you can manage, just try a little smile
Before you know it, baby, you'll come up shinin' again.

A frown has tears that linger
Long after pain departs.
But you can help it with a smile
Cause a smile has magic fingers
That tug the corners of your heart
With just a little smile.

If you just can't see it, come on an' wait a little while,
You know, baby, it ain't so bad as it sometimes seems.
Just try it, try it,
Yeah baby try it
Once just try 'n' give it a little smile
It might surprise you baby yeah what a smile means.

If you can't see it, come on, come on come on
Come on wait a little while
Baby all that stuff on the outside may not look so grand.
All ya gotta do is try a little smile baby
It's gonna change ya baby,
Gonna change the inside of the man.

"Whoa, dude," Rincon said after she hit the last cord. "What is with all this nice-girl stuff? What happened to our edgy bad girl?"

"I told you. I want to rock it a little slow and bluesy on this album. I'm thinking of calling it 'Singin' Life Soully'. I want the theme to be about coming back from the edge of darkness by finding the soul in music — smooth and slow. We can get back to the hard and fast stuff next time. We have a few new songs that rock the edge, so it's not like we won't have any hard rock on it. I kinda hear the original Eric Clapton 'Layla' playing in my head these days. I want that sort of sound for some of these numbers. And some 'Black Velvet'-style Alannah Myles. Slow doesn't mean I don't have an edge, Rincon."

"It's like sex, dude," Sticks commented. "It's good both ways — hard and fast, smooth and slow."

Rincon gave the drummer a long stare, then licked his lips and looked at Willa.

"Smooth and slow, huh?" he asked slowly.

Willa sang a bar of throaty "whoa whoa oh oh oh oh yeah yeah".

"I can dig it," Jonesy said. "I think we could do that with that southern-soul piece."

"Yeah, Jonesy. That's a good idea." Chloe had her eyes closed as though she was working on something. "I'm liking sax for 'Southern Soul'. Violin and keyboard for the 'Smile' piece."

"I'm liking the name," Willa said. "'Southern Soul'. I'll use that as a theme and it'll help me with the rest of the lyrics. So let's see what else you have for the other stuff I gave you."

They worked long into the night. Rincon's resistance faded when he realized that some of the new material gave him good opportunities to draw out long, mournful solos. Finally, Willa said she was tired and went back to the house. She had just climbed into bed with her writing tablet when Rincon walked in through the unlocked French door.

"Hey baby. You been a little distant. You needin' some surfin' at Rincon's site?" He climbed up onto the bed and sat cross-legged. She pulled the comforter up.

"Rincon.... We aren't such a good match anymore."

"Oh come on, baby. You're so uptight. Loosen up."

"We had some fun times, but that's all. I'm needing something a little more solid now."

"Why don't you let Rincon work a little magic?" He took the tablet from her and kissed her neck. She felt absolutely nothing. What had happened? She scooted across the bed and got up. She went to the French door, opened it.

"Good night, Rincon."

"Willa, you gotta chill, woman."

"Good night, Rincon."

"You don't mean it. You're just playin' hard to get. I like that." He moved close and put an arm firmly around her waist.

"That's it. You're leaving." Willa pulled away. Rincon grabbed her arm and jerked her back.

Suddenly, Jeb was in the doorway. "Son," he said slowly. "If I'm goin' t'keep my promise to the lady not t'hurt your hands, you'd better take them off her right now and get to bed."

Rincon backed away, held his hands up.

"No problem, big guy. We were just talking."

"Yeah. I seen that kind of talkin' before. But it don't happen here, understand?"

"Yeah, no problem." Rincon eased past him and was gone into the night.

"Thanks Jeb," Willa said.

"Are you sure you don't want me to hurt him?" Jeb asked.

"He's harmless," she insisted.

"Yeah. That's just plum clear to me."

They went to the Grange Hall to vote. Her dad left his cane in Ramon. Captain MacLeod visited with some of his fellow veterans — most of them nearly twice his age — charmed the ladies until they were blushing, and proudly placed his "I voted" sticker on his jacket. Afterwards they went for lunch at The Café, where Regi joined them.

"Hey, Captain," Regi said, scooting in beside him and giving him a very big kiss. "How's my favorite war hero?"

"Alive, thanks to you, sweetheart," Ronan told her. "I don't believe I thanked you."

"Not today, anyway."

Brooke came over to take their orders. Sara came out from the kitchen, covered with flour.

"I see the slackers finally did their civic duty," she teased, pointing to the "I Voted" stickers.

"Yup, Sara. Voted for the war hero. We vets have to stick together. Right, Willa, honey?"

"I'm probably the only person in this county who voted against him," she admitted.

"You what?" Ronan said.

"Sorry, Dad. I like them young and tall," she quipped.

Captain MacLeod sent a pleading look around the group. "Do you think I got a changeling at the hospital twenty-six years ago?"

"Yeah, Captain, they must have mistaken her for yours because she looks just like you," Regi answered.

"She doesn't think like me, though," he protested.

"Is that so...?" Sara asked. "I gotta get back to the pies. There'll be cranberry pear tart in a few minutes, if you're interested. And the beef pot pies are hot out of the oven."

"Do you have a kidney and beef pie?" he asked.

"Sure do."

"I'll take one of those."

"Me too," Willa said.

"See, Captain?" Regi said. "She *has* to be yours. No one else would eat that."

Jake Collins came in, alone this time.

"Sit with us, son," Captain MacLeod told him as he walked toward the counter. Collins slid in beside Willa, who glared at her dad over her sunglasses.

"Take those off, honey," he said. "You don't have any crazed fans in here."

"What?" Regi said. "You actually have fans in Idaho?"

"She does, in fact," Collins said. He took the Blackwater CD from his jacket pocket. "Would you mind signing this for me, Ms. MacLeod? I don't want to be a bother . . . ."

Willa gave Regi and her dad a great big toothy grin. "I do so have crazed fans at the Café — see?" She signed the cover.

"Where's Nokes and your dad?" Ronan asked.

"Nokes is out hiking somewhere. Scouting. He said something about looking around south of here. Dad and I had a conference call, and now he's working on a proposal. He might have to go back to Boise."

Willa sensed the admiration for his father in the young man's mind — and for her own father as well. Jake had a nice energy, she thought, level and respectful. She could tell he was flattered that her dad had asked him to sit with them. She glanced at him: his dark hair was tucked behind his ears and he had a good jaw line, though he hadn't shaved recently. The green plaid shirt was a Pendleton. His watch was Swiss Army.

"What do you shoot?" Willa asked him suddenly.

She almost laughed at his quizzical expression.

"Do you carry a Browning, like Nokes?" she clarified.

"No. Nothing like that. I have a Ruger. An ought-six. It's plenty of gun for me. I really prefer bow hunting, but this year I knew Dad wanted to go, so I didn't go for a bow tag. He got lucky. I didn't need to shoot anything anyway. I like fly fishing. Been doing a bit of that."

"If you have time this afternoon, you could come out and hang out for our practice session. We're working on some new stuff and it's a little slow going, but you're welcome if you want," Willa said.

"I'd like that, thanks. What's good today?" he asked when Brooke handed him the menu.

"Try the kidney pie, son," Ronan MacLeod told him.

"I'll do that," he told Brooke.

"Gyahhh, ick," Regi said. "You guys are all nuts. I have to go to work. Tell Nokes to stay out of Silverhorn Canyon."

"I'll remind him," Jake said with a smile.

Time, endless time,
as the granite wears smoother,
and the water cuts deeper
and my heart grows colder
waiting for the Morrìgan's promise.

Coér Mac Vyn

FEVER DREAMS

Tales of the Morrìgan crushed our childish dreams with night-mare and flushed every dark shadow with creatures of dread. The Raven Queen was the goddess of the Sithé, enemy of men, the battle goddess who slew kings for pleasure. It was she who severed the Sithé's ties to the Lia Fáil and wrenched the people from their ancient home to send them across the vast ocean when ice covered the world. I met the Morrìgan when I was in my eighteenth summer.

Kellwyc and I climbed the crags, leaping blindly from stone to stone, daring each other to climb higher without looking. It was the game my brother and I loved most. We reached the high meadows and raced across the yellow grass until our breath burned in our chests and we slowed, changing shape as we stumbled to the wet earth, laughing. A dark shadow fell across us then, and we went silent. The coldness of that shadow crept into our bones. A figure that bristled with armor stood against the sun, so that our eyes were blinded when we tried to look at it. The figure held a weapon in one hand, and fear clouded my breath. But it wasn't a Clan warrior; the weapon was a sword, and the figure was crowned with Sithé antlers.

We rolled to our backs; and only because we touched at shoulder and hip and our arms were locked did my brother and I not quiver in our terror.

Her voice cracked with terrible augury. "You are marked, Sithé," her raspy words declared in the language of the ancients.

Neither of us wanted to know which of us she meant, or how we were marked. I was too afraid to wonder.

"I hear your fear. You must face that fear or the Sithé will pass from this world."

The Morrìgan wore black armor ornamented with thorny vines and leaves. Two bristling ravens shaped the pauldrons on her shoulders, and a black cloak hung from their jeweled claws. The cloak was deeply cut at the hem, giving the impression of wing feathers when she raised her arms. Her gauntlets were spiked with tiny knives. She grasped each of us in turn in her spiny hand and dragged us to our knees. The cold metal dug painfully into my shoulder.

Her sword reached out and touched each of us; I felt the burning where the razor edge cut my cheek below my eye.

She raised the sword like a torch and her form grew, the horns on her head curling up and twisting into nightmare. "You will be the last Sithé," she said, her voice thundering like storm. Lightning cracked from a sky suddenly grown dark and blazed down the sword in worms of witch-fire.

"Face your fear or die, Sithé," she growled. Her shape was no longer remotely human. The half-shift she shaped was far worse than any nightmare I'd dreamed.

"When all hope is gone and you, the last, are alone, a child of the Sithé will come to the Silverhorn. You must have faith, beyond hope, beyond sorrow, beyond dream; you must wait. Your solitary life will linger like an omen, or a promise yet unkept. If you are not there when the Sithénna climbs Silverhorn Canyon, her soul will shatter and there will be no more Sithé in this world."

Soon thereafter, white men drifted to the mountains, and then more came, and more, battling with factions of the remaining Clans that split and dwindled into warring tribes. The fractured tribes turned on us in fear — except for the Story Keepers, who kept secret our sanctuary in the mountains. Neither Kellwyc nor I took a mate. Kellwyc was killed by a white hunter when he was one hundred and fifty summers. It was then that I knew the Morrìgan's prophetic words were meant for me. The older Sithé diminished; the young Sithé dwindled or drifted away, leaving the sanctuary for the changing human world. Despite the Morrìgan's warning, I could not shake my fear.

I began to visit New Britton, drawn there by human voices. The laughter of children drew me to the school, and for a little while I found comfort and warmth with the lonely school teacher. Then even she was gone. The voices of the clan faded like fires burning out; the last few bled away — killed by hunters, or just fleeing our dying world.

I was alone so long that I forgot the sound of human voices, forgot the words of humans. I met the new Mac Clæúd when he was younger; he was haunted, yes, but not driven by obsession as a Sithénna would be. He recognized me then, and took up the watch in his turn. I knew he watched. I felt him listening and waiting. I often longed to speak to him, but something stopped me.

Megan Magnes came to MacLeod Ranch when she was barely twenty, the young bride of Ronan MacLeod. The magic she sensed in the young captain and in the staggered cliffs of Silverhorn Canyon burned in her. Like the women she was descended from, Megan had a restless spirit and she could find no peace. She was haunted and obsessed — driven by the blood need of the Sithénna.

And I wondered whether and how she could be the one, for she was married and already carried a child. I wondered and watched, hearing the burning within her, and was haunted by her unfulfilled craving until it became an ache that cut my every breath. One day I could stand it no longer, and I appeared on the trail in front of her, touched her with an antler, and changed shape. When I touched her, she found the peace she sought; the sight of the Mac Nessas is very strong and needed very little to trigger clarity. It was I who gained unexpected insight: Megan was not the Sithénna of the Morrìgan's prophecy. When I touched Megan MacLeod, I heard the voice of the one I waited for.

From the Journal of Coér Mac Vyn

I have slept the dark sleep of loneliness
I have held nothing against my heart.
The emptiness is worse than death
There is no greater sorrow than an empty heart.

Coér Mac Vyn

THE MAN OF THE SILVERHORN

When the fever left him, Corwyn descended the canyon and crossed Silverhorn Creek. He could smell that the hunter had been in the canyon again, so out of precaution he walked the trail as a man. He stood beneath the fir tree at the trailhead for a while. There was no one nearby. Cautiously, he moved to the small rise where he could look down on the MacLeod dwelling. Usually a sithénna did not have to make the blood passage without guidance; he was torn between his need to return to the safety of the granite and his worry that Willa might need him.

She has a Story Keeper to help her, he told himself. He watched until the stars were hard and thick. The scent of her was on the fur of his coat; he ran his hand down the fur, bringing it to his face and breathing it in. One by one the house lights went out. He tried to sense her; he called her name in his heart. He heard someone coming then, but it wasn't Willa. He changed shape, and in just a few bounding moments returned to the granite fortress above Silverhorn Canyon. If she came to him again, he would not be able to send her away.

Jake Collins went back to the motel early to watch the election results with his father. He wasn't the guitarist that Rincon was, but apparently the band liked him. He'd figured out the sound board very quickly, and they taught him some of their songs so he could play along with them. Rincon sulked over it; he disappeared for a while, then came back in a better mood — which improved even more after Collins left. The band members watched the Republican candidate's concession speech and then continued their practice for another hour or so.

Willa finally left the studio and walked to the house. Sara had turned the lights in the house down and left a pie on the kitchen counter. Willa found her father asleep in his big chair, with Sunny keeping his lazy vigil on the floor at her father's feet. A half-empty beer bottle was on the table, but she sensed that her dad was sober. Apparently the new pain medication was doing some good. She wondered why Jeb hadn't put him to bed already. Ronan had been watching a movie; the Netflix menu was still on the screen. She turned the Netflix and the big screen off, woke him up, and made him go to bed. Sunny got up on the bed beside him.

"Why are you so good to your useless old man?" her dad grumbled.

"Because I love you," she said.

"Good movie, that Iron Man," he muttered as she pulled the down comforter over him.

"Yeah? I'll have to watch it."

"You need a better man than that egotistical pretty-boy guitarist."

"Shall I stay here with you?" she teased.

"Damn it, Willa. I'm going to have Jeb do this every night from now on."

"What? And deprive me of one of the few pleasures I get with a man?"

"Jake Collins is a nice young man."

"I would have to agree with you on that, even though I would rather not."

"I think he likes you," Ronan said.

"I think he likes you," she countered.

"Who is Corwyn?" he asked suddenly.

She didn't answer; she wasn't sure what to say. Her father took her arm.

"Who is Corwyn?" he insisted.

She stared at him.

"Do you know what a Sithé is?" she asked. The wild race of his pulse said that yes, he knew.

"Willa. There are some things best left alone."

She heard secrets in him, and saw someone she never knew stare out of his eyes.

"Willa," he pleaded, "it was long ago. We left that ancient life. We have another life here."

She opened her hand and showed him the line across her palm.

"Not for me," she said.

Her dad's terrible sorrow struck her. Tears welled in his ice-blue eyes. "He's a dangerous creature."

"He's a lonely man," she whispered. "A good man."

"Be careful, Willa. Please be careful. Please don't leave me." She heard this in an entirely different way than ever before: he was afraid for her life.

Willa set her half-written song aside and turned off the light. The darkness was not as dark as it used to be — she could see almost as though it were dusk. She heard a mouse in the wall. She'd have to get Jeb to put out poison again. She closed her eyes.

She dreamed that Corwyn stood on the hill above the house. He called her name. "Willa" echoed in her room as if he had spoken.

The clock said she had only been asleep for a few minutes. She threw off the comforter and got up, pulling on her black Thermawick leggings and a soft turtleneck sweater. She found her boots in the closet — the tall Uggs with the fur side in and a good walking tread. She put on her down coat and her knit cap with the braids on the ear flaps.

She picked up her heavy backpack and took it into the kitchen, where she made a fresh pot of coffee and put the pie Sara had made into a Tupperware pie-taker. She made some sandwiches and put everything in the top of the pack with a bottle of apricot brandy. When she put the pack on, she groaned.

Sticks was sitting on the hill above the house, smoking a joint. Willa scared him badly when she came up the hill in the dark.

"Shit, Willa," he yelled. 'What the fuck are you doing?" He was bundled in a heavy coat.

"Taking a walk," she said as she sat down beside him. 'What are you doing?"

"Just thinking. It's nice out here."

"Yeah, it is."

"Don't see stars like this very often. There was a big buck on the hill when I walked up here."

"Ahhh."

"How the hell did you grow up here and become so different from all these red-neck local girls in their cockroach killers?"

"I guess I'm just not like everyone else."

"No shit," he said with feeling. Willa knew that he liked her a lot, but she sensed that he was also a little afraid of her. They'd been friends a long time; he was the oldest member of Blackwater, and had been with her the longest. He offered her the joint. "Want some?"

"No thanks, Sticks."

"Rincon's pissed off. Letting that Collins dude come to practice set him off."

"I don't care," she said, a little tightly.

"Hey, you know something? Rincon can really shred. But we don't need him. If you don't want him around anymore, no one in the band's gonna get twisted over it. That Collins dude, he's straight money, but he could learn our stuff. He's got some chops. It ain't about the dude on the guitar, really. It's about you, and if you're done log-rolling with Rincon, give him his ticket."

"Logrolling. Is that what it was?"

"Come on, Willa. You never really dug the dude; you just liked hittin' the skin with him, and he likes livin' large. We all knew that. If it were me, I'd kiss his ass bye-bye."

"Are you sure you all would be down with that?"

"Oh, sister. We know who brings in the clams in this outfit. Rincon doesn't have the props for that like we do. He'll land on his feet with some warm-up band and they'll get some headliners off him. That is, if you're done playin' doctor with him. Seems like you've been done with that for a while."

"Yeah. I have." He offered her the joint again, but she waved it away.

"Hey, I didn't mean any offense. You're the elephant's instep as far as I'm concerned."

"None taken. Thanks."

"Somethin's been on your mind. Chloe says you're just not feeling well."

"I'm okay."

"You sure? Hey man, if you're lonely or wanta hook up, I'm always here. No strings, woman." She knew this was truth.

"I know, Sticks. But I'm cool."

"That Collins dude digs you. He's kinda your style."

"Thanks for the advice."

He saw the pack. "You goin' somewhere?"

"Yeah, I am." She stood up and brushed the grass off. "I might be gone for a day. Work on that song, okay?"

"The Silverhorn number? Dude, that's a weird song.... But it's gonna sell to the chicks."

"It kind of reminds me of that one by Alannah Myles, 'Family Secret' — or maybe 'Wildfire', the Michael Martin Murphy song."

"Uh-huh. You're a strange chick, Willa — you know that?"

"No one knows better than I do," she laughed.

"Hey, man. Is the Silverhorn where you're going? Is that for real?"

"Sticks.... There are some things even my best drummer doesn't need to know."

"Dude. Is that magic stuff for real?"

"How stoned are you right now?" she asked.

"Pretty fucking stoned."

"I want to try some magic."

"You're fucking with me now because you know I'm stoned."

"Maybe. But maybe I'll blow your mind. Don't tell anyone if I do, okay?"

"Hey woman, we've been tight for years. We've always been straight with each other."

"I know that, Sticks. That's why I trust you. Keep the band busy. Now, tell me if this works."

She thought about Corwyn. She pictured the ancient amulet on the cover of the book, with its circle of horns. The horns swirled in her mind, a living, pulsing symbol. She smelled the sting of pine on the slight breeze. She remembered the scent of him, of the Sithé, when her face was pressed against the fur of his neck. She felt the wind; it swirled around her legs and caught up tiny leaves and dry grass. It brushed Sticks' hair and flared the joint in his hand. A tiny ember circled up and away. She felt the wind in her blood, wanted to race it. Her heartbeat quickened.

"Shit," Sticks exclaimed. "It's working, whatever the fuck it is . . . ."

Willa lowered her head and carefully touched him with the tip of her antler.

"You're freakin' white!" he said, astonished.

Fire Rincon for me.

"Sweet," he said, as she bounded away.

She followed Corwyn's scent, tasting it in her mouth. It was recent and clear, like a line of light through the dusky woods. It took minutes to reach the creek above the bend; last week it had taken more than an hour. Each bound sucked the wind around her and burned like fire in her veins. She leaped down the slope. She held her breath as she cleared the creek, but it went beneath her as though it was nothing. She drew in the smell of him. Each bound took her higher up the east side. She entered the high cleft in the stone, and her eyes adjusted quickly to the sudden darkness. There was a small lamp flickering in an alcove; it gave just enough light to guide her down the corridor.

When she entered his chamber, Corwyn had risen from his pallet and faced the doorway. The room was warm, but the fire had burned low. He clasped the fur throw around his waist. Golden light flickered off his upper body; his eyes were heavy with sleep and his long hair was mussed. It seemed less silver in the dim lamp light.

"You're white!" he said, shocked.

Am I?

She thought about having two legs, not four, and was suddenly standing on them. She took off the heavy backpack, stripped off her boots and coat, and dropped them beside the pack. Feeling a little strange, she crossed the floor. There were skins beneath her bare feet. She stopped an arm's length from Corwyn.

"I've never seen a white Sithé," he commented.

"Maybe this will help," she said slyly.

She drew off her leggings, and then her sweater. He sucked in his breath.

"You have no undergarments," he said, surprised.

"It's called 'going commando'. How would you know about

undergarments, anyway?" She felt the cold on her breasts, felt them tighten. She began to shiver.

"I remember them as lacy and quite complicated, with buttons and hooks and ties."

"How long ago was that?" she laughed.

"More than a hundred years."

"Times have changed."

"Apparently."

He was speaking English. Modern English.

"How are you speaking this way?"

"I told you the gift of blood was a two-way giving. Was your fever very bad?"

"Pretty bad."

"I am sorry."

"Has it been more than a hundred years since you've been with a woman?"

He didn't answer. His eyes touched her everywhere.

"You are beautiful, Willa MacLeod," he said softly in his own language. "Like the moonlight. Like moonstones," he said in English.

His hair was wet and smelled of pine.

"I smell pine."

"It's the soap I make from pine sap."

"You bathed?" she asked, surprised.

"Don't men in your town bathe when they ask a woman to come to them?" She heard his heartbeat, felt his elevated pulse. She stepped closer.

"I don't know," she said.

She caught the musky man scent beneath the pine, and her own pulse quickened.

"You smell of mint," he said.

"Shampoo," she said mildly.

"And something foreign." His voice went husky.

"Black ginger soap. My favorite." He lowered his face to where her neck met her shoulder and breathed in.

"I like it," he whispered.

The heat of him touched her like hands. She panted slightly as the blood pulsed in her belly.

He let go of the fur throw. He was completely ready for her.

"You are beautiful," she breathed against his mouth. "Like silver." And she tasted the scent of him in her mouth, wanting all of him as he kissed her.

He pulled her down onto the furs. When he would have gone slowly, she wouldn't let him. She grasped him to her and snaked her long legs behind his, pulling him in, all of him, all the way.

His extraordinarily strong arms held her tightly against him and he moaned. He touched the inside of her like fire, and she cried out with an instant and unexpected climax. He buried his face against her hair and cried out. She felt the hot throb of his seed as it spilled from him.

"Oh gods," he whispered.

She felt his warm tears on her cheek and neck, and her own eyes welled up and tears slipped down the side of her face.

Corwyn held her like he would never let her go, his chest heaving with emotion. "I'm sorry," he muttered against her ear. "It's been so long. I would have gone slower."

"Why?" she asked. "Now we have plenty of time for next time." Neither of them moved; she thought she could die then and there in his arms, with his face against hers and his tears in her hair.

She woke sometime later when he moved.

"I have to go outside," he apologized.

"Jeez, don't you have indoor plumbing?"

"Turn right — next room."

She found it. The running water was warmed by the ashes from the fire. There was a bathtub against the other wall, some dark decorated metal thing that looked ancient.

She took the bottle of brandy from her pack.

She found two small silver cups near the water basin and brought them back to bed with her. Corwyn's arms came around her and she leaned into his embrace with a sigh.

"What is this?" he asked when she handed him a cup.

"A fine spirit for a fine celebration." She downed hers in one swallow.

He did the same and coughed with surprise at the heat of the brandy. She filled each cup again.

"To the strange and wonderful things I have found in my world," she said, and touched his cup with hers.

"To the beautiful thing that has come to my world," he said, and drank — this time without coughing.

She refilled their cups.

"To you, Willa MacLeod, who have filled my loneliness with your presence."

"To you, Coér Mac Vyn, who have given me the gift of yourself."

He went much, much slower this time.

Later, she awoke cradled against his heart. He must have known the moment she woke — he stirred at her back and kissed her ear, her neck, her shoulders. His hands cupped her breasts, felt them go hard against his palms. He responded in much the same way.

"Some things cannot be explained," he whispered against her ear.

"Like what?" she asked sleepily, snuggling into the cup his body made against her back, feeling his desire.

"That such a simple thing as a hand against a breast can stir so many things. That a woman can make a man both hard and soft at the same time. Now I will show you what a Sithé does when he is aroused." He moved her leg over his.

When Corwyn rose from the pallet the next time, Willa muttered in protest. She opened one sleepy eye when he touched her cheek. He changed from man shape to stag as she watched.

Come with me, Corwyn asked her. Bells chimed softly.

White Hart and Silver Stag, they ran across the snow in the high peaks until their breath came hard and sharp. When he stopped and turned to shake his antlers playfully at her, she asked foolishly, *I'm female. Why do I have antlers?*

It is the way of the Sithé, he answered. *It is part of why we were worshiped and now are hunted.*

The sudden fear made her change shape. She stood naked in the snow, shivering, until he changed shape beside her and wrapped her in his arms.

"I'm sorry I frightened you," he said. And she drew him down with her into the bitter snow. Then, after he had cried helplessly to the mute stars, she changed shape again and raced him until, breathless and with thundering hearts, they tumbled into his chamber and slept the rest of the morning away.

She awakened to find him watching her.

"Don't you ever sleep?" she muttered.

"I've slept alone for so long, I don't want to waste my moments with you on sleep."

She sat up. She pushed him down. When he reached for her, she shook her finger at him.

"No touching," she said wickedly. "My turn to show you what a rock star can do. You are not allowed to touch."

No man had ever fulfilled her as he did. He shuddered and moaned hoarsely when he was spent, and she finally let him hold her as she called his name over and over.

When she got out the pie and the sandwiches, he closed his eyes in ecstasy.

"Do I look as though I don't eat?" he asked with a laugh.

"No. I'm paying for your services with food."

He glanced up, startled, saw the mischief in her expression, and sighed.

"Your humor is — unabashed. I will have to get used to your unusual manner."

"'Unabashed'. I haven't heard that word since I read Jane Eyre. That's an old book, by the way, written back when women wore underwear like what you described."

"What would be a better word?"

"'Frank'. 'Frank' is unabashed, nowadays. 'Honest' might work. 'Unaffected', maybe."

"I will work on it."

"Where did you see underwear with hooks and buttons?" She cut the pie and looked around for a plate. He got up and handed her two plates — old silver pieces.

"I used to go to New Britton occasionally, before my brother was killed, and when there were still a number of us. There was a woman there. She was a teacher. She was smart and charming, but very lonely."

"What have you done since then?" She put a sandwich and a piece of pie on his plate and passed it to him. She got out the coffee.

"Done? What do you mean?"

"Physical needs. A Sithé has those, doesn't he? How do you satisfy the needs a man has?"

He actually blushed. He looked down at the plate.

"A man can take care of his physical needs by himself," he muttered. Then he raised his eyes to her face. "But he cannot fill his heart by himself."

"So what you're saying is that really, I'm not beautiful — I'm just all you've had in a hundred years."

"You're twisting my words. Or is my English wrong?" His expression was confused.

"No, you're English is fine. I'm messing with you."

He tried the pie, tried another bite. "Huckleberries? This is heaven, surely."

"Well. I was thinking heaven came earlier and this was just dessert."

"Are all women now like you — unaffected?"

"They're different nowadays, yeah, but not really like me. I'm worse, my dad says."

"Did you ask him about the Sithé?"

"Yes."

"What did he say?"

"He didn't have to say anything. His heart rate and the fear in him said enough."

"We met, when he was a boy."

"That's how he knew you."

"Yes. What is that black stuff?"

"Coffee. Want some?" She passed the thermos cup. He tasted it, made a face.

"It smells better than it tastes." He tried the sandwich. "And what is this?"

"Salami and cheese."

"It's good."

"Everything tastes good after sex," she said.

"Is that something you do often?" he asked.

"Which — fucking, or eating afterwards?"

He caught his breath. "Isn't that a bad word? I know how it would translate, and I wouldn't tell you. What I meant was, is speaking your mind something you do often?" He saw the horror on her face. She blushed this time, but recovered quickly.

"I'm sorry," she said. "I will have to work on my 'unaffected' humor, too. I forgot you're an old guy and might be easily offended by my youthful language." She danced away when he reached to catch her.

She rummaged in her backpack and pulled out an iPod. She found the latest recording of Blackwater and put the headset on him.

"Can you play it again?" he asked after a few minutes. She showed him how it worked. She used the time while he listened to study him. He looked younger, his hair a little darker. The hair down his chest was more black than silver.

"Is this you?" he asked.

"Yes."

"It is very rhythmic and wild. Oddly melodic for as rough and strident as it sounds. The slow song, the ballad about the stars, is haunting and sad. Are you always sad? Did someone hurt you?"

"I've always been like that. Sad things are cumulative — fodder for my creativity. I've had a few affairs that weren't great, but I've never fallen in love with anyone, so I've never had my heart broken. I love my dad — that's different. I love Regi and Sara." She told him about her friends.

"It is good to have a strong sisterhood," he commented.

"Why is your hair darker? What did you do?"

He held up his scarred palm, which was still healing. "You have shared with me some of your young magic. You wouldn't want to have to..." He paused. She knew what he wanted to say. "... To lie with an old guy," he finished lamely.

She blushed again. She stood there, gazing at him. He was so forgiving. She fell in love with him that moment.

So he wouldn't see her expression, she picked up the pie and set it near the water basin. He took her wrist, pulling her to the table. He brushed the plates onto the floor.

"I've seen that look — my mother looked at my father like that," he whispered. "I only have one answer for it." Slowly, and methodically he showed her that he was not such an old guy after all.

I lived with the myth, and lived by the myth
until the myth became
the never-ending story of my life.

RM

LOOKING
FOR WILLA

H er cellphone rang — Regi's ring, "She's A Lady". Willa
stared at it. She was still amazed that it worked up in
Silverhorn Canyon.

"What is that?" Corwyn asked.

"A plastic shackle," she growled. "One of the wonders you have
missed living up here alone like Howard Hughes. A very serious
waste of time, more often than not."

"What does it do?

"Keeps me in touch with my sisterhood," she grumped, and
accepted the call. She put it on speakerphone.

"Regi — "

"Willa!" Corwyn started at the sound of Regi's voice. "Where are
you? Your dad called here. You've been gone since last night. The
young guy's president."

"I heard that before I left, Regi. No one's surprised."

"Sticks said you went for a walk."

"Was that all he said?"

"Mostly. All that anyone believed, anyway. I think he must have been stoned."

"He was."

"Where are you?" Regi wasn't giving up.

"Who's asking?"

"Willa, it's just me. Regi. Remember me? I'm the one that puts up with your shit."

"Is anyone there with you?" Willa asked.

"Yeah. Search and Rescue. The county Mounties. The governor. Hell no, Willa. Sticks told everyone you were fine, and everyone is pretending to believe him. Your dad is worried, though — I can tell. He started drinking this morning. Sara put a stop to it — hid all the booze."

"Poor Dad."

"Are you okay, sweetie?"

"Yes."

"Where are you?"

"Raz. I'm fine. I'm better than fine." She smiled at Corwyn. "No one needs to worry. And no one needs to know where I am. After all, a girl can have a secret tryst now and then."

"Dang rock-girl. Are you with a guy? Who? Jake Collins?"

She didn't answer.

"Willa?"

"Regi?"

"But Sticks said he saw you at the ranch."

Willa didn't answer. Regi's silence said that she was thinking. Then Regi said, "Oh God."

The silence dragged.

"Are you coming home?" she asked quietly.

"Maybe. If you leave me alone for a while," Willa said, in a voice that Regi was more familiar with.

"Willa, go ahead and turn off your phone. I'll tell them you're fine, and they don't have to bother you with calls or messages."

Thoughtfully, Willa put her phone down on the table. Corwyn picked it up.

"If I had one of these," he said, "could I talk with you when you were somewhere else?"

"Would you want to?" she asked.

"Yes."

"I'll get you one."

"They are like magic."

"No, Corwyn. They are not magic. They are mostly a big waste of time."

"It seems things in the world have gotten very interesting."

"In some ways," she agreed. "Communication by telephone started back when women still wore the sort of underwear you remember. These things are everywhere in the world I live in now, and there is no magic there. The only magic I have ever known is you, and the secret of the Silverhorn. I suppose there is other old magic some-where in this big, confusing, scary world, but I don't know about it. All I know is this." She gestured around.

"What will you do with this paradox, Willa MacLeod?"

"I don't know. Would you come to my world, Corwyn?"

"I don't know that I could. Would you come to mine, Willa?"

"I already have."

"But you will leave."

"Yes."

"Will you come back?"

"How could I not?"

"Are you afraid of the magic?"

"No. But my father is."

"You have not seen anyone die because of it."

"Are you afraid of the magic, Corwyn?"

"Yes."

"Now I am afraid."

"Come, my Moonlight. Come and lie with me and let me hold you against my heart that has been empty for too long. We have this moment. If we never have another, we have this. It is everything."

They finished the pie and the brandy for dinner. Then the White Hart and the Silver Stag raced across the snow of the high country, and climbed the Silverhorn Crags until their knees grew weak and even their thick deer hides could not keep out the cold. When they came back winded, shape-shifting in a swirl of snow, Willa heard again the bells in Corwyn's hair as he shook the frost from it.

"Why bells?" she asked, falling onto the furs of his bed, laughing as ice clattered to the floor from her hair.

He hesitated.

"Well?"

"It was something we always wore. So ancient humans would know a Sithé from a deer."

"Oh." She turned on her stomach.

Corwyn ran his fingers lightly down her body, stopping in surprise at the small of her back. He rose to his knees. "What is this?" he asked, touching the mark there.

"A tattoo," she replied.

"That is obvious. I have one. But do women have tattoos? It was once a warrior thing." He peered closely at it. The brush of his fingers made her shiver. She got goosebumps.

"It's the cool thing to do these days," she said. "But for me, it's a totem."

"It is a stag," he said softly.

"Yes. It's the Silverhorn Stag."

He kissed the spot. "Then it was you who called me," he said against her skin, "not the other way around."

"No. I was just answering, the only way I knew how."

"Here's another way, my Moonlight."

She emptied her backpack on the floor. She placed a box of granola bars on the table, along with a jar of almond butter and a package of crackers. Corwyn's expression was quizzical.

"You're too thin," Willa said, grinning. He stood up and turned around.

"Do you think so?" he asked.

She sucked in her breath. He was lean and well-muscled from all his years of climbing up the stones and racing across the snow; his waist was narrow.

"No," she purred. She took out two books. One was an almanac; the other was a collection of contemporary poetry.

"Here's some reading that might help you catch up."

"Who is Jake Collins?" he asked.

"He came with the other hunter I told you about, the one I caught in the canyon. He's kind of a nice guy, actually. Plays the guitar."

"Why would Regi ask if you were with him?"

"Probably because she thinks he would be good for me."

"Would he?"

"Maybe. If the circumstances were different."

"Who is Howard Hughes?"

"A wealthy guy who used his money for odd projects. He loved airplanes and women. He became a very weird recluse when he got old. They say he got frozen in a cryogenics lab when he died."

"You will explain that."

"It might be in the Almanac. You can read English, can't you?"

He nodded. "I was able to read your note, after the fever passed. Who is president?"

"A young senator from New Mexico is the first Native American president of the United States."

"Really? From the Totem Clans?"

"He's only like a quarter Native American, actually. But it's a big deal for some people. He's very eloquent and well-educated. I think the rest of the world will like him better than our last president. He reminds me a little of Thomas Jefferson — smart, worldly."

"What is this?" He held the turquoise cougar totem.

"A totem for good hunting. That's what the carver told me."

"Who is Sticks?"

"The drummer for Blackwater. He's been with me the longest of anyone in the band. He's kind of like one of the sisterhood, only he's a guy. I can tell him things I can't tell anyone else."

"Did you tell him about me?"

"Sort of. He gives me guy-type advice — like a brother. I changed in front of him, to see if I could. That's how I knew I was white as a Sithé."

She pulled a black sport bra and leggings from her pack and put them on.

"Is this underwear?" he asked, fingering them.

"Well, kind of."

"I think I liked the buttons and lace better."

"Corwyn," she laughed. "You are all man."

"I hope that is a good thing."

"Yes. It is."

"Not just an old guy, then?"

"Age has nothing to do with it."

She put on her leggings and sweater.

"It's my birthday the first week of December," she told him. "I'll be twenty-seven. I thought that was old."

Corwyn chuckled as he put on his fur coat.

"Is that wolf skins?" she said, feeling the coat. It was incredibly thick and soft underneath the guard hairs.

"They started coming back about twenty years ago, killing the deer and elk. Their pelts are very fine, don't you think? They are quite warm."

"You know, the wolves are protected here — you can get into big trouble for killing them."

"Why?"

"Because a lot of people in this country think all animals should be protected."

"Protected from what?"

"From people killing them."

"Why don't they protect the deer and elk?" he asked, incredulous. "Why would they protect a vicious predator?"

"I'm not sure. Maybe so that when there get to be too many stupid people, there will be enough wolves to eat their children."

"Well, Willa MacLeod, that's a bit on the bloodthirsty side. Do I detect a warrior's anger?"

She jerked on her boots and put on her coat. "People are ridiculous. The Indians were right: they speak with forked tongue." She rubbed the fur of his coat. "Hardly anyone makes fur coats anymore. It's considered uncool. They make fake ones instead."

Corwyn took a set of tiny bells from a box and wove them into her hair.

"You should wear these," he said. "They have a special magic. They will become part of you."

When they stepped out, it was snowing. They shape-shifted to cross the creek, and then changed back. Corwyn didn't think it was safe; he told her about the hunter's being in the canyon again.

"That Nokes is trouble," she grumbled. They walked in silence. The world was a hush of white. Their footfalls made no sound on the white trail, but left two pairs of tracks in the snow. There was no sound except for their breathing and an occasional bell chime. Their breath came white, like smoke.

"Will you come to the house?" she asked when they stopped on the hill.

"No," he said quietly.

"Will you ever come?"

"I don't know. Will you come back to me, Willa?"

"I'll get you a phone. I'll be back in a few days."

"It will feel like a hundred years."

When he kissed her, she tasted the scent of him; her throat closed and her eyes teared up.

"Good," Corwyn smiled. "It is already too long for you." He turned and went back, retracing their tracks in the snow.

She watched until the snow obscured him.

When Willa entered the house, the door blew open with a little extra force and the napkins swirled off the kitchen table. Sunny greeted her with his happy dog dance and then sniffed her all over. Ronan MacLeod sat at the table, and Sara was fixing breakfast. Willa removed the Tupperware and the thermos from the pack and placed them by the sink, poured herself a cup of coffee, and sat down. No one spoke.

"Why didn't he come down to the house?" her father finally asked.

"He is afraid," she said carefully.

"He is wise, then," Sara said. "I hear bells."

"They will chime a little," Willa said. and moved her hair for them to see them. "Nokes has been in the canyon again."

"God damn that man," her father cursed. "I'll have Jeb do patrols. We'll turn on the electric fence again." He looked closely at the bells. "Those bells can't protect you. You know it isn't safe. He is the last of his kind, Willa. It would be better to just let the legend die."

"You can't believe that," she said, stricken.

Ronan saw her expression and knew he was defeated. "No. I don't really believe that. I am just so afraid of losing you. We could move somewhere — somewhere people don't hunt deer."

"Move away from the Silverhorn? You know that he wouldn't leave."

"Your band members will be in for breakfast soon," Sara said. "Maybe you want to change?"

"Good idea." Willa stood up with her coffee and grabbed her backpack. "You look better," she told her dad.

"I had to stop drinking in case I had to go out and find you," he grumbled.

"Shall I get you a brandy to celebrate my safe homecoming?"

"There has never been a more irreverent, disrespectful child than you," he said with a laugh.

She leaned over and kissed him. "And there has never been a more handsome, brave dad," she said brightly.

She didn't want to wash the scent of Corwyn from her skin, but she took a hot shower anyway. She put on corduroys and a sweatshirt and went back to the kitchen.

"Willa!" Chloe said. "We were worried about you."

Sticks looked very pleased with life. "I told them not to worry, that you had a hot date."

Rincon did not look pleased, but he made an attempt at charm. "Sugar," he said, moving in when she refilled her coffee, "where ya been? I've been missin' you, girl."

"Rincon, get your hands off me."

"Aw, come on baby. Don't be like that."

"Back off," she snarled.

"Shit, dude. Don't get hostile."

"Rincon," she said, "do you like the music we play? That's what we do, remember? We're a band."

"I like some of it, but not all that slow, bluesy, country-sounding shit."

"Sticks, Jonesy? Do you like the music we play?"

Jonesy was startled. "Sure, Willa. I like it."

"You know I dig your stuff, woman," Sticks said. "Your tunes are otherworldly."

"What about you Chloe?"

"I love it! It's so much fun. I love it all. I feel privileged to be part of Blackwater."

"Me too," Neil said. "But I'm easy. I even like country."

"There you go, Rincon. What's wrong with this picture?" She heard what he was thinking and it made her even angrier.

"Did Sticks have a little discussion with you about it?" she continued.

"Yeah, man. He was saying I needed to find musicians I could lock with better."

"What do you think?"

"I think I like Blackwater."

"What if I told you I was going country?"

"No way, dude. You wouldn't do that."

"What if I did? Would you still like the music?"

"Naw. Country's not my thing."

"Well, we may not be going country, but we're slowin' it down a bit, going to get a little bluesy. I don't think you're a good fit for us anymore."

'Are you firin' me, Willa?"

"No, because Sticks already did that."

"Yeah, he was raggin' on me, man, but I wanted to talk with you. It would have been nice to do it alone."

"Then you shouldn't have acted like an ass in front my family, my friends, and my band. You put me on the spot, Rincon, and

I don't dig that. I don't dig that you have no respect. I don't need that from anyone. It's time for us to part ways. You're not a good fit for this band anymore. You need a younger group."

Jeb came in the back door and stood there, listening to the interchange with interest.

"What? You got some cowboy dude to ride now, so you're givin' me the mitten?"

Willa's dad stood up, his face like thunder. "Watch your mouth, son," he warned.

"Yeah, well where did your bitch daughter go for two nights, anyway?" Rincon continued. "Off fuckin' that Jake dude?"

Jeb came up behind Rincon, picked him up out of his chair, turned him around, and knocked him out cold with a hard right. He looked at Willa apologetically. "I didn't touch his hands."

"Get his things," Ronan told Jeb, "and put them in his car. Take him out of here. When he comes to, tell him Willa will send him his check. He won't talk to my daughter like that if he values his hands."

"...Well," Willa said, sitting down with coffee and sausages. "That's one problem solved. Probably the easiest one. Anyone have any objections?"

"No way, woman," Sticks said. "We were hoping you'd see the light one of these days."

"They say," Chloe began slowly, "that a full cup cannot be filled."

"Huh?" Sticks asked.

"It's like coffee," Jonesy said.

Everyone stared at him. Jonesy hardly ever said anything.

"If your cup is full, even if it's cold there's no room for a hot refill."

"Can't you just microwave it?" Sticks asked.

Willa laughed until her sides hurt. She pretended she didn't see her father watching her intently.

"I have a new song," she told them. "It's a strange one. I was singing it in a dream. I don't know if we can make it into a rock song. It's odd, for sure. I only have the first part — it's all I could remember when I woke up." She sang softly:

> My name is Lydia and I walk the floor
> Down through this old house to the front door
> I used to be mistress here but that was before
> When the young men came knocking on that front door.
>
> I am the ghost of Greenmoss Hall!
> Can you hear me sighing?
> I was the last girl at the ball
> Did you see me dying?

"Willa, that's just strange," Chloe commented.

"Yeah. I thought so too," she said.

"I like it," Jonesy said. "It's weird enough to be interesting."

"Like Willa," Sticks muttered.

She is the Raven Queen.
Wherever the battle goes she follows.
She brings death to Kings,
and victory to the arm of the maiden.

THAT WHICH
STOPS THE
BREATH

Willa's father had a follow-up appointment in Boise with Dr. McInally. Ramon the Escalade took them there; it was snowing, but the SUV handled the roads better than any car she'd driven before.

"How is our patient?" Jamie McInally asked when the nurse showed them in.

"Better," Ronan said enthusiastically.

"Truly better," Willa agreed.

"No problems?"

Her father glanced at her, then shook his head.

"What was that look?" the doctor asked.

"Willa had a fever," Ronan said.

"Dad!" she scolded.

"Well, fevers are common."

"Not a hundred six degrees they aren't," her father countered.

"That is a little high," McInally agreed. "Do you feel all right now?"

"Fine. Dad's just trying to distract you."

"We could run a blood test to see what it was," the doctor said.

"I'm fine," she insisted.

"I'm going to have the nurse re-run the Captain's blood samples. We need to see what's going on with that knee inflammation and what, if anything the medication is doing." The nurse took her father down the hall.

"I like the CD," Dr. McInally told Willa. "Are you working on anything new?"

"Yes, as a matter of fact. I fired our lead guitarist, though."

"He'll be a little hard to replace," McInally mused.

"Musically, yeah, but we won't miss him."

"So — we have to adjust your father's medication back down now, to find the right level for long-term pain control. We don't want to keep him on this high a dose; instead, we want to find the lowest possible dose that will keep the pain under control. I started him the high dosage to give him some instant relief. We'll work on it from here."

"Okay. About that blood sample. Can you check for unusual immunities, or viruses that aren't common?"

"For you or for your dad?" McInally asked.

"For me."

"Do you think you were exposed to something out of the ordinary?"

"Yeah. I was."

"I can run an AIDS test if you want."

"It isn't AIDS, Dr. McInally. It isn't an STD either. It might be something that affects DNA."

"That would be highly unusual...."

"So prove me wrong," she said.

"I can order the tests," Dr. McInally said, writing out the instructions.

"Thanks."

"People watch the National Geographic channel and think they have Pharaoh's Tomb Disease. I get that all the time. I'll let you know if we find something unusual."

"Cool," she said.

She took her dad to the mall for a haircut and some shopping. He sent her away and said he'd call when he was ready for her to meet him; he made it clear that he didn't want her to wait with him. Willa went downstairs to Victoria's Secret.

"I want something lacy, with ribbons and buttons," she told the clerk. "My guy isn't into sport bras and bike shorts."

The woman laughed and helped her find something black, trimmed in pale pink. Willa bought more than she'd intended.

"I should stick to shopping online," she told the cashier when she paid the bill.

Her dad called, and she went upstairs to fetch him. He used his cane to walk, but his gait was pretty even today. He eyed her shopping bag. She caught him smiling.

"What?" she said.

"Even tough girls get soft when they find a real man," he commented, and began whistling a quick tune.

"I have no idea how anyone thinks these things are comfortable to wear," she groused.

"Honey, they aren't for wearing." He grinned.

She blushed. He stopped and stared at her; he turned her face to the light.

"Are you blushing?"

"Dad, come on. You're being nosy."

"You never cared before." He watched the color deepen in her cheeks.

"Dad. Please!" She put her arm through his and led him to the Communications Pit Stop. She made him help her pick a phone for Corwyn, and got him a 911FindMe unit while they were there. The manager showed them how it worked and activated it for them, and if he thought she was crazy buying so many extra batteries for the phone, he was polite enough not to say so.

"Hey," the young man said suddenly, when he ran her credit card. His name tag said Justin. He was nice looking, college age, knew his phones. "Aren't you the singer from Blackwater?"

"Yeah. I am," Willa said, putting her dark glasses back on.

"Oh man," Justin said. "I really dig that song, 'Waitin'. The guitar player is awesome."

"Thanks," she said. "Unfortunately, we're looking for a replacement for him."

"Bummer, man. Wow. But, you have that cool chick on the sax. She didn't leave, did she?"

"No, no. She's still part of the band. Chloe. The guy on lead guitar — he didn't like my music."

"Whoa. That's not cool. Hey, I have tickets to the show at BSU. In the nosebleed section, but no biggie."

"Wow, thanks," she said. She took out one of her business cards, turned it over, wrote "seat upgrade" on it, and signed her name. "Bring this. This will get two of you down front. I like my fans — they keep the lights on. I'll introduce you to Chloe."

Justin called his co-workers over. "Guys, this is the lead singer from Blackwater — Willa MacLeod!"

She signed autographs. One of the staffers had a CD that she signed. Her presence drew a crowd of mall-goers and she wound up signing shoppers' bags and CD's that some fans bought when they discovered she was there. She turned to look for her dad. He was sitting on the bench outside the Com Pit.

The crowd finally thinned out, and she managed to get away. "That was unexpected," she said. "I'm sorry. Let's get out of here." She pulled up the hood on her coat and took his arm.

In Ramon on the drive home, Willa concentrated on the snowy road.

"I guess having a hit song is making you a little more visible," Ronan commented.

"I'm so sorry. I had no idea it would be like that."

"I rather enjoyed it," he admitted. "Do I get a card for your concert?"

"Do you want to come?"

"If it's not a bother."

"Let's find someone to go with you, okay?"

"Yeah, sure. Jeb would do."

"Dad. We can't torture Jeb. We need him."

He laughed. "You know, I've asked this question before. The answer was always no." He took a breath.

"Maybe you shouldn't ask."

"You can't live two lives."

"I already do," she reminded him.

"Three, then."

"I do have some practice at it. But you're right."

"You know, I don't like it when you agree with me. I feel much more comfortable when you're being Wicked Willa. This agreeable person is someone I don't know, and I don't know if I like what she's thinking."

"How do you know what I'm thinking?"

"Because it's probably what I would be thinking."

She licked her lips, breathed out. The wicked smile returned.

"So, my lecherous dad is thinking how I'm going to look in my new black and pink Victoria's Secret outfit?"

"Damn it, Willa!" Exasperated, he leaned his head back against the seat.

"Wicked Willa, huh?" she muttered.

When they got back to the ranch, Willa joined the band and Jake Collins, who were already practicing. They would have worked through dinner, but Sara sent Jeb for them and put a big batch of lasagna on the table. Jake joined them.

"What do you do to keep this woman here cooking for you, Willa?" Jake asked.

"I pay her double what the government pays her, so she moonlights here on their time."

"Willa MacLeod, don't you ever say that in town," Sara hissed. "You know the Agency job is part-time, anyway — or at least it only pays part-time wages."

"Don't worry, Sara — no one listens to Willa anyway," her dad said. "People in this town have been hearing her say outrageous things since she was a kid. They all just smile and nod their heads. I don't even think they hear her anymore."

"Speaking of that, I have a new handle," Willa announced. "Dad says I am Wicked Willa."

"Dude," Sticks said, "I like that."

"We could change our name to Wicked Willa and the Blackwater Gang."

"I *don't* like that," he said.

"Then we better get back to work, or our name will be mud," she said. She wanted to get a lot done so she could slip away back to the Silverhorn soon.

When we crossed the water we were strong and full of
dreams. I never imagined that I would outlive
everyone and everything, even the magic
— everything but the hope.

Coêr Mac Vyn

The Stuff of Dreams

Corwyn read until his eyes grew tired in the lamplight. He put the book down and sighed; so many things reminded him of her now. He read a poem of Joy Harjo twice: "But you must have grown out of / a thousand years dreaming / just like I could never imagine you." Those words seemed meant just for Willa, as surely as if Corwyn had written them himself. Now the emptiness within his place was all the more empty for her having been there. He saw her hand on the silver cups. When the hard edge of the pine table pressed against him, he remembered the white, smooth skin on the inside of her thigh. The scent of her in the fur throw roused him from sleep, hungry as he had never dreamed of being. When he closed his hands, she was his whispered prayer.

She is busy, he reminded himself, and tried to be the same. He went looking for his cache of furs. He arranged them by color, and, choosing the dark pelts and one white one, he began a new coat. When it grew dark on the third day, he couldn't stand it any longer. He stripped naked and let the change come. At the cliff's edge, feeling a daring he hadn't felt since the youthful days of rivalry with his brother, he sprang up the granite, ledge to ledge, instead of taking the trail. He galloped across the fields of snow until his hoof-falls became a rhythm that drummed his blood and set his lungs on fire. Later, after he bathed, he laced on his tall boots to keep the snow out and drew on his fur coat; then the Silver Stag leaped wildly down the sharp cliffs in the dark, trusting his instinct and memory to find footing he couldn't see.

Sticks sat again on the hill above the ranch, watching the moon paint enchantment across the snow. He heard footfalls and tried to be as still as the tree he leaned against. He had been seeing things everywhere, and hearing things he shouldn't; the whole world was weird, and he didn't have to be stoned to notice. The wind swirled snow around him and he heard bells. Footsteps crunched and halted just feet from him. A huge silver buck stood there, his antlers forming a circular crown that blazed like witch-fire. Sticks stopped breathing, but in doing so he must have made a sound — for the stag turned his heart-shaped face toward him. The edges of the creature blurred, and where Sticks had seen a buck, a man now stood ankle-deep in the snow. The antlers Sticks thought he saw above the man's head faded like some ghost image, and all Sticks saw was the blaze of tree branches brush-stroked with moonlight. Sticks' mouth dropped open.

"You're Sticks," the man said in a husky voice.

Sticks nodded dumbly.

"I am Corwyn. I live in the Silverhorn."

"Far out," Sticks managed. Corwyn sat down.

"You're silver. Willa was white," Sticks commented. He lit up his pipe and offered it to Corwyn.

"What is that?" Corwyn asked. Sticks withdrew his hand; Willa would have his head.

"Nothing you would be interested in, man," he said.

"The Totem Clans used to smoke a plant in their pipes called wild-weed. It gave them visions. The Sithé did not share this practice with them."

"You're a Sithé, I take it."

"At the moment," Corwyn said, "I am just a man who cannot pass another night alone. I have been bewitched by a woman."

"Welcome to my world, dude. And it's a good shittin' thing you showed up, because Willa's been raggin' on us like a demon-woman. That woman's a harpy when she wants something. Maybe you better go douse her fire, or whatever it is she needs. I think she was planning on hiking up the canyon soon. Not soon enough, I'm thinkin'."

"I will take your advice, Sticks." Corwyn stood up.

"Hey, Corwyn," Sticks said. "You don't have a sister by any chance, do you?"

"My sister died long ago. I am the only one of my people left."

"That's a bummer."

"Yes."

Corwyn went down the hill, catching the scent of her in his mouth.

Willa decided the black bustier would make a great top to wear under a vest or jacket when she did a show. It showed a lot of skin and made her appear better-endowed than she really was. She smoothed on her black leather pants and zipped them. Then she ruined the whole effect with a black-and-pink plaid flannel shirt.

She placed her pack on the bed and stuffed some clothes around what was already packed. Distantly, she heard Sunny bark. Then she heard someone on the porch, and figured it was Jeb leaving for the night. She took Corwyn's new phone from the charger, and gathered the extra charged batteries.

When the French door opened, she caught his scent on the breath of wind that swirled in. "Corwyn," she breathed.

He closed the door and shook the hood from his head. Very clearly, he heard what she called him in her mind, and the tension in him eased. She dropped the phone and batteries on the table and wrapped her arms around him. His coat was freezing.

"Wow. You're like Old Man Winter." She pulled his coat open and slipped into the warmth underneath. She buried her face against him and just breathed in the smell of him. She felt his heartbeat quicken. "Did you miss me?"

"As though I never had a life before you. How can that be?" he mused.

"Like you said, life is a paradox."

Behind her, Sunny barked, and came into her room wagging his tail. He sniffed Corwyn all over. He showed special interest in the coat.

"Ah-hem," her father said from the doorway. "Are you leaving or arriving?"

"Both," she replied. "I was leaving, but Corwyn got here first."

Her dad stepped into the room.

"Ronan MacLeod," her father said, extending his hand to Corwyn.

"Coér Mac Vyn. We met once, long ago. You were a boy." Corwyn clasped her father's hand and gripped his elbow with his left hand, while her father did likewise. She sensed ritual.

"Are you staying?" Ronan asked. "You're welcome to, Sithé. You are welcome here."

Tears started in Willa's eyes at the love she heard in her father.

Corwyn bent his head. There was immense humility in his sigh. He gazed back at her father. "Thank you. I don't know."

"My daughter is all I have. Have a care with that."

"I understand that, Ronan MacLeod. As you know."

"We understand each other, then. I bid you a good night. Good night, honey."

Her father left, shutting the door behind him.

"He is full of pain," Corwyn said.

"Yes."

"Have you told him about your mother?"

"No. Not yet."

"Maybe I will do that."

"Maybe you should."

She hung Corwyn's wolf-pelt coat on the clothes tree. He sat down in the tall-backed armchair and watched her move around her room. She placed a snifter of something amber beside his hand, and removed his boots. She touched the stereo controls to shuffle through soft instrumental selections and adjusted the LED light controls. She turned on the gas fireplace and removed her pack from the bed. Corwyn sipped the liqueur and his eyes drooped, lulled by the music, the warmth, and the contentedness of watching her graceful flow within her element. When she stepped close to shut the blinds, he caught her around the waist.

"Enough, woman. Come here."

She leaned down and tasted his lips, kissed him lightly, kissed him again, then again. He levered himself out of the chair, pulled her against him, and kissed her with such hungry intensity that she murmured softly. She unbuttoned the top button of her flannel shirt. He paused to watch. She took her time, raising her eyes after she freed the button; his gaze was riveted as her hands fell to the second button. Slowly she pushed it through its buttonhole. He licked his lips. Willa smelled pine soap on him. Her fingers touched the third button and eased it through the buttonhole. He was mesmerized; he couldn't tear his eyes from her hands. Her fingers found the fourth button; his hands covered hers then, moved them aside so he could unbutton the last two buttons himself.

He stripped the shirt off.

"Gods," he said. "What is this?" He ran his fingertips over the black lace appreciatively, then up to the white breasts, her neck, her jaw, and drew her soul out as he kissed her.

"Ahhh," he breathed as her hands slid up his ribs and drew his shirt off. His fingers found the tiny hooks on her bustier and began to unhook them urgently. He pushed them both back, step by step, until the edge of the bed bumped her.

He cursed under his breath in frustration.

"Untie it first," she told him. He found the bow at the back and pulled the ends loose. She ran her fingers over his chest and his nipples hardened.

"My Moonlight," he murmured in his own tongue. "I have never wanted anything as I want you. I am a man on fire."

She pulled him down with her. He unfastened the last hooks of her bustier all at once, and stripped her leather jeans from her long legs. He paused when he saw what she wore beneath.

I like those, he said in her mind.

When he came to her, he was indeed a man on fire.

She pressed the controls to turn off the lights and the music and turn down the fireplace. He had fallen asleep after, and slept as though exhausted. Maybe he'd climbed the mountain that day. He looked thinner. Maybe he wasn't eating. She drew the comforter over them both and his arms came around her, cupping her with his body, his chest against her back, his knees bent into hers, his sleeping breath on her shoulder.

The grey light woke her and she sat up cross-legged to watch him sleep. On his chest was a long scar from the nipple down his ribs to where his waist narrowed. Beneath his eye, a small, thin scar slanted toward his ear. On the inside of his forearm was a mark that looked like a tattoo of the circle of horns — in his open palm, the blood-rite scar was still red. The ceremonial knife in its amulet hung from the chain around his neck. The chain was heavy and the links were hand-wrought, and, though darkened, looked to be silver.

The hard planes of his face did not seem so ancient as when she had first seen him, and the small lines were relaxed by sleep. He hadn't shaved, and the shadow of beard defined his jaw. The muscles in his calves and arms were those of an athlete — well-formed and brawny. There was another long scar that twisted ropelike down his thigh. She touched it with her fingertip.

His breathing changed. She traced the scar on his thigh upward, touching him, exploring, curious. He grew hard beneath her hand.

She laughed when she realized he was watching her.

"Did you find something that interests you, my Moonlight?" he asked in his husky voice. She answered him without words.

She showed him how the shower worked. That took a long time and ran the hot water out in Willa's wing of the house.

She was dressed when he came out wrapped in a towel. He had shaved and pulled his hair into a knot at his neck.

"I should have looked long ago for the magical house where the Sithé lived. I would have found it at the foot of my own mountain," Corwyn said, gesturing around the room.

Intentionally, Willa had turned the TV on. He stopped, stared.

"What is this?" he asked.

"It is another invention, called a television or TV. We are watching the news — we can see things that happen all over the world right here in this picture. *And —*" she added, "people make picture stories for entertainment — like a whole book acted out for others to watch. We call them movies. If you stay, we will watch one later. I'll show you what they are like." She flicked on the NetFlix button on the remote and scrolled through the movie selections until she found the Iron Man preview and played it for him.

"You said there was no magic in your world," he muttered.

"This isn't magic. It's contrived, all made up. It isn't real. They fake it to look like magic."

"But, Willa MacLeod, what is the unreal, if it isn't magic?"

"This is like the magic that a magician makes when he uses sleight of hand for entertainment." She held up her scarred palm. "*This* is true magic."

"For me," he said, "it is life."

She bit her lip. She rummaged in her pack and laid jeans and shorts, a T-shirt and a soft chamois shirt on the bed.

"I got these for you. You are a little bigger than my dad, so I guessed if they would fit. You can try them if you like. Or not, if you would be uncomfortable."

He touched them. She had washed them so everything would be soft. He picked up the shorts and T-shirt.

"Are these undergarments?"

"Yeah, sort of. You can go commando, though, if you'd rather. It's a choice these days. I just thought you'd like the option."

"Did you think I would need these?"

"I was hoping you would come to my world," she said, her heart beating fast, "even if only to visit. I thought you might need them if you did. They are comfortable, I think. You would blend in that way." Her voice trailed off. "And...."

He read in her mind what she didn't finish saying.

"...and not be afraid," he finished for her.

"Yes," she whispered.

"You have driven the fear from my heart, Willa MacLeod." He put on the undershorts, adjusted and smoothed them. "These are like a loin cloth, the way they hold a man."

"Well, okay then," she muttered, suddenly feeling hot.

When he was dressed, she showed him the mirror.

"Not how I imagined I would look," he said.

"You ought to try changing shape in front of it."

"You have done that?" he asked.

"Oh, yeah," she said. He looked at her twice because there was something strange in the way she said it. Suddenly, she realized that she could block him from reading her thoughts. She kept her eyes fixed on his face.

He took off the moonstone earrings and handed them back to her.

"They are too fancy for such simple clothes, and I know you had a hard time parting with them," he said.

Willa rummaged in her jewelry box. "Try any of these." She dropped two tiny gold loops into his palm, and a handful of studs. Her stomach growled. "Sara Blackhawk will have breakfast made. The band may make it in to eat, eventually. They don't get up early, except for Sticks. Do you want to eat with everyone? Or would you rather I bring food in here?"

The look he gave her made her want to take off the clothes he had finally put on. He heard her thought. He laughed, and the care and loneliness dropped away from him.

"Let's eat first. Then you can take them off. I think we should go run across the snow. There is a meadow I would show you. In that magical place, it looks as though the Great Sithé of my ancestors poured out a basket of diamonds that burn in the light. Like you, Moonlight." What she said in her mind made him forget that he hadn't eaten. She slipped the moonstone earrings on.

"Maybe we should take the clothes back off," he suggested, but she moved away from him.

"You said 'later'. Be careful what you ask for," she said wickedly as she opened the door and led him to the kitchen.

Sara, Ronan MacLeod, and Sticks acted as though it were an everyday occurrence that Willa should walk into the kitchen with a man, but Jonesy's eyes just about popped out of his head. Habitually late risers, Neil and Chloe were absent as usual.

Corwyn took the chair next to Ronan MacLeod, which Willa's father had pushed out for him. Willa poured coffee, held up the pot.

"Coffee?" she asked him.

"I don't think I can," he said apologetically.

"I'll take some," Sticks said.

"And me," her dad said.

"It smells so much better than it tastes," Corwyn said.

"I'll make you tea," Willa said. "I have one I think you will like." She got a ginger-mint teabag and set the steaming cup by his hand. He touched her fingers for reassurance.

"Everyone drinks coffee these days, man," Sticks said. "It grows on you. Then you want it all the time. Like Sara's cooking."

"I never tasted anything so wonderful as that huckleberry pie," Corwyn agreed. "The berries smell enticing in the summer — their fragrance is powerful. You can catch the aroma of them from a long way off. But to pick very many takes long hours in the heat. To have a whole pie of them is a small wonder."

"It's Willa's favorite. In the summer, we buy huckleberries from anyone who will sell us some. Willa often pays too much, just to have plenty." Sara Blackwell studied Corwyn without seeming to. Willa sensed her wonder, and the great will power she used to try to conceal her thoughts from them both.

"Ahhh!" Corwyn said. "The pie was more than just food, then," he said as if ascertaining something momentous. He and Willa exchanged a charged look.

"I don't have pie this morning," Sara said. "You might like to try something different."

Silence stretched. Everyone seemed afraid to speak.

Willa brought their plates and took the seat next to Corwyn.

"It's kind of biscuits and gravy — but fancier. Sara makes it with white sauce and sherry, and ham and bacon with hardboiled eggs and little tiny mushrooms. The red thingies are called pimentos. There's lots more if you're still hungry."

Beneath the table, he squeezed her knee gratefully — she had given him information so he wouldn't appear ignorant. Not that it really mattered with anyone sitting at this table.

"After breakfast, would you like to see the ranch, Corwyn?" her father asked. "I thought you and I could go."

"He doesn't drive, Dad," Willa reminded him quickly.

"Jeb will drive us. I want to show Corwyn the ranch boundaries and the security system. I'm sure he will be interested in your horses, but if you would rather show him those, I'll leave them for you and just show him the cattle. I kinda figured you might like to get some studio time in this morning so you would be free later."

A tear dropped on her cheek.

Corwyn brushed it away with his thumb. "You must have something in your eye," he said softly.

"Yeah." She glared at Jonesy and Sticks. "Do you suppose we can roust Chloe and Neil out of bed and maybe get Collins out here? Or does he want to keep playing with us?"

"I think he wants to," Jonesy said. "He isn't sure he's what you want."

"I like him," Willa admitted. "I heard him on the Taylor yesterday. He's got a nice style with the acoustic guitar. And he does an adequate job on the electric — it's a different sound, but I think it works. How 'bout you guys? What do you think?"

"The dude's got some stuff," Sticks said. "He's a square deal — no floss."

"I'll show him some things. I learned a lot from Rincon," Jonesy said. "I don't know if he has the time for us, though — I mean after he goes back to work."

"Let's just let it ride," Willa said. "He'll work out for the gig at Boise State. You guys gotta teach him some songs. Maybe you can do that this afternoon and evening — the next few, even. Anything he can't learn, Chloe can manage on the sax or the violin. And I want Chloe to use the hip-harp on the Silverhorn song. OK, Chloe? Let's bag the recording this morning — let's just work on that one song — the 'smile' one. We can finish up the recording after the gig."

"Where you gonna be this afternoon?"

"Corwyn wanted to show me some diamonds," she answered. Everyone froze. Sunny's sleepy breathing was suddenly very loud.

"... You gettin' married?" Sticks finally asked.

"Whoa, drummer-boy. These diamonds are ice and snow."

"You're a weird chick, Willa. Ya know that?"

"No one knows it better than I do, Sticks," she laughed.

Captain Ronan MacLeod used his cane since the snow made walking more difficult. He and Corwyn walked from the truck to the gate. Ronan showed him how to turn off the electric current if he wanted to pass. They gazed down across the pasture where the cattle were contentedly lying in the hay that Jeb had spread out in a line earlier that morning.

"My ancestors came down the mountain to protect the clan. There were few of the Sithé remaining by then. They made a choice, and it was a wise one. We've been happy here. We understood that the Age of the Sithé was over, and we chose to transition into the new world."

"You have watched the gates a long time," Corwyn said. "Your daughter does not know."

"Most of the MacLeods drifted away. Only this family remained here. The knowledge was passed only to the sons. We were a small and very secret society."

"What will you do, Ronan MacLeod, with no son to pass the knowledge to?"

"You, Corwyn, are the last Sithé. It occurs to me that our guardianship is over, that it is time to let the past die."

Corwyn turned over Ronan's words.

"...Time for me to die?" he asked finally.

"To come down the mountain."

"I am not the last Sithé. There is another now."

"I couldn't keep her from searching for you," Ronan said sadly. "She has desired the myth her entire life; especially after her mother vanished."

"She is pure Sithé. That's why the 'myth' calls to her. Her blood desired the rite of passage."

"How can she be pure Sithé? The MacLeod blood is diluted many times over."

"Because you married one whose Sithé blood was more pure than yours. Your daughter is a throwback to our ancestors. Her blood is as pure as mine."

"How can that be?" Ronan's hair in this light was as white as Willa's, his eyes the same hard blue as all the MacLeods before him. Corwyn felt the pain in him, physical and emotional, like a sharp blade. Life, for Ronan MacLeod, was a struggle with pain and with daily choices that were not made easily. The bright light in him was his vision of Willa.

"When Kiervyn Mac Nessa was killed by a hunter, Rìgan Mac Nessa took her daughter and left the mountain. I was a much younger man then. There were still a few of us left. Rìgan went mad with grief and fled to New Britton. Her many-times-great-granddaughter Megan was your wife. Somehow the blood had not yet thinned. You know how it works. The Mac Nessas had the sight — the Magnes women were not 'crazy'."

"It must have been very difficult for them," Ronan agreed compassionately. "I never realized. Do you .... Do you know what happened to Megan?"

He turned to walk along the fence toward the barn. Jeb started the truck and followed slowly. Corwyn took Ronan's arm to keep him from slipping.

"Yes," Corwyn said slowly.

Ronan turned toward him slightly, gripping Corwyn's arm that steadied him. "She's alive?" he asked. For just a moment, hope bloomed.

Corwyn shook his head. He felt the man's hope and grief like a sharp blade in his chest. Sorrow touched his voice then. "I am sorry, Ronan MacLeod. She is not alive. She came back to the mountain to die. She thought she could offer her blood so that you might live. She didn't understand the rite of passage. It was an accident. I didn't find her until it was too late to save her, until she had bled almost to death. She lies now with her family."

"I wish I'd known." Ronan was crying. "Someday ... will you take me there?"

"Yes, Ronan MacLeod. I will take you."

"Does Willa know?"

"I have taken her there."

"We all have too many secrets," Ronan said wistfully.

"It is the way of life for the Sithé," Corwyn said. "But I have no secrets that I won't share with her. She is the last daughter of the Sithé. She holds my heart in her hands."

They reached the barn. The horses nickered at them.

"You have nothing to offer — no life, no family, nothing but a dream of the past."

"She has a life and a family. I will give her my dream. Then we will both be complete."

"It's time to give it up, Corwyn. You have nothing left. Come down the mountain."

"I don't know if I can, Ronan MacLeod. I am older than your world."

"You are young enough for my daughter. How old are you?"

"Ten times her age."

"Really? Well, that's good. She does like older men."

Corwyn glanced sharply at him, saw the small smile. "Ah. You jest." The fear that he would displease Ronan began to ease just a little.

"Do you love her?" her father asked him.

"With every minuscule part of me."

"Then the decision is already made. Bring your heart home. Let the past die."

"I don't know if I can."

"You will, Coér Mac Vyn. Listen to your heart."

Corwyn and Willa climbed past the high peaks, their coats silver and white, crowned with fire. The day was breathless with sharp cold, the sky cloudless and dark blue. They ran for a long time. Finally, they crested a ridge whose teeth gnawed the feet of the sky. Below them, a round depression in the mountains cupped snow and light as though it were an offering. As Corwyn had promised, the snow sparked with tiny diamonds — millions of them glittering over a vast field. They plunged down the slope; around them, the reflections cast lightbows that burned their eyes.

They surprised a herd of elk. Ten brown creatures raised their heads and ten pairs of eyes stared at them. The Silver Stag and the White Hart raced toward the elk, who spooked and turned to gallop away. The Sithé raced them, heard the animals panting with fear and exhilaration. Hart and Stag caught the elk and ran with them until the elk tired and fell behind.

A howl broke the stark silence of snow. Another joined it, and then many more.

We must leave, he told her urgently.

Several wolves broke cover ahead of them and chased them across the snow, eventually falling behind when the two deer leaped down the granite cliffs. Corwyn and Willa changed shape when they reached the fir tree at the trailhead and ran, laughing, down the hill to the studio.

A swirl of snow scattered the music sheets, and tiny bells rang. Chloe's lips parted in wonder.

Corwyn clearly heard the chord that Willa struck in Sticks, a clash of sound when they walked through the door. "Sweet," Sticks said.

"Nice," Jake Collins exclaimed. "That's what I would call blowing in!"

"This is Corwyn," Willa said. "Corwyn, you haven't met Jake, Chloe, and Neil."

"Corwyn and Willa went to look at diamonds this afternoon," Sticks said slyly.

"What?" Chloe and Neil said together.

Willa made it across the studio in five long strides. She took the drumsticks from the Sticks.

"Drummer-boy, you are a very bad boy," she said with a wicked smile. She straddled his legs with hers and sat on his lap and kissed him on the mouth. She could feel his heart hammer under her fingers. "We went to see a snowfield that looks like diamonds and we were almost eaten by wolves." Sticks was breathing hard.

"What?" Jake said.

Willa got up, handed Sticks back his drumsticks, and gave him a look that silenced him.

"Yeah. Wolves. Nasty, scary things with teeth and evil eyes."

"But you had guns, right?"

"We forgot to take them," she answered lightly, picking up her guitar. "Did you practice? Let's go, let's hear it. Let's do 'Waitin'. I'm singing this one now — sorry, Sticks. Chloe, I want the violin on this one to help Jake with the lead. Neil can handle the keyboard — give us a bass line there. I'll do the acoustic rhythm. Jonesy, help Jake out too. Can we do this?"

Corwyn found a spot to sit on top of a table, crossed his legs, and leaned against the wall.

Neil started the lead-in.

Willa sang the song to Corwyn and meant it. When she got to the final chorus she stalked across the studio, shoved the guitar behind her back, and sang the end of the song to his face in her throaty alto.

> *Take me with you sugar*
> *Make me burn with fire*
> *Keep me burnin' baby,*
> *Take me higher,*

'Cause I been waitin', waitin', bring it to me sugar,
Don't keep me waitin'
I hear your footsteps baby crossin' the floor
And when you touch me baby
I ain't waitin', waitin', I ain't waitin' no no baby
Ain't waitin for the waitin' no more.
Hey hey, come on come on
No waitin', baby, yeah yeah
Waitin' no more
Yeah yeah yeah.

Corwyn was mesmerized by her eyes and her body language when she sang the words. The band members' thoughts were a jumble of amazement and exultation. The last chord had hardly slid into the fade when Sticks did a little drum roll.

"May I present, ladies and gentlemen, wicked Willa MacLeod, Blackwater's star. Woo-yeah!"

"That's gonna work," Jonesy breathed.

"Oh yeah," Chloe said. "That is going to work all night long. Nice. Is Corwyn coming to the concert? Maybe that would be a good thing."

"Maybe," Willa said. "Let's try 'Wild Cat'. Did you guys work on that?" This was Sticks' song. Jake and Sticks began the fade-in; Chloe came in with the violin.

Willa started humming the background vocal while Sticks and Jonesy whispered in an undertone. Sticks threaded into the song. He sang the verses alone, and the band joined in on the chorus with lots of vocal harmony.

She is a wild cat. She is on fire.
You can't hold her, you can't let go.

She burns as she takes you higher,
Eats your heart and steals your soul.

You can't see, you can't breathe.
Nothin' holds you but you can't leave
As you burn for the wild cat.

She brings you brilliance, she brings you light
She brings desire like you never knew.
When she turns, she leaves you night,
And a terrible darkness that covers you.

You can't see, you can't breathe,
Nothin' holds you but you can't leave
As you burn burn burn
for the wild cat.

She can't be caged, she's never kind.
She loves you fiercely, but strips you bare.
She'll scratch your eyes out, leave you blind.
She ain't good for you, and she don't care.

You can't see now, and you ain't breathin'
Nothin' binding keeps you from leavin'
But you burn, burn, burn,
for the wild cat.

Sticks' rough voice always sounded sexy on this song; he whispered the last line again as the guitars faded and Willa hummed a haunting vocal background.

"That was good," Willa told Jake. She turned off her guitar, took it off her shoulder, and put it in its stand.

"We have to go now. Get the other bread-and-butter songs down. We can work it out, for sure. Maybe we can add a few new ones before next week. Jake, are you down with playing with us at the BSU gig?"

"Yeah, sure. I can do that."

"You have to do something for me though. Keep Nokes off this place and out of Silverhorn Canyon. He was there two days ago. He has to cross this land to get there. He can't do that. He can't hunt here. He *will* stay the hell out or I will have him arrested — or worse. Can you do that for me?"

"He was here? He said he was going south."

"He was here. Tell him to stay out. It isn't debatable." She put on her coat.

Jake followed them out into the snow.

"I honestly thought he went south. My dad and I were busy. I don't know what to say."

"Jake, I get it. You aren't his keeper. But you need to know he's a liar. He isn't what he seems. How are you even friends?"

"We grew up together — went to school, played football. We've been friends a long time."

"It's time to find new friends."

"Maybe I have."

"Tell him — he comes on our land, I might shoot him."

One of the most basic conditions of love
is that someone wonders where you are
when you don't come home.

RM

Hunters of the
Silverhorn

Tired, they watched Iron Man. Her legs ached from running, even though that had been in a different shape. She only wanted Corwyn to hold her so that he filled every breath and she could taste him. She felt like she would dissolve into completeness and become light, and the rise and fall of his breath became a mantra for her heartbeat. Together, they were one whole; Willa had no idea how she had ever existed without him. She thought she finally understood yin-yang, because she could no longer tell where she ended and Corwyn began.

"How did you live alone so long?" she asked, pausing the movie.

He protested, and then heard what she was really asking. "It was only time, waiting to be whole."

"How could you stand it?"

"Each moment brought this one closer. The promise, the hope kept me alive."

"Will you go back to the mountain?"

"I have to go hunting," he said.

"For what?"

"For wolves."

"Don't tell Regi."

"Will I meet her?"

"She's coming out this afternoon."

"Does she know who...?"

"You are? Sort of — yes. She doesn't believe any of it."

"Ahhh."

"When will you go...hunting?"

"Soon. Tomorrow, maybe."

"Is it dangerous? Maybe I should come with you."

"Go to your practice."

"Will you come back?"

"How could I not?" he said, repeating her words from before.

"What about your fear of being away from your fortress?"

"Perhaps, Willa MacLeod, I was most afraid that I would die alone with an empty heart. Perhaps I feared that I would die before you answered the promise. I don't even know anymore — nothing else seems important. Nothing is as it seemed."

She turned the movie back on. He kissed her neck and ear. Then the door opened.

"Am I interrupting something?" Regi asked. "Should I come back later?"

Regi stopped moving and breathing when their blue eyes looked up. They both felt her realize: *They are not of my world.*

"Come watch the movie with us," Willa said. "I don't want to pause it again, or Corwyn will take the remote away. And he doesn't know how to use it yet."

"I'm Regi," she muttered, nervous and self-conscious. "I can't use a remote either."

Willa could sense Regi's surprise that Corwyn wasn't older — except for his silver hair and his eyes, he appeared younger than Captain MacLeod. *Willa has those old eyes too — she had them even when she was a kid.*

"Old eyes, huh?" Willa muttered, repeating Regi's thought back to her.

"Damn it, Willa," Regi said. "Get out of my head!"

"I'm Corwyn. Coér Mac Vyn. I am glad that Willa has a good sister like you," Corwyn said. His smile erased Regi's annoyance.

Regi smiled back at him, unsure what to say. *He's a lot like Willa. But he doesn't look like her father,* she thought wryly, remembering their conversation at The Café. *Does he love her? Is he going to make her happy, or is this all going to be some kind of awful tragedy for everyone?* She resisted the urge to ask.

"Pause it," Corwyn whispered in Willa's ear.

Corwyn touched her, and Willa leaned in to his caress. Willa could feel the thrill these small movements gave Regi. She paused the movie.

Corwyn rested his pale eyes on Regi's face.

"You should say what is in your heart, Regi Zumwalt. If you say it with love, it will not matter if the words are troubled. I *am* a little like Willa and her father because we descended from the same people long ago — a people called Sithé. I pray that no tragedy comes to any of us, on my account or anyone else's. And yes, I love her — how could I not love her?" His voice grew husky. He closed his eyes.

"Corwyn — you'll make Regi uncomfortable."

"Oh — like *you* haven't been doing that all your life," Regi quipped.

"What are you two going to do for an encore?"

"We're working on that," said Willa.

"Kill some wolves," Corwyn growled.

"What?" Regi said. "I can't hear that."

"Corwyn! I told you not to say that in front of Regi. She's a Fish and Game officer. She'll arrest you."

"She will have to catch me at it, will she not? You know, they chased us across the snow for many miles this morning. They are deadly creatures — the butchers of the mountains. Willa says they are protected there. It is a little disturbing that the world has become a place that protects such predators."

"They . . . ." Regi began.

Willa interrupted. "I hear a debate coming. Arguing with Regi is like smashing your head against a stone. Do we want to finish the movie, or argue with her?"

"The movie, my Moonlight," Corwyn conceded.

Willa felt Regi go mushy inside. She caught her friend's eyes and said, wickedly, "He's not *all* soft."

"Yeah, yeah, baloney."

Willa pulled her friend onto the bed next to her and they watched the movie together, arm in arm. Regi managed to put the movie on pause when both Corwyn and Willa fell asleep.

She went to the kitchen. Sara had dinner cooking. Captain MacLeod and Sunny were not there.

"Now *that's* going to be hard to live with," Regi told Sara, pouring herself a drink.

"I seem to remember a time when you were a very giddy bride, my dear. Think about it. It is the wonder of the human world, Regi. Despite their huge differences in age and culture, they've found magic together. We have terror and wars around the globe; we have crazy politics, trade wars, half the country not on speaking terms with the other half; we have a planet teetering towards environmental crisis; but still, the way of a man with a woman is a mystery and a wonder that can displace all care — it can surprise you, make you believe in the unbelievable, and give you hope that we will all survive somehow. It's one of life's miracles."

"Well. Aren't *you* feeling all understanding and philosophical? It's just too weird, Sara!"

"Some things cannot fit into your definition of the world, Regi. Or mine. Willa's a strange girl. Did you expect her to have a normal life?"

"Actually, no. I just didn't expect her to find a happy abnormal life. I guess I sort of saw her staying as she has always been — weird, edgy, troubled, searching, chasing the myth. I was glad she didn't become a drug addict or — you know — like her grandmother. She's so smart and...and...and non-temporal. I didn't expect her to catch a frickin' myth and bring it home."

"No. That doesn't happen in our world, does it, Regi?"

"Well, it shouldn't...but I guess it does. Do you think, in the bigger balance of things, something like this is...is...ummm...allowed?"

"Is what allowed?" Ronan MacLeod asked, coming in the door. Sunny ran up to Regi, wagging his tail, and promptly lay down by her chair.

"I guess I was asking whether one age is allowed to spill over into another. There's an old Ray Bradbury story, 'Sound of Thunder' — a time travel story. Someone brings something back with them — a dead bug? — when they return from a trip to the age of the dinosaurs. It was just a little accident, but it changed the whole world."

"Are you asking if they will somehow screw up reality? I don't think anyone's got a time machine around here." Ronan looked thoughtful.

"But it's an accident he's here."

"Maybe not so much."

"I'm afraid for them." Regi was troubled. "I just wonder if the world we know will allow them to exist together unmolested."

"I'll tell you this, Regi Zumwalt. I'll do everything in my power to see that it does. That's my ancestral duty."

"Dinner's ready," Sara said mildly. "Who's ringing the bell?"

"I'll do it," Regi said. "Shall I go wake them?"

"They'll hear it. If they don't, they're too tired to eat."

When Willa woke the next morning, Corwyn was gone. He had taken the rifle she laid out, and two boxes of ammo. Willa went to the porch and saw Corwyn's bootprints in the new snow. She didn't know if she should be concerned. She spent the day practicing with the band and trying not to think about it. He had lived three hundred years. He would be fine.

Corwyn climbed the granite to his high chamber. The fire had long gone cold and the rooms had grown chill, as though no one had ever lived there. He built a fire and banked it to last the day out. He put on the leathers he hunted in and tied his hunting boots over his knees. He took his pack and his crossbow, his knives, and the rifle Willa had lent him. He picked up the turquoise cougar from the table and put it in his pocket. Then he shape-shifted and climbed the mountain. When he came to the field of diamonds, he saw that the wolves had killed two of the elk. Blood stained the snow where the beasts still haggled over the flesh. This was no time to be in deer-shape: he changed, positioning himself above the wolves to pick them off.

When he had killed five of them, the rest grew wary and skulked into the trees. They tried to track him, to scent his location, but he shifted position each time they attempted to get downwind of him. Finally they went back to their kill, and he picked off four more before the remaining five seemed to figure out his general location and began stalking him.

Wolves are among the cleverest and most savage hunters. They respond as much to the thrill of the chase as they do to hunger; they are killers by nature. The five wolves split up. Two approached him from the woods to Corwyn's left. Two came from the jagged boulders on his right. He lost sight of the fifth. Corwyn picked off one of the wolves as it came over the top of a boulder. But the shot gave the others his exact location, and they began to move in at a run. He shot another as it emerged from the woods. The one remaining in the rocks stayed low. The one galloping toward him from the trees came so fast he barely had time to aim. He dropped it at twenty yards. With no time to reload the rifle, he pulled the crossbow up, waiting for the other wolf to emerge from the boulders.

He never heard the fifth wolf until it sprang at his back. He went down in the snow beneath the weight of the animal. The wolf's fur smelled of blood and musk — he was an old one, a pack leader. When Corwyn tried to fend him off, he locked his teeth on Corwyn's arm; this wolf was too smart to go for the neck and leave his prey's hands free. Corwyn groped for his knife, but the wolf was too strong and heavy for him to maneuver, and it began to drag him along the ground. Corwyn felt the animal's teeth meet bone. He knew he had only seconds before the other wolf would be on him as well, and together they would tear him apart.

Corwyn heard the high-pitched, unworldly scream of a wild cat over the snarling of the wolf and the sound of his own ragged breath. He knew fear, but shoved it away. The wolf shook him while its guttural snarls waged a mental battle with him — the old creature sought to unnerve his prey before he dismembered him. Corwyn anticipated the other pair of jaws that would grasp his other arm at any moment — but nothing came. He finally found his knife. Snow and ice burned his face as the wolf shook him, tearing his upper arm. The animal wasn't just heavy and strong — he was fast. Corwyn dislodged him, but he came back so quickly that Corwyn barely had time to pull the knife out of its sheath. When the wolf seized his thigh, Corwyn brought the point of the knife down hard, just behind the wolf's ear. He followed it with the weight of his body. The knife went in, touched bone, went further, and Corwyn twisted his hand. The wolf was dead before his jaws unclamped and he slid to the snow.

Quickly Corwyn looked for the last wolf. This one — a bitch, smaller than the wolf he had killed, but still big — was locked in battle with a tawny animal. In wonder, Corwyn realized that it was a cougar. With two quick moves, the cougar launched forward in the snow, lifted its front paws, and made a lightning-fast swipe on each side of the wolf's head. The blows took out the she-wolf's eyes; the next swipe ripped out the bitch's throat. The huge cat sat down in the snow and screamed in triumph, then began delicately to lick its paws clean.

Corwyn touched the totem in his pocket, and the cougar gazed at him with burning yellow eyes. He was a full-grown male, probably weighing a little more than Corwyn did. Corwyn wondered if he would now become prey for this new, larger predator. But the cougar's shape wavered, grew taller . . . and in place of the tawny cat there stood an old warrior.

"You called for help, Sithé," the man said. He strode forward. He was in full buckskins, with fur boots, coat, and headgear, mink tails and eagle feathers braided into his white hair, and a cougar-skin cape draped over his wide shoulders. The beading down the breast of his shirt and the sides of his leggings depicted magnificent plains animals. He looked to be Piegan Blackfoot, but his dress was similar to Siksika, or maybe Kainah.

"Even a Sithé should not hunt wolves alone," he said.

Corwyn was dizzy. Blood oozed from his thigh and ran profusely from his arm. He had to be hallucinating. There had been no Cougar Clan for hundreds of years.

"We all have secrets, Sithé. You are not the only magic left in the world. We totem people have a few tricks left. Has it not occurred to you that the Sithé dwindled from this world in part because they shaped an animal that is prey? This is a world of predators now, and the ancient magic of your forefathers has become a myth. But magic hides in more places than your high fortress."

"That's like something she said. . . ." Corwyn mumbled.

"We've watched you hiding on your mountain. We have honored the pact of our ancestors: You have had your silence and your sanctuary. In turn, you protect the elk and the deer. You have done us a service. The wolves deplete our food source. Now, let me see what I can do for your wounds. I do not think you could run all the way to your fortress without losing too much of your life blood." He removed his cape, laid it on the snow, and eased Corwyn down.

"I am Joseph Yellowgrass. The old spirits still know you, Heart of the Wind — Coér Mac Vyn. Let's take a look at the damage that sly old dog did."

The wound on the thigh was a deep bite, but had not opened a vein. Joseph cleaned it and packed it with snow to stop the bleeding. The arm was far worse. The skin was shredded down to the bone, and the bleeding was profuse. Joseph cleaned the wound and closed it with thin sinew threaded on a needle. When the bleeding was under control, he removed the snow pack and bound Corwyn's arm with herbs and strips of cloth. He erected a low shelter and built a fire. He wrapped Corwyn in the wolf-fur coat.

The old warrior cut a haunch from one of the dead elk and put it to roast over the fire. Then he stripped the pelts from the dead wolves.

"The Fish and Game woman . . . she said the wolves are protected," Corwyn said.

"I will make certain their bodies are not visible from the air before we leave. The Fish and Game people don't come here by foot. If there's nothing to see from an airplane, no one will be the wiser. I would like some of the pelts, Sithé, if you would share them."

"My life is worth all of them, Joseph Yellowgrass."

"No more than half," the old man laughed. "You will need the others for a new coat."

Yellowgrass gathered the wolf skins and worked on them while Corwyn slept. He kept watch through the night, but no more of the beasts came to the kill.

Corwyn woke at dawn. Yellowgrass had stoked the fire. He gave Corwyn a bitter tea that made him gag. The lines in his dark, flat face told Corwyn that he smiled a lot. His eyes were wise and kind.

"You will live, Sithé. It is good, or my hearth-mate would not let me come home for the winter."

"And who is your hearth-mate, healer? Why would she take an interest in me?"

"Because the child of her heart, her adopted daughter Willa White Hart would then be the only Sithé left in the world. Willa would probably die of grief and loneliness — as have so many of her mothers before her. Already she worries that you have not returned to her. She will come for you before long."

He gave Corwyn the last of the bitter tea. Corwyn closed his eyes. Nothing, indeed, was as it seemed. He slept.

When he woke, the fire had burned to ashes and he grasped the cougar totem in the hand of his uninjured arm. Corwyn was sheltered under a cover of pine boughs and wrapped in his wolf-skin coat. He lay on a cougar hide, and his weapons were carefully placed close by. Seven fresh wolf hides were laid out on the snow to cure. He sat up. A chunk of roasted elk wrapped in a bit of cloth had been left where he would find it. He ate all of it and drank the cold tea that he found next to it.

When he moved painfully to gather his things for the long trek back, he saw only cougar prints in the snow around his shelter and the elk carcasses. Of the bodies of the wolves there was no sign. He turned for home with a new mystery in his heart.

When Corwyn didn't come home the first night, Willa missed him, but didn't worry overmuch. The band practiced hard all day and late into the evening; they would be ready for the gig at BSU, and Willa was relieved. Jake Collins was enthusiastic and tried hard to bring himself up to their level of music. He had enough skill that when he let go of his rigidness and allowed a little of the magic in, he was actually quite good. She hoped the thrill and stage-fright of a real gig would bring out even more of the music in him and he would find his groove.

Lonely, she went to her father's sitting room after the practice finally ended. Ronan MacLeod was still awake.

"Willa!" he said, surprised. He paused the video. Sunny looked up and his tail thumped the floor. On the desk was an open journal and a writing tablet. The computer had a Word page showing on the screen.

"You've been writing!" she said, surprised.

"I've meant to do it for many years. The story of the Silverhorn needs to be written, if only for us to remember. I have a lot in my heart and my memory that you should know. Corwyn has helped me to clarify some things that were a mystery before."

"I didn't know you ever wanted to write."

"I started a journal when I was younger, before the war. It seemed important then. After I came back, other things pushed it from my mind. It's like therapy, you know. Writing…. It can untangle things that you can't seem to sort out in your head or feelings. Maybe you know that."

"Yeah. I do." She sat down.

"It's been awhile since you used your chair." He gestured to the recliner beside his.

"I've been busy — tangled up in my head and heart," she laughed.

"Seems like maybe things are a little less tangled, but no less complicated, these days."

"No. That's not true," she said. "My life has become simple. All the mystery, the strangeness that kept me isolated from everyone, everything — even myself — all that's gone now. I understand who I am. It makes things very simple." She looked around. There was no beer on the side table.

"Hey, you want a beer?" she asked. "Or a nightcap?"

"I'll have one, if you have one. Whatever's your pleasure."

"Cognac? Or Crown?"

"Crown."

She set the glass by his hand. "You aren't drinking much these days," she commented.

"So many things have taken away the need. The new meds help, a lot. But Corwyn.... When we walked the ranch the other day, he told me about your mother, where she is. That helped."

"I'm sorry I didn't tell you."

"Now you're apologizing. Remember what you tell me about that? You probably didn't make the decision lightly, so don't go back on it now."

"Thanks. Corwyn thought he should do it."

"You're right," Ronan said thoughtfully.

"About...?"

"He's a good man. I'm not saying he isn't dangerous, or a danger to you. But he's a good man." Ronan rubbed his chin, shook his head. "He...."

"He what?"

"He showed me...what it's like to change, to become Sithé. We lost a lot when the MacLeods came down the mountain."

She started to protest, but he waved her silent.

"But we gained something greater — we gained a new life, a present, and a presence in the changing world. We came forward in time and lost the magic. The others, they kept the magic and stayed in the past. They faded away. After a while, they didn't have anything left — not even love. At least I have had a life, and love, even a purpose, although it wasn't always clear to me. Now I understand why it was so confusing."

"Yeah. I get that, for sure."

"But there's more." His tone made her glance up at him. "He touched me. You know, with the magic. I can see now — see what's inside, hear what people are thinking. Probably not as clearly or consistently as you do; he said the magic wouldn't be quite like what a pure Sithé has."

"Probably more than Sticks, though," she laughed.

"What? Did you mess with that poor kid?"

"Yeah. I was punishing him for being so guileless."

"Sticks adores you, you know."

"Yeah."

"When Corwyn touched me, it took away my pain. Not just the physical pain, but the pain in my heart and in my mind. Perhaps it's because I can see inside myself now."

Willa couldn't help the tears that ran down her cheeks.

"So .... I can't come up with any reason to not like Corwyn, even though I would like to have one. Actually, I feel as though I've known him for a long time. Perhaps we always had a connection; it's as though I always felt his presence. Maybe it was the presence of the thing the clan MacLeod left behind. We did that on purpose, made a decision and a sacrifice so the ones who remained would be safeguarded."

"I love you," Willa said.

"I know. It worried me for many years that you were too attached to me as a father figure. There aren't any child-rearing books that deal with a kid like you. Do you realize that you never had a childhood crush or a teenage puppy-love phase? You completely missed all the things that drive normal parents crazy. That doesn't mean you didn't drive me crazy — it just that you weren't in the books. Oh, I knew you had an affair or two — but you never even pretended that you really liked the poor guys. I was afraid you might have liked Rincon, because he was probably the least likable of the ones I knew about. But when you didn't, I was almost disappointed. You were always waiting — obsessed with the Silverhorn. You can't know what that does to a parent."

"I'm sorry."

"Damn it, Willa. Stop that." He got a very wicked gleam in his eye, one she hadn't seen in a long, long time. "Actually, I'm relieved beyond measure now."

The way he paused, she knew he was baiting her, like she did with him. She played along. "Relieved? Why?"

"I don't have to worry anymore that I will wake up to find you in bed with me, like you always threatened."

"What would be so bad about that?" she asked, grinning wickedly herself.

"I might take you seriously," he said, his face a mirror of hers.

"Ohh. I'd like that," she quipped.

"Shit. Don't you have a man now?"

"He didn't come back today."

"Give him time, Willa. He has some heavy decisions he's brooding on. He'll make them."

The next day dawned clear and brittle cold. Willa made coffee to serve with the cardamom coffee cake Sara had left for them. Sara had taken the day off—the Agency was after her for the final contract proposals and she had left to present them in person. Jake had committed to join his friend Nokes for some scouting, so the band decided to take the day off. Chloe and Neil wanted to go to Boise to shop, and they actually got up early for once, and left. Willa sent them with a small shopping list of her own.

"Stay the night if it gets late," she told them, slipping them some extra cash. "Don't drive after the roads ice up."

Jonesy talked Jeb into taking him fishing in the ranch reservoir, after Willa had teased him with her stories of late-season lunkers she had caught at exactly this time of year. He came to breakfast animated as he rarely was.

"What bait do you use?" he asked.

"Worms and anise oil, with a little fake maggot on the end to make it visible. Use the worm threader and you won't lose so many worms," she told him. "Jeb knows what to use — he'll show you how. I keep extra poles and gear in the tack room for my friends to use. He'll get what you need after he finishes the chores. You don't need to go super-early this time of year — the fish will feed when it's warmer. I just replaced the line on all the rigs, so you shouldn't have to worry about a big one breaking your line." After she said that, Jonesey could hardly eat, and left to go help Jeb with the chores.

"Willa, look what you've done!" her father scolded. "The poor guy is positively obsessed with the idea he's going to catch a huge fish.

You shouldn't be so cruel. He's such a quiet, nice young buck — you just prey on that sort of thing."

"Dude," Sticks agreed, "she is the wickedest of women. There has never been a crueler woman in all the world."

"Sticks," Willa grumbled, "you wouldn't know cruel if it slapped your ass awake."

"Woman, I would know it was you if that happened. Don't make me those kind of promises." He turned to her father. "Do you see how she does me? She is badass cruel, dude, cruel."

Her dad chuckled. It was so rare to see his eyes sparkle that way; but she caught a tentative sense of worry as well.

"Did Corwyn make it back?" he asked carefully.

"No."

"Do you know where he went?"

"He went hunting yesterday," she admitted. She tried not to let him read her concern.

"Hunting? For what? Birds?"

She dropped her eyes.

"For what, Willa?" he asked gruffly.

"Wolves."

"Shit."

"Dude, what's wrong with hunting wolves? Willa told us the wolves chased her and Corwyn for miles."

"When?" Ronan growled. Willa heard the fear rise in him again. She glared at Sticks and he just shrugged.

"Willa?"

"Day before yesterday. We were in the high country. It was a large pack."

Her father turned to Sticks. "If you breathe a word of this in

Regi's presence, you will never smoke pot again for the rest of your very short life."

"Whoa, dude. I did not hear a thing." Sticks was completely surprised. "Dude. I know now where Willa learned to be so cruel." Her dad laughed outright. Willa caught Sticks' sly little smile before he covered it with contrite innocence.

"Should you be worried?" Ronan asked.

"I don't know. He's no novice at what he does, but I didn't think he would be gone so long. I lent him the .444. I think I'll go up the mountain and check it out."

She felt her father want to protest.

"You shouldn't go alone," he tried.

"I've been going places alone since I was a kid."

There was no answer for that.

"I'll come," Sticks suggested.

"Yeah, right," she scoffed.

He followed her to her room.

"I mean it — I'll come with you, Willa." Sticks was serious.

"You can't run in the snow."

"Well, can't you carry me or something? Shit, dude, you turn big as a horse — freakin' white nightmare with horns. Fuckin' kick-ass deer, man. Do lady deer even have horns?"

She laughed so hard, tears ran down her face. She sat down on the bed and buried her face in her hands. Maybe because Sticks was a stoner he believed things more readily than people who could never imagine a warp to the world. Rincon would never have believed it. In the end, she took him so he wouldn't follow her and run into trouble by himself. She gave him her rifle to carry, easing the sling so it would fit across his chest.

Sticks held on and closed his eyes. She knew his eyes were closed because of how he flopped around.

Open your eyes, or you will fall off! she told him.

When they reached the high shelf, she shape-shifted so quickly that Sticks fell off her. There was only one set of tracks into the passage and back out: Corwyn hadn't returned from his hunt. He'd changed his clothes, taken the crossbow, and banked the fire. It was out now, but the stones were still warm and there was a lingering warmth in the room. The cougar totem was gone from the table. While Sticks turned in a surprised circle, Willa set a new the fire and banked it to last.

"Do you want to stay here, or come further with me? It will be colder further up the mountain."

"I'll come."

There were furs across the bed; it looked as though Corwyn was making something, but it wasn't anything identifiable yet. She rummaged in a wooden chest and found an old fur coat; she thought it was beaver. It was large and fit over Sticks' other coat with room to spare.

When they leaped up the granite, Sticks held on and again refused to open his eyes until they reached level ground.

She raced across the brilliant snowfield. Corwyn's track was clear and his scent, though faint, was a line she could follow with her eyes shut.

She had run for two hours when Sticks grunted. "There," he shouted. Across a wide, steep hillside, a dark shape was visible in the snow.

It was Corwyn. He lay face-up on a pile of furs. When Willa reached him, she quickly reshaped herself, tumbling Sticks into the snow.

"You have to stop doing that, woman," Sticks complained.

She touched Corwyn. He had a tawny skin draped over him. His lips were blue with cold and his skin was chilled, but he was alive. His wolf coat was torn and he was spattered with blood. The bandages on his arm were soaked in fresh blood.

"Corwyn," she croaked, her voice shredded by cold and breathless running. "Corwyn!"

His lips moved.

"Corwyn, can you hear me?" she said, very close to his ear.

"M...light," he whispered, trying to raise his hand.

"Oh God," she breathed. "Don't you leave me," she said firmly, holding back panic, trying not to cry.

She drew out her cellphone. Amazingly, it showed two bars. Apparently the network still had her back, she thought wryly. She held down the second preset. Her dad answered after one ring.

"Willa. Where are you?"

"I don't know. Somewhere behind Silverhorn Peak, probably ten or twelve miles northeast. I don't think we can make it back on our own. Corwyn's hurt and he's lost a lot of blood. What should I do?"

"Is he responsive?"

"Not very. He muttered something, but I don't think he's really conscious."

"Can you tell what happened?"

"Looks like he got torn up by wolves. He's lying on a pile of fresh pelts."

"How did he survive?"

"I don't know. He's been bandaged. But he's bleeding. What should I do?"

"Can you carry him?"

"I don't think so. Not far. He's bleeding too badly. Maybe I need to do something about that first. He's terribly cold."

"What sort of terrain are you in?"

"It's the open face of a high ridge."

"Can you get him somewhere flat?"

"Yeah. I think we can do that."

"Who's we?"

"Sticks is with me."

"Okay, good. Get him somewhere flat. Keep him warm. Do you have water?"

"Yes."

"Give him water. The warmer, the better. Get him warm. See if you can get him to respond. Hang tough for a spell, sweetheart. Let me see what I can do to get you out of there."

Willa shifted and with Sticks' help, she got Corwyn onto her back. Sticks clambered along beside the White Hart in the snow to keep Corwyn from tumbling off. They reached a high, flat meadow and eased Corwyn to the snow. She made another trip to bring their gear and the fur pelts. She shifted back to human, then she and Sticks dug a depression in the snow and lined it with fur. She got Corwyn laid out, with his arm where the snow could prop it up. She covered him with more furs and the cougar-skin cape. They got him to take a little water, but he didn't respond when she called his name.

"Sticks — we have to keep him warm. You crawl in on one side, I'll crawl in on the other. Our body heat will warm the furs."

She took the injured side and pulled Corwyn against her carefully. She felt his heartbeat.

"He's gonna be okay, Willa," Sticks said helplessly. "...But what the fuck are we gonna do?"

"Wait for my dad to call me back. He's got a lot of contacts with veterans in the area — maybe he can get one of his friends to come get us."

"Why can't you just call for Life Flight?"

"Life Flight won't come unless a paramedic or someone with medical qualifications is with the patient to request it."

"Really?" Sticks asked.

"Yeah. When I was in high school, three of my friends got caught in an avalanche. My one friend dug out the other two. They tried to do CPR on his younger brother. He had a satellite phone and called for Life Flight. The two kids couldn't revive his brother, but the Life Flight center said the paramedics had to reach them before they would send the chopper. It took five hours for Search and Rescue to reach the boys. My friend's brother was dead by then — long dead."

"That's fucked up, man."

"Think about it, Sticks. We can't call Life Flight for Corwyn anyway. He doesn't even have a Social Security number."

"Lie about it, Willa. Tell them he's an illegal alien. They give medical care to illegals all the time."

The absurdity hit her and she began to laugh. Her phone played Home on the Range.

"Do you have your GPS app turned on?" her dad asked.

"It's on."

"Here's the deal. My friend, Colonel Tracy Ford, is with the Reserve. They're bringing a chopper to get you. He needs to coordinate with your phone to get your location. They were already airborne on an exercise, and they're on their way to you now. They'll bring you down to the ranch. I'll take care of this end. Hang in there, sweetheart. We'll get you down."

"Thanks Dad." Tears leaked from her eyes.

Corwyn stirred against her. They were very warm now. In her mind she heard him say, *Don't cry, Moonlight.*

In 1974 gray wolves in the Northern Rockies,
the northern Great Lakes, the Southwest,
and in Texas were listed as endangered under
the Endangered Species Act.

FRIENDS ALONG
THE WAY

Rotor-wash spun sharp flakes of snow, and Willa buried her face in her coat as the pulse of the blades beat against her. The Blackhawk came down on the white expanse, and four soldiers in camo gear leaped to the snow. One was a medic.

The senior officer emerged last of the four. "Ms. MacLeod, I'm Colonel Ford. I was with your father in the Gulf. He's a true hero." He took her hand. "We're going to get you out of here."

The medic started Corwyn on a saline drip, then the men loaded Corwyn and everything else into the chopper, helping her and Sticks in. Within minutes they were airborne.

As they lifted away, the colonel looked down.

"How the hell did you get here, anyway?"

"We ran," she said.

"No way," one of the soldiers, a corporal, said.

"If you weren't Ronan MacLeod's daughter, I wouldn't think it was possible," the colonel said. "But then — you are, and you're here."

The medic came forward. He leaned close so she could hear.

"Blood pressure's coming up, and we're getting him warmed up. His heart rate is better. He'll need emergency care, but I think he's going to make it. Who sutured his arm?"

"I don't know," she shouted. "He was bandaged and unresponsive when we found him."

"Not a bad job for sinew — kind of crude materials, but some skill there. I don't think he could have done that himself. Wolves tore him up pretty bad. I think the doctor from your clinic will be at the ranch when we reach the drop point."

"We're just a few minutes out, Ms. MacLeod," Colonel Ford said. "I understand you're in a rock band."

"Yeah," she said. "Blackwater. Sticks here is my drummer." She gestured to Sticks. He grinned and waved.

"Hoo, yeah," one of the enlisted men said and tapped fists with another. "We knew it. Sir, she's the lead singer, sir."

"You guys like Blackwater?" she shouted.

"Yes, ma'am! We sure do, ma'am!"

"Ms. MacLeod," the medic touched her shoulder. "The patient is responding. He asked for you."

"Excuse me, Colonel, guys...." she said.

"Ma'am."

She went to Corwyn. She kissed his hands and held them against her cheeks.

Don't cry, he told her. *I'm not leaving*. He closed his eyes.

The chopper came around and began to descend, landing in front of the bunkhouse where there was a large, open parking area.

Her father and Dr. Lossman were waiting. Colonel Ford went straight to Captain MacLeod when they debarked, while the men unloaded the patient and the gear. Willa asked them to wait a moment and ran to the studio. She came back as the soldiers were boarding.

"Colonel," she said, "would you and your men be interested in copies of our CD? I've signed them."

"Thank you ma'am," the soldiers said, taking the CD's.

She held up four strips of paper. "And how 'bout tickets to our concert next week at BSU? Four of them, up front seating."

"Oooo yeah! That's what I'm talking about. Thank you ma'am," the Sergeant Major said.

She handed the tickets to Colonel Ford. "Thank you, Colonel. A thousand thank-you's."

"Glad to be of service, Ms MacLeod. Your father saved my life, you know." He saluted her father, climbed aboard, and the Blackhawk took off.

They took Corwyn to the closest bunkhouse, where Dr. Lossman examined him.

"He needs emergency care," the doctor said. "He's stabilized, but he probably needs blood. We absolutely have to go in and work on that torn-up arm. I don't know who stitched the wounds, but the area needs to be reconstructed and re-closed with dissolving stitches. The risk of infection is high. The wound wouldn't heal cleanly anyway, as I'm sure the sinew wasn't sterile. If we don't do all that, the scarring and damage after it heals will be substantial."

"No blood transfusion," her father told the doctor. "He has a rare type. You won't be able to match it. Saline would be safer."

"We can do that. I'd like to Life Flight him, considering the blood loss, the tissue damage, and the borderline vitals. The medic got his pressure back up, but it may not stay that way."

"Any possibility we could just treat him here, doc?" her father asked. Willa began to relax; Dad was in charge, protecting the Clan.

"That would go seriously against my Hippocratic oath and my medical ethics. Who is he, Captain MacLeod?"

"Coér Mac Vyn. Corwyn. Our families go way back."

Willa looked up. "He's...uhh...my boyfriend. We're engaged." Corwyn squeezed her hand and she saw his eyes gleam. She leaned close. "They're going to insist on taking you to the hospital, Corwyn. What shall I do?"

"Willa...." he whispered.

"Should I let them treat you? Are you okay with that?"

Come with me.

"I don't know if they'll let me. I'm not a relative."

Yes you are. Didn't I hear you say we are betrothed?

She blushed. It took great effort not to drop her eyes.

I like it when you do that. Corwyn closed his eyes. Dr. Lossman took his blood pressure again.

"Willa, his pressure is dropping. Why don't you want him to go to the hospital?"

"Ah. He's sort of...not in the system. Doesn't have a Social Security number, driver's license, anything like that. Native," she improvised. "Kinda reclusive. I can pay cash for his treatment. Can we let some things slide?"

"He's American, isn't he?"

"Very much so."

"There are some ways around the paperwork. Let me take care of that. We'll run it through the clinic. Will that help?"

They waited for her decision. Corwyn squeezed her hand.

"Okay. But only if I can go with him. I might match his blood type, or I could be a donor for his type. Sometimes, he doesn't understand our English so well." She squeezed Corwyn's hand back.

Sticks stuck his head in the door.

"How's the patient?"

"We're going to Life Flight him," Willa said.

"Bummer. Will that be cool, man?"

"It's cool," she said. "I'll go with."

"Dude, Jonesy caught a monster fish!"

Dr. McInally found Willa asleep with her head on the bed next to the patient, the sleeping man's fingers laced in hers. He paused in the doorway. The man had strong, clean features, and though he was weathered and dark from the sun, he was not obviously Native American. McInally wasn't sure, but he thought that to be officially Native American, the proportion of native blood had to be at least one quarter. Maybe the percentage was less? It wasn't important, the doctor decided. The patient's long silver hair was plaited in two braids and had something in it — were they bells? He couldn't quite tell. The stud in one ear was dark blue and tiny, and there was a gold loop in the other.

Who was he to Willa MacLeod? McInally wondered. He was not closely related, that was certain. He didn't think the man was part of Blackwater. It was the blood that was so impossible. The transfusion had worked perfectly — that was the strange part. Their blood type matched, and was the same as Willa's father; but Willa and the patient both had some additional very strange blood markers that her father didn't have. It was the talk of the lab.

Wryly, Dr. McInally thought that if the lab folks saw the subjects, they would have fully expected something unusual. He cleared his throat.

Two disturbingly intense pairs of pale blue eyes met his.

"You are extraordinarily alert for someone on heavy pain medication," McInally said. "I'm Doctor Jamie McInally, Mister...uhh...Macvyn. Ms. MacLeod and I have already met." He came to the bed and Corwyn took his hand firmly. Willa stood up and paced the room.

"Call me Corwyn," Corwyn said in his own language.

McInally looked quizzically at Willa.

"He says to call him Corwyn," she explained.

"Can we dispense with that for now, Corwyn? Willa?" the doctor said. "I don't care if you don't have ID. Nothing would surprise me after having seen your blood work. But it would be so much simpler to speak English here." The doctor closed the door to the hallway.

"So. Let's talk about the injuries. The surgeon reconstructed the tissue in your upper arm. The tearing was severe, but he managed to reattach everything. We may lose some of the skin over the next weeks, but we're hoping a skin graft won't be necessary. Keeping the area clean is very important, and the high-dose antibiotics we gave you will help to avoid infection. The wound had been cleaned up remarkably well, and whoever originally stitched it and dressed it had considerable skill. It probably saved your arm, Corwyn."

"There were some tiny fractures to the bone, probably from the animal's canine teeth; nothing that could be addressed, so the surgeon just removed the small bone fragments. The bone will heal on its own, but will be quite painful for a while. It is absolutely vital that you stay on the I.V. antibiotics for at least five days. If infection were to develop in the bone, we would have a much more serious problem. That means you will have to stay here at least four more days. After that, you will be on an oral antibiotic for another twenty days. The arm will have to be immobile for a while — at least until the stitches take. We'll use a soft wrap and a sling when you leave here."

He perused the chart again. "The leg seems not to be much of an issue — puncture wounds for the most part, and some bruising. No frostbite; that's lucky. It looks as though the animal shook you pretty savagely and had powerful jaws with a lot of teeth. I would guess he was a very large wolf. We did a brain scan to be certain we didn't have any issues with bruising in the brain; normally we call that shaken-baby syndrome. Everything looked okay."

McInally looked up. "Do you understand, Corwyn?"

Corwyn blinked. "Yes," he answered quietly.

"Good. I've seen some maulings. A lot of dogs and children — usually these are on the face, or we have issues with shaking. I had a bear mauling that was pretty bad. Bears do more biting than tearing, and they use their claws to rake the victim. But I've never seen quite this sort of tearing.... Of course, we don't get many wolf attacks. If we were to believe the biologists and the media, wolves don't attack humans. Of course, we all know they're full of crap. Would you like to tell me about it? Off the record, of course. It must be quite a story."

"Wolves are cunning and deadly killers," Corwyn remarked. "They will often eat their victims alive — they do that with elk — tear strips off the haunches while the animal runs. But just as often, they will kill for pleasure — for entertainment. Unlike most animals, they don't kill only because they are hungry. With me, they were angry. I was fortunate that another hunter came along when he did."

"So there was more than one wolf?"

"Only one was able to get to me."

"You weren't hunting wolves, were you?"

"No. Of course not!" Willa interjected.

"They were hunting me," Corwyn said. "I defended myself."

"They? How many were there?"

"Wolves hunt together. There were fourteen to begin with. The last five were the problem."

"What happened to the other hunter?"

"He dressed my wounds and vanished."

"Did you know him?"

Corwyn hesitated. "No."

Clearly, Dr. McInally thought that Corwyn probably did know more than that. He closed the chart and looked up at them, although he seemed to find their eyes rather disquieting.

"Your blood work came back, Ms MacLeod. You showed no antibodies to any unusual viruses we know about. Your blood type is slightly rare, but it matches your father and Corwyn here and it's nothing all that strange. There were, however, some very extraordinary markers that your father doesn't have. We don't know what they are, but this could possibly account for the fever you had — antibodies to something we don't know how to test for, or — who knows? Blood testing isn't always an exact science, but most of the time it's pretty blue-collar. We just don't know in your case. I would have let it be one of those mysteries that you see every so often when you're a doctor, until Corwyn came in as a patient. You, Corwyn, have the same blood type and the very same weird blood markers that I saw in Willa's tests. Do you know if you are related?"

"We come from the same ancestral people — it was relatively far back," Corwyn said. "We are close and not close. Different family, same tribe."

"And what tribe is that, Ms. MacLeod?"

"Do you really want to know?" she asked.

"Well, naturally I am curious. I can't imagine that you are Native American descendants. I'm not looking to doubt you — your blood tells a very mysterious story, so I would believe something remarkable, actually. But most Native American people have Type A blood, so that sort of leaves you two out of that possibility. Perhaps this is a blood type that has all but vanished from the modern world. I would be interested in what you might know. Off the record." He smiled reassuringly.

"It's pre-Celtic," she said cautiously. "I don't know much more than that."

"Listen. I'm a doctor. I'm trained to think that certain things are so and others can't be. Most of the time, everything falls conveniently into one box or the other. But I see strange things sometimes that aren't mentioned in any textbook or published study. I want to give you the best care I can, not make trouble. I'm not going to call National Geographic or anything; I'm fine having a mystery all to myself. Maybe I can be of some help to you that way." His gaze did not waver or drop, and Willa trusted him.

"My dad, Corwyn, and I are all that remains of a pre-Hibernian people who migrated here during or just after the last Ice Age. My dad isn't full blooded. It's complicated."

"I imagine. Did these people have a name?"

"Sithé," Corwyn said softly.

"Someday, maybe, you can tell me the whole story. I would love to hear it. The scientist in me has got his ears perked like an eager dog. But now, the doctor in me will be content to deal with the present. We know at least that transfusing you with anything other than Willa or her father's blood would have probably been deadly. Let's leave it at that and just get you well enough to go home."

"Does he have to stay so long?" Willa asked. "Can't we take him home and keep him on the IVs and hire a nurse or something? I can afford it."

"Listen, with these wounds I'm amazed he isn't in more critical condition. So we aren't having this discussion until he's been on those antibiotics for at least forty-eight hours."

"Okay," she conceded.

"I promise no one will bother you. Mind you, that wouldn't be the case if you didn't have money to pay for hospital care. Fortunately, that's not an issue. I'll stay on the case. I can switch my shifts around so I take days off after Corwyn's released."

"Okay."

"Other than descending from some extinct people — how else are you connected?"

Corwyn took Willa's hand. The look that passed between them could not be misinterpreted.

"Okay, then. Got that straight," the doctor said.

Paler be they than daunting death
the sleek slim deer
the tall tense deer.

E. E. Cummings

SINGING IT HOME

W illa was reminded that she had other pressing obligations when Sticks sent her a message. It was a photo of Jonesy holding a thirty-inch lake trout that he said weighed eighteen pounds. She showed it to Corwyn. Jonesy was undemonstrative by nature, so his big smile said that this was a major triumph.

"Sticks is a good friend," Corwyn said. "I am surprised you were not more than friends."

"With Sticks?" she laughed.

"He loves you very deeply."

"*Sticks?*" she said, flabbergasted. "I know he thinks I'm sexy — but it's all in fun."

"For Sticks, it is more than that. He was very angry about your last lover."

"He was?" She was blushing again. "How do you know that?"

"I hear this in him."

"I don't hear it. Why don't I hear it?"

"He doesn't want you to."

"So," she asked, "is he angry over you, too?"

"Not at all. He's pleased. He knows that I like him."

She was mystified. And hungry. Her stomach growled; she missed Sara's cooking. She thought about ordering in. She didn't have wheels here at the hospital, so she couldn't go out to get anything.

The phone rang "She's a Lady".

"Regi," she answered, putting it on speaker-phone.

"What's the matter, sweetie?"

"I haven't said anything yet. How would you know something was the matter?"

"Well, maybe because you got Life-Flighted to the hospital, I thought that just possibly something might be ever-so-slightly the matter."

"Other than the fact that a wolf tried to kill Corwyn and I'm stuck here at the hospital without a car so I can't go get anything to eat and I miss my dad and I need to be practicing for the gig next week…we're perfectly OK."

"Good, you're fine then. I got good news for you, sweetie. I'm in Ramon with your dad, and we are on our way over to you. I have a care package from Sara. I can't fix the band thing, but Jeb's taking them fishing. Apparently your guitar player — Jonesy, is it? — he caught a monster in your reservoir, and everyone has forgotten all about practice. Sticks was so torn between coming with us and fishing, it was pitiful — but the fishing won out. Actually, your dad told him to stay and keep an eye on the place, and Sticks couldn't have been happier."

"Wow! Great."

"We'll be there in half an hour. How's Corwyn?"

"He'll be fine."

"Tell me when we get there. I gotta drive."

Sara had sent sandwiches, apples, water, a large thermos of coffee, and another one filled with mint tea. There was a package of huckleberry muffins, and homemade ham croissants. Willa set the basket on the counter and got out the croissants.

"Who wants some?" she asked. She was the only taker.

"Corwyn?" she asked, raising the pastry.

He shook his head. If he wouldn't eat, he wasn't feeling well.

"How's the patient?" her dad asked.

"Two pints of my blood and some saline later, better. Surgery on his arm took five hours. They have him on high-dose antibiotics and pain meds. The wolf fractured the bone a little, and they very much don't want a bone infection."

"No problem with the blood?" her dad asked carefully.

"Nope. I was a perfect match. We're the talk of the lab."

"Soooo, Corwyn…" Regi began, "aside from the seven wolves — whose pelts I did not see, by the way — how many wolves were there?"

"Fourteen altogether."

"What happened to the others?"

"Dead."

"You're lucky you aren't dead," she grumbled. "You know that you can't hunt wolves in the Silverhorn."

"They were hunting me. And Willa."

"Officially, wolves don't hunt people."

"Please tell that to the wolves."

"If I fly over the area, what will I see?"

"Wolf kill. Two dead elk and a lot of tracks."

"What kind of tracks?"

"Elk, wolf, human, deer, and cougar. And whatever else turned up after I left." He sighed and closed his eyes.

"Maybe it will snow…." Regi said hopefully. "Who sewed you up?"

"Joseph Yellowgrass, Sara Blackhawk's husband." Willa's head whipped around.

"How did he get there?" Regi asked.

"Ask him."

"The media is clamoring for info. What should I tell them?"

"As little as possible," Willa said.

"No argument there! The wolf thing is a big issue. Let's take some photos."

"Now?" asked Willa.

"Yeah."

Willa hadn't seen Corwyn's wounds yet. When she did, she left the room. Regi found her in the waiting room, crying.

"You better come back. Corwyn's concerned. And the Channel 2 folks are bugging me. I didn't tell them anything, but they're gonna figure it out and be here any minute. You might need to talk to the hospital about some security. Officially, this was a wolf attack on a lone back-country snow-shoer. I'm not saying that there was more than one wolf, and I am definitely not saying what happened to the wolf— not to anyone: media, my agency, or otherwise. If you can stick to the same story, that would help a lot."

"Okay."

"Do me a big favor. Talk that man out of hunting wolves."

"I'm never going to let him go alone again."

"I do not want to hear this. I am not listening."

"I didn't say anything."

"Sticks said you're getting married."

"Really? Did he say when and to whom?"

"That's my girl."

Willa thought Corwyn was finally asleep.

"Do you wish to talk about the betrothal?" he muttered.

"What betrothal?" Willa said. They were alone at last, after hours of people — friends, media, nurses, doctors — and questions that they answered vaguely or not at all. Regi's ever-patient husband Kenne came to pick up Regi and Ronan, leaving Ramon at the hospital for Willa.

"Ahhhh. So your talk of our impending marriage was a ruse for the doctors. I wondered if perhaps customs had changed so much that women did the asking in your world."

Willa bit her lip. "I was scared," she said.

"So was I."

"You are not going hunting alone again," she said.

"So. Are you coming up the mountain, or am I coming down?"

"Down. Both. Down, mostly."

"I thought that might be so. Is that what you wish?"

"Yes."

"As a myth or as a man?"

She thought about this awhile. "Are they separate things?"

"For you, they might be."

"As a man, then, if I have to make a choice."

"Ah. How will your father take this?"

"I believe I clearly heard him say that you were welcome at the ranch."

"Yes. Indeed he did, Willa MacLeod. Is this the custom, then?"

"What do you mean?"

"For men and women simply to live together and share a bed? Do they not get married these days? Your father and mother were married, were they not?"

She couldn't remember any man who so consistently made her blush.

"People get married when they love each other. Have families. Nothing has changed. Young people do live together a lot — sexual values in this society aren't rigid, and divorce is very common but often messy. So they live together and then, when they don't get along or they get tired of one another, they move out and live together with someone else for a while. We have something of a temporary society."

"One which protects predators. That is very disturbing. Have you lived with another man before, Willa?"

"No. Just my dad. I've never needed a man."

"Ah. Then you wish to share your bed with me on a temporary basis, and have me go back up the mountain, or somewhere else, when you get tired of me or become angry with me?"

"Fuck."

"How should I translate that, Willa MacLeod?"

Willa blushed, speechless. She stood up and walked to the window so Corwyn wouldn't see her tears.

"I don't know your customs, Willa. I only wish to understand."

She turned around. "I can't imagine, ever, ever, ever, ever, ever wanting to live without you. How hard is that to understand?"

"That is very clear."

Willa and Regi went shopping while Ronan and Sticks sat with Corwyn. Willa didn't like to leave him alone.

"You gave us a little scare, Coér Mac Vyn," Ronan said.

"That would be sort of putting it mildly, dude. Willa was scared shitless, man."

"It is a strange world you live in now, where predators are protected, and men and women have casual relations."

Sticks choked.

"Yes it is, son," Ronan said.

"Is 'son' not still a term for a younger man, Ronan MacLeod?"

"Yes it is. Sorry. You just seem younger than me, somehow. That's pretty strange, isn't it?"

"And how do I seem as perhaps a...man for your daughter?"

"I'm not sure I understand."

"I'm a little more traditional than Willa. I would like to have a more traditional partnership."

"I told you, dude. 'Here comes the bride...!'" Sticks sang, almost on key.

"Are you coming down the mountain, my friend?" Ronan asked.

"I thought it might be advisable."

"I think you would be a fine man for my daughter."

"I don't understand how the traditions are, Ronan."

"What traditions, son?"

Corwyn smiled. It was a good sign, being called 'son' by this man.

"It appears that things have changed much of late. I don't know how to ask her."

"That's easy, dude," Sticks said. "You buy her an engagement ring, get down on one knee, and say 'Willa, will you marry me?' Or maybe something more like how you would say it, man. That 'Moonlight' thing really gets her."

Corwyn looked at Ronan.

"That's about it," Ronan agreed.

"You don't think she needs a younger man, then?"

"Well, she always wanted a father figure...."

"What does that mean?"

"Nothing. Nothing. I'm sorry. Bad joke. I've lived with her so long I'm becoming insolent like her."

"Maybe, Ronan MacLeod, she is like you."

"That's a compliment, Corwyn," Ronan mused.

"Dude. You're not old, man. She's like, a real woman, you know. She doesn't need a baby, like that Rincon joker. How old are you anyway? Like thirty-eight or something? Forty?" Sticks scrutinized him. "She ain't no chickadee, you know. She's got a birthday comin' — she's gettin' up to woman-land from baby-land, you know?"

Corwyn laughed. "I am much older than she is, believe me."

"What? Do you think she's going to care, dude?"

"As you said, Corwyn, she's not very traditional," Ronan added.

"Is giving a birthing-day gift still a tradition today?"

"It is," Ronan said.

"And what day is that for Willa?"

"December third," he replied. "Right after Thanksgiving."

Corwyn closed his eyes and sank against the pillows. His color was good, but he was tired.

"What is an engagement ring?"

"A diamond, dude," Stick said. "A big rock. Ice. Chicks dig 'em."

"Where does a man get one?" Corwyn asked, puzzled.

Regi and Willa came in the door then, laughing. A little breeze struck them and Corwyn heard the bells. He smiled contentedly.

"Let Sticks and me take care of it, son," Ronan told him.

Dr. McInally entered the room hesitantly, and visibly braced himself before making eye contact.

"Hey," Willa said. "The good doctor! How's it going today with the patient?"

He relaxed. "You're pretty happy, I see. Am I intruding on something?"

"Yeah, a little. I got you something," she said. She picked up an envelope from the dinner tray and waved it. She handed it to him. "Open it!"

The doctor pulled out three tickets. "Are these tickets to your concert?" he asked.

"Front row, center."

"Wow. I don't know what to say."

"They come with a condition."

"Okay. . . ." McInally said tentatively.

"Hey. You're going to like this, because I know you came in here to tell me that Corwyn can't leave yet."

His expression was so suspicious that Willa laughed — a big, open guffaw.

"You have to take Corwyn and my dad to the concert. It's in three days. You want to keep him here at least two more, I know. This way, you can keep him three. My band's coming to Boise so we can practice. My dad will come over here and sit with Corwyn — they seem to like each other, why, I don't have a clue. You probably scheduled your time off around when you planned to let Corwyn go home, so I figure you'll be free that night. So how 'bout it? Is it a deal — he stays here three days, then you get to babysit for one night? You can even drive my car if you like."

"I have a perfectly good car, thank you very much. But yes, it's a deal."

Willa felt incredibly relieved. "I wanted him to come to the show, but I was afraid it would be too much. I'll pay for your time, Dr. McInally."

"No, no." He waved the tickets. "This will do."

"My dad's buying dinner. Can Corwyn leave the hospital in the morning, so he can go to the hotel with my dad? You can pick them up there."

"That works for me," McInally said.

"...So what did you want to tell us?" she asked.

"That I didn't want Corwyn to leave until he finished the five days of antibiotics."

"That's it?"

"Yup."

Willa probed his thoughts to be sure. "Why did you seem so reluctant to come in the door, then?" she asked.

"Did I?" he asked. But clearly he thought, *because telling you anything you don't want to hear scares the hell out of me.*

"I guess I was imagining things," she said.

Willa started the concert on autopilot. They were solid without a doubt, and when they began the acoustic set they started to really catch fire. Willa's voice was big and deep with emotion, and the crowd heard that. Jake Collins went off the hook about then — she decided maybe he thought he was better on the acoustic guitar than on electric. He wasn't, but believing sometimes makes miracles. They gave the new song, "Southern Soul", its first public performance — and the crowd came to its feet for it.

She let "Smile" take them into the final set. They continued with two early hits, "Down the Street" and "Killin' Time". She felt the crowd waiting — the students in the audience were mostly familiar with Blackwater's music, so they knew what songs to expect. She looked down. She could make out her dad's and Corwyn's faces even though the lights were very bright in her eyes.

"Thank you all for coming tonight," she told the crowd. She took off her jacket; she'd worn the black lacy bustier under it. She heard a chorus of whistles. She picked up the Taylor and buttoned the end strap. She strummed it, did the little riff from "Waitin'". The audience got very quiet.

"You know, we have a new face with us tonight. Some of you might have noticed that our lead guitarist, Rincon, is not with us. The ladies certainly noticed." The women in the crowd hooted and whistled and everyone laughed. Neil started a very soft chord sequence on the keyboards.

"Rincon's one hell of a guitar player, but when I told him that I wanted him to play some steel guitar, he decided to go find a new band." The crowd was silent.

"So I want to introduce our new lead guitarist. He told me he would try to play the steel guitar, but he didn't make me any promises." She strummed a chord and did a little slip with it. "I can do it if I have to, so no biggie," she laughed and the crowd roared.

"Anyway, on the ancient Stratocaster tonight, and sometimes on my sweet little Taylor six, is the newest member of Blackwater,

Jake Collins!" She let go of the guitar and raised her hands to clap along with the audience.

"Come on ladies. Can't you welcome him a little more enthusiastically — he's a hunk, don't you think?" She waved her hand at him with a flourish and Jake bowed. The women screamed and the crowd roared.

She played another few bars of "Waitin'".

"I also want to say a little thank you tonight to four guys who helped us out last week." She walked to the edge of the stage.

"Do you all see these guys down here in the front row dressed in camo?" The crowd was quiet; this was a rock crowd, not a country crowd that automatically cheered men in uniform.

"These guys are Blackhawk crew in the Army Reserve," she said to them, gesturing with her hand. "Hey, Colonel Ford, would you and your crew stand up please? Come on, you sexy guys, don't be shy. They are gonna love you like I do — come on, stand up for me, please!" They did, looking a little shy.

"Thank you, Colonel, I'll try not to embarrass you anymore." They sat down.

"Do you know — these guys aren't just out there saving our country — these four guys saved my life last week." There was a smattering of applause. "Yeah. My special guy was gonna die in the mountains 'cause he got hurt, and these guys came and just plucked us up, me and Sticks" — there was hearty cheering — "and my man. I wouldn't be here tonight if not for these brave guys, so I want you all to tell them what that means to you, okay?" This time the crowd cheered loudly.

"I don't know if I thanked you that day, Colonel Ford, Lieutenant Brackowitz, Sergeant Major Howard, and Corporal Britos — 'cause

I just don't remember much about that day. But I want you to know how grateful I am. And everyone here wants you to know how grateful they are that I am here tonight, thanks to you!" The crowd agreed.

"Now I know you all think that this next song was Rincon's song...." The crowd went wild.

"But...." she waited until the place got quiet, "really, it's mine. And I'm singing it tonight for someone very, very special."

Neil and Chloe launched into the lead-in for "Waitin'". The crowd rose to its feet.

"He's here tonight," she shouted over the roar, "so you all let him know if I sing it right!"

Blackwater brought the house down with "Waitin'". After they left the stage, they had to wait for five minutes backstage for the crowd to settle into demanding the encore. When they ran back onstage, no one was sitting, but the crowd went instantly quiet.

The lighters and flashlights looked like stars when the house lights dimmed. Willa sang "Night is When the Stars Die", and they rolled it into three choruses. The song faded with just the big Guild and the harmonica.

"Good night Boise," she said. "We love you!"

The crowd brought them back for a curtain call, and they held hands and bowed.

A little later, the arena manager came to the dressing room where they were packing up. Corwyn and her dad had already gone back to the hotel.

"There's a huge crowd of students, man," he said. "Every one of them bought a CD! You guys wouldn't feel like signing autographs, would you? I mean, we get these bands in here all the time and when the show's over, they split, man. But you're like the hometown thing. You don't have to do it — it's not in the contract or anything, and you sure aren't obligated. I just wondered if you might want to."

She looked at the band. "Are you guys up for that?"

"Sure Willa. This is your gig. If you want to, we'll do it," Neil said.

"We gotta have security, man," Sticks said. "Those dogs'll be all over Willa."

"We'll take care of that, ma'am," someone said. The Blackhawk crew stood there.

"Okay. We'll do it," she agreed.

And much later, when they finally got back to the hotel, she was too tired to even talk. Corwyn stayed up most of the night, watching her sleep.

If the deep night is haunted, it is I
Who am the ghost: not the tall trees
Not the white moonlight slanting down like rain,
Filling the hollows with bright pools of silver.

Robert Hillyer

RUNNING WITH
THE WIND

She supposed they would have to adopt Sticks, now that he was part of their secret. Everyone except for Sticks went straight home from Boise to spend Thanksgiving with their families. The band would return on Monday to get back into the studio and finish the new tracks. Sticks came back to the ranch with them.

New snow blanketed the valley and the mountains. Everything was white and virginal; the ranch sparkled like a Christmas card. Willa was so glad to be home that she wept.

She wanted to run. She wanted to change shape and run and run and run and run until her breath was knife-sharp with cold and exertion. She wanted Corwyn to run with her.

"Can you run?" she asked. The stitches were the dissolving kind — surely they would be okay.

"I don't know. I can walk, maybe. I can hop." She looked so vibrant; he didn't want to disappoint her.

"You can watch and I will run," she said with a laugh.

She tied his boots and helped him into his coat. It had been mended. Hand in hand they walked up the hill.

"We need snowshoes for this," she complained.

Sticks was sitting under the tree. They stopped.

"Hey," he said. "No badass deer with scary horns? What's up with that?"

"Corwyn doesn't know if he can make the shift. We were going to test it someplace a little less visible. You want to come?"

"No way, dude. I'm going to stay within shouting distance of help, thanks. Have fun!" he called after them.

At the trailhead, she shifted. *I will carry you.*

Corwyn grasped the lower branches of her antlers. His weight didn't faze her. She ran. The trail was knee deep with snow. There was one deer print on it, nothing more. When she reached the bend in the creek, a cougar track crossed the trail, heading downward. Willa bounded down the slope and leaped the creek. On the ledge high up the mountain, she waited for Corwyn to slide off before she shifted.

Someone had been there. The low fire had burned almost to ash, but the chamber was still warm. Corwyn stoked the coals. On the table was a pile of furs. Corwyn turned one over.

"These are the wolf pelts I brought back with me," he said. "Someone cured them."

Willa picked them up and dumped them in the corner.

"I haven't forgiven you yet for that. I mean, tell me, Corwyn —

don't you think that if you shaped a wolf you would be a little safer out there?"

"I don't know how to shape anything but the Stag. I don't know if it's possible. I don't know that anyone shapes the wolf except for those who change with the moon-tide."

"You mean, like werewolves? Are you serious?"

"Very much so. We don't love the full moon so much."

"The world is a little hard on prey animals. It's a Darwinian thing. Why did such genetics even happen?"

"We are not so meek and helpless as you might imagine. In ancient times, the Sithé warriors went to battle in half-shift."

"Half-shift?" A little thrill went through her.

"You have seen pictures of that. Men with antlers and swords. The magic is strong when a Sithé half-shifts, and so Sithé warriors are far less vulnerable than when fully in human or deer shape. It was the Morrígan who gave the Sithé power in half-shift."

"So why didn't you do this half-shift to do your wolf-hunting?"

"I never fully learned it. I don't know how to prevent my shape from shifting all the way. Knowledge of this used to be passed on as part of the rite of passage, but at some point the knowledge was lost. I can only hold half-shift for a few seconds before the shift goes all the way. This was one of the reasons we began to diminish."

"I see."

He took off his coat and boots and made tea. Willa walked around the room, touching things. She stopped by the fire — there was terrible restlessness in her. She shucked her coat and boots. She tried shifting slowly, tried to hold the shape when the antlers crowned her but she was still woman. She held the shape for almost a half a minute. Then a great heat built up inside, and she shifted the rest of the way. Corwyn walked to her, stroked her face and withers.

"There has never been another white Sithé — not that any story tells. There was a red one once who was a famous warrior. And a black one who had a black soul."

She touched his face with her nose. He thought about shifting. She heard the thought and re-shaped herself. He felt her hands on his chest. She unbuttoned his new shirt and carefully took it off. His arm was yellow and green where the bruising was visible above and below the protective wrap. She stepped back. She unbuttoned her jeans and stepped on the cuffs to pull them off. Her hands went to the buttons on her long shirt. As she unbuttoned it, she backed away from him. He followed. She dropped the shirt. She was wearing something red and black and amazing underneath.

Corwyn drew her against him with his good arm and dropped his face to the spot where her neck met her shoulder. He breathed in the scent of her. Then his breath caught, and he stiffened.

"What?" she asked, alarmed.

"I cannot come to you this night, Willa MacLeod."

"Why? What's wrong? Is your arm hurting?"

She stepped closer. He stepped back. She stepped close again. He closed his eyes.

"Willa, Moonlight. I cannot. If I give you my seed this night, it will produce fruit. You are — most fertile. I know by the scent. It dizzies me like a potent wine."

She considered this. Her fingertip touched his nipple, and it hardened.

"Willa," he breathed.

She unbuttoned his Levis and slipped them down.

"What was it you told me? We have this moment. It's all we have."

"But...." he tried to move back, but she moved with him. He said, "We are the last of our people. We are, as you say, prey in a world that protects predators. We should let it end with us."

"Corwyn. It's so much simpler than you want to make it. If it's meant to end with us, then it will. If not, then perhaps we must find the way to half-shift. Or to shape something that isn't prey. Or to shape nothing at all but our love. I want what you will give me this night."

He breathed out slowly and inhaled the scent of her, tasting it, savoring it. It compelled him so forcefully that had he been able to use two arms, he would have taken her where she stood.

Her hands slipped his shorts down. With her foot, she slipped them all the way off. She pushed him back and he stumbled into the chair behind him. She straddled him and eased him in past the lacy thing she had on. It was like sliding into a pool of warm water. His powerful arm wrapped her waist and held her.

"Willa, my Moonlight. Are you certain?" he asked hoarsely.

In answer, she touched his lips with hers, softly, like a snowflake, then longer, then with her tongue and her mouth in such a manner that he cried her name over and over until her name was nothing but the ending syllable.

They lay in the furs and watched the fire burn low. Finally, she got up and stoked it. When she came back, she kneeled over him and felt his skin with her lips, everywhere that she could reach, soft, whispery moth-wing kisses until he was mad with the aroma of her fruitfulness and the brush of her tongue on his burning skin. He rolled her beneath him.

Willa moaned with each breath. His seed spilled; she felt the heat of it inside, and she sensed the life spark in her belly like a small light turning on. It was a long time before she could stop calling his name.

"I have lived longer than the lives of three men," he said against her ear, "and yet I can still be surprised."

"By what?" she asked sleepily.

"By what a woman can do to a man. Nothing can bring a man to his knees so completely as when a woman takes his gift of life. It is a wondrous defeat."

It snowed again in the night. When they came down the mountain the next morning, Corwyn brought his snowshoes with him. After the White Hart carried him across the creek and up to the trail, she shifted and followed him as he cut the trail down the mountain. The trees were white, the woods hushed. The creek was noisy in all that silence. Willa was distracted. The sense of the new life inside her pervaded her awareness. She rested her hand over the flat of her belly and walked along feeling strange, and oddly connected to something circular.

Corwyn must have asked her a question. He stopped and turned around. When she realized he had turned to watch her and she saw the look on his face, she felt foolish and embarrassed. He strode back to her, lifting her hands to his face.

"If you spend the next nine months with that look of bewildered amazement on your face, I don't know that I will be able to get anything done other than to sit and watch you," he said.

Her laughter made the snow slide off the branches and down the back of her coat.

"What else do you have to do? It'll be a cold day in hell before I let you go hunting again."

Sticks and Ronan were at the kitchen table when they walked in. Sara was putting the Thanksgiving turkey into the oven. They shook the snow from their hair in a shower of bells. Willa poured coffee, changed her mind, made tea, changed her mind, gave Corwyn the tea, and took the coffee for herself after all. Sara eyed her suspiciously. She cut coffee cake for both of them.

"We were telling Sara about the concert," Ronan said. "I still can't believe that was my little girl up there. What did you think of it, Corwyn?"

"The music is still strange to me — oddly melodic and poetic, while at the same time it is discordant and...heathen? The odder thing still is that I am compelled by it. It is very sensual and arousing."

"Dude," Sticks said, "I'm not sure you can even talk like that in mixed company."

"That does lend an entirely new perspective to the showman's advice for stage-fright — you know, imagining everyone in the audience naked," Willa joked.

Corwyn choked on his tea. Her dad had to swallow a chuckle.

"You are a wicked, wicked woman," Sticks said.

"You must remember, Sticks," Corwyn said, "I was on pain medication. It adds to the sense of unreality."

"Really?" the drummer asked.

"Stop it, Sticks," Willa scolded.

"That was cool with the Blackhawk dudes, though."

"Was it okay?" she asked.

"Willa.... We have never done a better gig, man. You were badass. That thing you had on with all the little hooks and ties. Whoa, baby. And that deep voice of yours is even more kick-ass than it used to be. You had all those boys having wide-awake wet dreams in public."

"Nonsense, to quote Regi," Willa said. "How would you know?"

Sticks just looked at her. She heard what he thought, and her cheeks flamed.

"I know how that would translate into my native tongue, and I think that maybe you aren't supposed to say those things in front of the ladies."

"You *were* more than a little provocative," her father agreed.

"That's what sells," she said.

"I know that is part of it," Corwyn said. "Sticks is right. But Willa's songs are very beautiful."

Later, Willa caught Sara alone as she was getting into her car; understandably, Sara's family wanted their mom to spend the rest of the day with them. Regi and Kenne were coming out to the ranch.

"The turkey will be ready at four," Sara reminded her. "Everything else should go into the oven at three-ish. You will know."

Willa handed Sara the cougar cape that Joseph Yellowgrass had draped over Corwyn on the mountain.

"Tell him 'thank you.' I understand now why you believe so strongly in magic, Sara Blackhawk." Willa opened her hand; the cougar totem lay in her palm, an offering. Sara took the hand she loved in both of hers and closed Willa's fingers over the tiny turquoise carving.

"Keep it safe," she said. "Yellowgrass will do the same for you."

Every heart sings a song, incomplete,
until another heart whispers back.

Plato

DAYS OF THE
HART

Corwyn was healing faster than expected. Willa thought it was the nature of the magic; she figured that was why he wasn't dead — probably many times over. He spent hours with her father, or walked the ranch on snowshoes. He often disappeared during the band's studio time, coming back for dinner.

When Jake returned from Boise with Nokes, they took rooms at the motel. She would have let Jake stay in the bunkhouse with the band, but she'd made it clear Nokes was not welcome. Jake hunted the Aspen Breaks in the morning with Nokes, and came out to the ranch to work the sound board or lay down lead tracks in the afternoon.

Wednesday dawned brilliant, the coldest day of the season so far. The morning low dropped to six degrees Fahrenheit just before the sun rose over the ridge. Corwyn left early on his snowshoes, and Jeb and her dad were out with the cattle. Sara got busy in the kitchen.

"I'm making a nice lunch for you and the band today," she said, "since it's your birthday."

Willa humored them all; they were clearly up to something.

The band didn't knock off for lunch until 12:30.

"Look at the time," Chloe said. "Sara insisted we come in for lunch by 1:00, since she's fixing something special. I want to shower. Willa, can we finish up later?"

"Sure, sure. No problem. I'll go pretend that I don't know something's up and see you inside at 1:00." She wanted to change out of her leggings and sweatshirt. If they were planning something nice, she didn't want to look like the barn help.

She put on her black leather jeans. Then she decided on the black lace top with all the hooks, but toned it down with a white cotton shirt that she left unbuttoned, along with a big necklace that softened the blow of the revealing neckline. It still felt kind of daring. She looked in the mirror. *Who is that sexy woman who looks so happy?* she wondered. Her hand went to her lower abdomen, sensing an unfocused response from the tiny glimmer of life. She wet her hands and re-spiked her hair. The bells jingled and her moonstone earrings gleamed.

She walked into the big, timbered living room.

"*Surprise!*" everyone screamed, throwing streamers all over the room. The place was full. The band was all there, of course, along with Jeb and her dad, and all of Sara's family — even her husband, Joseph Yellowgrass. Regi was there with Kenne, and Dr. Lossman had brought the staff from the clinic. The only person missing was Corwyn, but he walked in as she was pulling streamers from her hair. He hesitated at the door. Their eyes met — hers shining with amusement, and his pausing in appreciation.

Sara had made a giant pot of San-Francisco-style cioppino, knowing Willa loved it. Willa heaped a bowl full of clams and crab legs and other seafood, and piled the top with sourdough bread. She ate until she could barely breathe, and then blew out the candles on her cake. Sara had decorated the Creole Chocolate Cake to look like a gold record.

Neil handed Willa a letter. Quizzically, she took it out from the record-company envelope and read the first paragraph: *Blackwater* had sold a million copies.

"Oh my god," she laughed. "We did it! You guys, we did it! Holy cow, what a birthday present." She hugged the band members, pausing to give Sticks a very lazy kiss. She loved to hear what he said in his mind when she did that. *So this was what they were up to*, she thought. *Surprising me with the gold-record letter. I didn't guess that one!*

Sticks took a guitar case from behind the couch and set it on the table. It had a red bow around it. She opened it; inside was a lovely, big-bodied Gibson SJ200 Custom. *This, I did guess*, she thought wryly.

"This can go with Neil and the band equipment. It's too freakin' expensive and too much work for you to have to fly with your guitars. I know you like the Taylor, but I thought you might like to try one of these — they're badass guitars."

Neil took another case with a bigger bow from behind the couch. She opened it. It was a Guild F512 in black with the new D-TAR pick-up system. She whistled.

"Nice. I didn't know they came in black."

"They don't. It was a special order," Neil said.

"They're from all of us, Willa," Chloe said. "Even Jake pitched in." Jake gave a little salute.

Willa opened Regi's present next. She whistled again. Regi had gotten her a beautiful soft black leather notebook that folded closed like an envelope, with a silver buckle engraved with her name. Inside, it held two tablets and a couple of very pretty pens.

Sara gave her an envelope. In it was an unlimited coupon for huckleberry pie.

Her dad handed her another envelope. She read the home-made card, wiping away tears. "Here's something special when you need a break from your bothersome dad. I love you, Dad," it read. There were two vouchers for round-trip airline tickets to pretty much anywhere.

"Jeez, Dad. Is this a hint? Are you trying to get rid of me?" She gave him a big kiss. She opened all the other cards and thanked everyone — most had given her gift cards for various stores they knew she liked. Sticks gave her one for Victoria's Secret — and blushed when she favored him with another big kiss.

"We all liked the last thing you picked up there," he said, waving a hand in the general direction of her outfit. He handed her a glass of champagne.

"Can I have an orange juice instead?" she asked, and he poured one for her. Corwyn, who had stood quietly inside the door, stepped forward. The way her dad and Sticks watched him gave her some warning. He had something made of fur over his arm.

"I made you something," he said, and displayed a full-length coat. He helped her put it on. She ran her hands down the soft front plackets.

"I have had these pelts for many years — they are not protected, so Regi will not have to arrest me," he said with a smile. "These are black mink. The white trim on the hood is from a fox."

Then, he handed her a pair of boots sewn with the fur side in. She sat down and pulled them on. She tried to decide how the ties worked.

He knelt and took the ties from her hands. "Here, let me show you," he said, tying the boots just under her knee and rolling the cuff down. "They will tie higher if you need them to. They will keep out the snow." His hand rested on her knee and she smiled at him, feeling relaxed and happy. He reached into his coat pocket.

"Willa," he said. She caught her breath at his expression.

"I have spent a very long time alone," he said, and took a deep breath. "My heart was empty."

The room grew very still suddenly. He held a ring in his fingers.

"With you, I am complete. Will you marry me, my Moonlight?"

No one moved. Everyone could hear the chime of tiny bells as Willa nodded her head, speechless. She shimmered, as though she might shift shape, but the pressure from his hand on her knee kept her in her own form. She placed her hand over his for reassurance, and he drew it to him. He slipped the ring on her finger. Willa went to her knees in front of him and kissed him. Her father finally cleared his throat, very loudly.

"A toast, then!" he said, and Sticks passed around more glasses of champagne.

"To the birthday girl and my future son-in-law!" Ronan raised his glass. Everyone followed suit. Willa raised hers but she only pretended to sip it. It was a very long time before her heart quit racing.

When she stood alone in the sunshine by the kitchen door, Joseph Yellowgrass came to her and closed her hand over something. She opened her hand: in it was the carved crystal stag she had found on the mountain. It now had a clever locking silver band around it so it could hang from a chain.

"White Hart," he said. "This is also a totem — a very ancient and powerful one. Keep it near. Maybe you will find a way to use it. The turquoise cougar should stay with the Silver Stag; perhaps I could set it for him one day, as I have done with yours."

Regi burst into the kitchen and grabbed Willa's arm. "Okay sweetie, let's see it," she chided, grabbing Willa's left hand. Joseph Yellowgrass slipped out the door; through the window Willa watched him lope up the snowy hill.

After all that, a quiet dinner of leftovers was bound to be a bit anticlimactic — and welcome.

"Have you talked about when?" Ronan asked.

"Tomorrow?" Willa said hopefully.

"Tomorrow?!" Sara was indignant. "You can't have a proper wedding by tomorrow!"

"Why not? It's kind of a nice birthday present, don't you think?"

"People would be offended."

"Like who? My record company? Everyone who matters is here already. Or could be by tomorrow."

"What's the hurry?" Regi asked.

"Why wait?"

"A girl needs a beautiful wedding." Sara had that don't-argue-with-me look.

"Sara, I have everything I need." They locked gazes. Neither dropped her eyes. Willa got up and went to the woman she loved and put her arms around her.

"Sara — I have never been a normal girl. I have always wanted...no, *needed* to think outside the box. Now I need you to see me like I know you can, outside the box. It should be easy for you unless you don't want to. Just think differently about this. It isn't about putting on a show for family, which I don't have — other than what's right here. It isn't about getting presents, which I don't need. It isn't about waiting until I can afford it, or I'm old enough, or Corwyn quits his job or gets a job, or the weather or the economy improves. It's about something that is far deeper and has been waiting far longer than is humanly possible. There's no good reason that we should wait any longer than it takes to put a party together."

Sara sighed. "You have to have a cake and a wedding dress. There will be no argument about that. Someday, when your children or grandchildren look at the pictures, you will be a beautiful bride. That may take two days. Or three."

"Then we'll do it Sunday. That way, no one has to take off from work. The seventh is a good day." She turned to Corwyn. "Unless you wanted to wait."

He chuckled. He glanced at her father, then Sara, then Regi, and finally at Sticks.

"Hey, dude. Don't look at me. I'm not arguing with that badass, scary white woman. She's on a mission. You are on your own, man."

"I've already waited. The traditions that I recall required only that the men showed up when the women scheduled the event. As far as I can recall, I have no prior commitments this Sunday." Corwyn's expression was deadpan.

Ronan snickered. Willa started to giggle. It was infectious.

Willa pointed at Regi. "You: Bridesmaids — all one of them. Silver dress." She pointed at Sticks. "You: Best Man. In a suit. Dad, Corwyn: black suits, white tie. Sara: white cake, white and silver trim."

"And you?" Regi asked.

"White dress. No frills, no bows, no lace — like a white lily." She saw Corwyn's frown. "I'll use Sticks' gift card for something to go underneath. White calla lilies and red poinsettias for the flowers. Silver leaves. That's it. Planning over. Oh — Chloe and Neil: Music."

Everyone was staring at her.

"What? What have I forgotten?" She looked puzzled. "Ahhh. Booze? Yes. Champagne? Yes. Dinner? Hmm...no. Too much work. Just lots of good hors d'oeuvres. We'll send Jeb to deliver a few hand-written invitations and put a little card announcement in our Christmas cards to everyone else. Simple. No gifts. So what else did I forget?"

"...To make a big deal out of it?" Chloe asked.

"Yeah. I'll work on that. I don't want a big deal, I want Corwyn. But now, I'm super tired. Do you all need a memo, or can you remember all that?"

"I told you the chick was on a mission. Scary, man."

Willa and Corwyn's wedding would have been easy had she given in and gone with a traditional dress. When she and Regi couldn't find what she wanted in Boise, Willa refused to compromise. She drew a picture of what she wanted, photographed her drawing, and emailed the picture to her record company in New York.

"Willa MacLeod," said her producer on the phone, "why didn't we know you are getting married?"

"He just proposed yesterday."

"How long have you known him? What's his name — Cor McVin? Who is he, anyway? What does he do? Isn't this a bit hasty?"

"I've known him as long as I can remember. Our families go way back." She hesitated. "He does magic."

"Huh. Like David Copperfield?" he asked. Before she could reply, he said, "Well, good for you. So you need a dress. Nothing but the best for our beautiful white-haired rock star. Let me put Lisella on the line. She'll get you your dress."

Lisella called her back four hours later with the results of her search. "Makes a girl want to get married!" she said. "I found a dress for you that's perfect for a couple of reasons. Atelier Aimée has some incredible collections. Your drawing is more like their prêt-à-porter stuff — simple lines, less skirt and frill. But here's the deal. They have a little dress in their A Collection, it's called the Clorinda-4. I'm sending a picture to your phone right now. It's a frothy little thing — not much fabric, but whoa baby, is it pretty. It's maybe a little more frilly than you wanted, but it's going to be the most beautiful dress on you. They agreed to take the pastel roses off the shoulder and put callas and poinsettias, or silver leaves and something, instead. They have one right here in your size already."

Willa looked at the photo and knew it was her dress.

"Now here's the best deal. I'm sending another pic. This is the dress for your friend Regi. It isn't silver. I couldn't find a thing in silver that wasn't — umm, how should I put it? — something you couldn't wait to get out of. This dress is called Cortina from the Emé Emé Collection at Atelier. It's red, not silver ... but your friend won't want to take it off. Well, maybe she will," Lisella said with a wink in her voice.

"Because these two dresses are here ready to go and already in your sizes, and because you might get onto the cover of *Rolling Stone* in your dress, they're gonna give us both dresses for next to nothing. We'll cover it." Lisella waited.

"Okay...." Willa said finally. "I'll take it with the callas and poinsettias, then. How long? How will I get them?"

"I'll wait for them while they change the flowers. They have the most beautiful silk flowers, oh my god. I'll make certain the flowers look right, then I'll bring the dresses to you tonight. Can I get to your ranch easily?"

"You can't even fly into Boise at night."

"Yeah, I know. With all the connections, I'll be traveling all night and I'll get into Boise tomorrow. I'll rent a car there. I'll be bringing some people . . . ."

"How many people?"

"Four, besides me. Can do?"

"Who?"

"Photographers, make-up artist, a journalist or maybe two. We can't have this a secret."

"Jeez."

"Come on honey, you're the cat's meow of the rock world right now. We know you want it low key. That's why there are only gonna be five of us — or maybe six."

"Okay," Willa said. She wanted to change shape and run across the snow until she couldn't breathe. "Okay. Wear warm clothes. It's snowing here."

"Can I bring anything else?"

"Yeah, some ballet slippers that will match the dresses. That's about it. How will you find the place?"

"Willa, honey. That's what GPS is for."

On Friday and again on Saturday, the MacLeod ranch was invaded by photographers and journalists. Supposedly there were just two of each, but every time Willa turned around at least one photographer was right behind her, and neither the band nor the ranch residents were left alone. They were in the studio. They followed Jeb around the ranch. Jonesy took them to the fishing hole to show them where he'd caught Moby Dick. They worried her dad with questions, and pumped Sara for stories about Willa, all the while getting in the way in the kitchen. And they wanted most of all to catch shots of Corwyn and Willa together, but she did her best to give them the slip. Finally, Sticks managed to entice the whole group into a guided tour. Willa and Corwyn slipped away and went up the mountain, barely waiting until they were out of sight of the ranch to change shape and run. She had to wait for him because the snow was deep and he went slowly, still favoring his injury.

They lay naked on the furs on Corwyn's pallet and watched the fire burn to ashes in the granite hearth. He ran his fingers down her back and kissed the stag tattoo.

"I promised your father to bring him to see your mother," he said finally.

"When?" she asked, turning over.

"After tomorrow. Monday, probably. Or even tomorrow evening. It is so cold here now — it's better to go there in summer, but he understands that."

He fingered the leaping crystal stag totem that she wore around her neck. He traced a line with it, up her neck and across her lips. She opened her mouth and took it gently in her teeth. Light leapt from the carving and blazed so brilliantly, Corwyn closed his eyes.

Heat washed through her. Willa felt compelled to shape the Hart, began to shape the crown of antlers, and stopped. She was in half-shift. She held it.

She sensed that she could hold the half-shift endlessly now. Power imbued her with hunger. The infinitesimal new awareness within her was terrified. Mentally, she calmed it. Corwyn put his hands on her belly and kissed the spot over the place where the tiny life resided. He soothed it with his spirit and a sang song she had never heard — one that had wind and bells in it.

His mouth came over hers and the magic in the totem raced through Corwyn as well. He shaped the Sithé of the half-shift; his hunger was even greater than hers. Together they discovered the Sithé Fire — something Corwyn remembered his father mentioning only once, as a nearly forgotten legend. The power and heat of it made them both a little afraid when it threatened to spiral beyond their control. Panting and spent, Willa let the crystal stag slip out of her mouth.

He took the palm of his scarred hand and placed it against her own.

"Blood calls to blood," he said. "I pledge you my life, my arm, and my crown."

The words rang of ritual. She understood that this was Corwyn's wedding vow.

I read the legends and scoffed,
and yet I kept the watch.
The legend says the blood of the stag gives life.
How far does that law extend?

RM

Heart's Rest

In the middle of the night, the Silver Stag and the White Hart climbed the Silverhorn Crags. High into the wilderness, they raced the moonlight across the snow until their breath froze and floated away in splinters of frost. There was no more weakness in Corwyn's limb; the power of the half-shift had burned it away. They pulled the wind in their wake, weaving a spiral from shards of snow that reached into the brittle stars.

Corwyn and Willa came down the mountain before dawn, shifted, left their snowshoes on the porch outside Willa's room, and fell asleep at first light. Today was Sunday, and the restless house stirred with guests worried by the absence of the star players of the wedding. Sticks came into their room far too early and dragged Corwyn from Willa's arms, pretending to be deaf to their protests.

"It is very bad luck, dude. You are just gonna have to cool your jets until later. Maybe we should go up the hill for a little calm-down treatment. Those two women are making some mean coffee, man, and they are women on a mission. You and I are getting out of here before they show up."

Regi and Sara brought coffee, tension, and hurry with them when they rousted Willa from the down comforter.

"Where have you been?!" Regi asked, her eyes glinting with annoyance. "Everyone was in a complete panic last night because you two vanished."

"We stayed at Corwyn's place," Willa mumbled. "It was quieter."

"That's what your father said. The *Rolling Stone* guys wanted to know where that was. When your dad pointed to the top of the mountain, they asked how to get there. Sticks said, 'You have to walk, man.' Of course they didn't believe any of it. I think they thought we were hiding you."

"You wanted an early wedding. We have three hours," Sara said.

"I shouldn't have spent the night running across the snow...." Willa muttered.

"Yeah, I bet that's what you did," Regi said lewdly.

"Will you wear that totem?" Sara asked, fingering the stag on its chain around Willa's neck.

"Yes. Something old," Willa said. "Do you want to see some old magic?"

Both her friends went still. She sensed doubt and excitement wrestling in their minds. She placed the totem in her mouth. The lambency in the crystal flashed. She allowed her shape to half-shift, just for a moment. They stared at her, awestruck, imagining she was a dream.

"You are a myth," Sara whispered.

"You can't *do* that," Regi said. "I take back what I said. You are not normal. How can you do that?"

"She is a myth," Sara repeated.

The makeup artist buzzed in, and Willa quickly shaped herself back to human as he did a double-take. He proclaimed Willa a *goddess* and set out to perform his own magic.

Sticks came in to check with the women on timing; when he emerged and re-joined the band in the bunkhouse, he described the scene in the dressing room: "Man," he said, shaking his head, "we got Queer Guy and the White Elf Queen in there — Willa is a vision and the makeup artist's completely in love and he hasn't even heard her sing. The *Rolling Stone* photographers are having wet dreams. Even Regi is amazing — there is a woman under that uniform, who'da thought? Dudes, my head is spinning. And watch out, the Queer Guy is coming to fix us next."

Sticks' phone rang. It was Neil.

"Rincon's here. He's coming your way."

"Dude — who invited him?"

"The *Stone* feature writer."

"Freakin' busybodies."

The door opened. Sticks and Corwyn were dressing. Corwyn had on his black slacks and was putting on his white shirt. When the boyish-looking blond guy came in the room, Corwyn knew exactly who it was; he heard the thoughts in Rincon's mind: Rincon hated snow. He hated the ranch. He wanted to ruin the day so he would feel better. He wanted to humiliate this guy who thought he could take Willa away from him.

Rincon hesitated at the door. Corwyn felt Sticks' alarm, and gripped his arm reassuringly.

"Dude…." Sticks whispered.

"I know who he is," Corwyn said quietly. He stepped to Rincon and put out his hand. Reluctantly, Rincon took it.

"I'm Coér Mac Vyn," Corwyn said. "You must be one of Willa's friends." He stepped back and Sticks scrambled to help Corwyn with his cufflinks.

"Rincon. I'm Rincon, man. Didn't she tell you about me?" He studied the scars on Corwyn's chest, the trim waist, the long hair.

"The former lead guitarist, yes?" Corwyn appraised him.

"Yeah. Willa and me, we hooked up pretty good. She must have taken it hard when I left, to jump in the sack with some old dude."

Sticks scowled and lunged toward Rincon, but Corwyn caught his wrist. *Patience, my friend*, he told him.

"Taken what hard, Rincon Young? A very fitting name for you, by the way," Corwyn added. "What did such a woman need to be concerned over?"

Sticks did up Corwyn's second cufflink, still glowering.

"That I was busy, dude. A little surfin'. Waves and babes — you know." He walked around the room, watched himself in the mirror. "She was into exclusives, you know. She didn't own me, man."

"That is very fortunate, Rincon Young."

"Why's that?"

"Because it means she is free to own me."

"That chick's complicated."

"Yes, Rincon, she is extremely complicated. So am I. That's why I love her. I hope you can stay for the wedding."

The makeup artist breezed in. "Well, well, well, well, well," he said walking around Rincon, "what have we here? Are we eating in, or is this takeout?" he asked, stroking Rincon's arm. Rincon jerked it away and slammed out the door.

"What did you bad men *do* to that sweet boy? I don't think he liked you," he said, pushing Corwyn into a chair.

Sticks said, "I don't like him, dude. Nobody does. He overdoes it with everything."

"Ohhhh. My kind of boy! Now, what are we doing with you, Mr. Buff Guy?" He walked around Corwyn, rubbing his chin. "We have Tolkien's Queen of the Elves in there, and out here, Strider in the Rough."

"What is your name?" Corwyn asked.

"Emelio. *I* am Emelio and *you* are a lucky man. You are about to marry a goddess. The Ice Queen! Perfection in confection! But look at you. A bit rough around the edges."

"Emelio. Do you cut hair?" Emelio's smile got big, and he bowed. "I can work all *kinds* of miracles."

Corwyn reached up and began to untwine a string of silver bells from his hair.

"I heard that you were a magician," Emelio said. "This is lovely magic." He touched the bells and they chimed faintly. He shook out a cape and fastened it around Corwyn's neck.

"Now let's see what magic *Emelio* can work!"

When Emelio stepped back, Corwyn had lost centuries from his appearance, along with an arm's length of hair. Corwyn twined the bells back into his remaining hair; Sticks tried but couldn't see how they vanished. There was magic, and there was magic.

Willa's dad leaned close. "I always thought you were beautiful. I was mistaken. Whatever you were before pales when compared to this exquisite vision on my arm. Prepare yourself. Your Corwyn has had a transformation too."

She placed a hand on her abdomen and breathed. So tiny and inconsequential — barely considered life, according to those who had credentials to speak of such things — yet she sensed a sharing of excitement; she felt the listening. She listened to the listening.

Where is she? her father wondered, watching her. Her eyes were closed, her arm was in his; her hand was cupped at her waist. *What is she listening to?*

She opened those pale eyes and he startled.

"I am listening to the next Sithé, your grandchild. This day is exciting for both of us."

She felt it — the river of cold laced with fear that went through him. Then the joy — bright, hot, joy.

"It can't be long. How long?" he asked.

"Fourteen days."

"Does he know?"

"Corwyn knows."

"Are you certain?"

"Absolutely."

"Here," Regi said as she brought in the flowers. "Don't stain the dress. That's why they're wrapped in satin and ribbons. You're absolutely certain about what?"

"That Dad should be holding a shotgun."

"What?" she asked, distracted, straightening the flowers of Willa's dress, straightening the gathered skirts of her own. Then: "… *What?* Oh my God. Baloney. Really? Oh my God. Oh God, don't tell the reporters! Do not breathe a word. Those people are absolutely relentless. Take your flowers, sweetie. You've never looked lovelier. You know that Corwyn had a little makeover. Don't let it startle you. That gay guy did a major Queer Eye on him. He's a

stud — Corwyn, I mean." She took a breath. "Well, I imagine . . . ."
she added. "Are those guys going to start the music? What the hell
is wrong? Maybe . . . ."

"Raz." Willa gave her friend a little shake. "Breathe. Everything's
fine. Breathe." She took her friend's hands and kissed them. Then
she took her father's arm again.

"Rincon is here," Regi added, as if to make certain that Willa
would be as nervous as she was.

"Why?" Willa asked — and the music started.

Corwyn turned to watch Willa walk toward him on her father's
arm. Corwyn had stepped forward in time for her, from someone living centuries in the past into a sudden present he had never
prepared for. He took her hand. His eyes asked her approval. She
smiled. She never heard the words the minister spoke. She heard
what Corwyn was repeating in his heart: *my life, my arm, my crown.*

Corwyn kissed her. The stag totem sparked. For a moment Willa
saw a vague image of the antler crown appear on Corwyn's brow
and knew it crowned her as well. The guests murmured. Cameras
flashed. When she glanced up to see everyone's reaction, she saw
Rincon. Lisella was hanging on his arm, but his gaze was on her
and her husband.

For a long time afterward, Corwyn kept an arm around her waist,
as if the feel of her affirmed that she was real — that his new life was
real and the decades without voice, without a companion, the endless
hours entombed in the mountain had no hold on him any longer.

The feature writer for the *Stone* cornered them at last.

"Tell me, how did you do that interesting thing at the kiss? Some sort of trick with the lighting?"

"No, that's just how we really look," she said, leaning against Corwyn. He stiffened momentarily — out of instinct, she supposed.

"Right," the guy said. "Some kind of magic trick, obviously. Never tell the tricks of the trade, eh?" Willa couldn't remember his name — Jeff, Jack? — something with a J, anyway.

"So, tell me. Have you two known each other all your lives? I mean, here in this little town, did you like hang out as families, or something? I know you didn't go to school together — there's a little bit of an age difference."

"Our families were connected," she replied. "It goes way back. I knew about Corwyn all my life."

"But," J-whatever insisted, "you haven't really been an item all that long now, have you?"

"I was waiting," Corwyn said mildly, "until she got un-busy enough to notice me."

"I understand you are a magician," the reporter asked. "Exactly what sort of magic do you do?"

Corwyn smiled lazily. Willa didn't sense any fear in him at all. He reached into his hair and removed the string of tiny bells. He laid them in the reporter's hand. Then he put them back into his hair; they vanished. Corwyn then pulled the bells from Willa's hair, put them back — and they too disappeared.

"Interesting. Very clever. Good sleight of hand. I couldn't see how you did that. Do you work anywhere?"

"I am retired," Corwyn said. "Willa has the big life. I am a simple man. It works for us."

"How do you feel about her spending time with the band, traveling, and all that?"

"It's what she does, who she is."

"Didn't you have something going with one of your band members for a while?" J asked Willa.

Willa leaned in close. "Please don't tell him I dumped him for an older man. He's so young. I wouldn't want his ego to be permanently damaged." She grinned wickedly. Sticks came up to them then, thinking that they needed to be rescued from the writer's clutches.

"Now, Sticks and I," Willa continued smoothly, "we still have our thing going. I just couldn't give them both up."

Sticks' jaw dropped a little, but Willa gave him "the look" and a mental nudge.

"Oh man," he said, picking up her cue, "did you give up the baby, woman? Who's gonna keep you happy all night now when Corwyn and I are gettin' our beauty sleep?"

"All right, I get the hint," the reporter laughed.

"Today is not the day, my friend," Corwyn told him, "to bring up the past. Today is the beginning of life for us. Nothing before today matters."

"Does that mean you won't be going on tour?" J-whatever asked.

"What it means," Willa said, "is we are working on our next album. I can't think about touring right now — not for a while. I want to put out some music that has meaning, soul. I don't want to just write stuff because that's what we do. I want the songs, and the whole album, to have weight, to make people think, maybe remember something in their own life that the music and the words speak to. There was a song at the end of one of the Hobbit movies, by Ed Sheeran — "I See Fire". I was spellbound. I want my music to be spellbinding like that, and just as unforgettable when you wake up the next day." She sang a few bars from the song: "Oh, misty eye of the mountain below. Keep careful watch of my brothers' souls."

"I don't think I've heard it," the writer confessed.

"Music should stick in your head, and play in your soul all the time. OK, how about that song by Jason Isbell, "So girl, leave your boots by the bed, we ain't leaving this room, 'til someone needs medical help, or the magnolias bloom...." That's the kind of music I want to do now. Corwyn is music in my soul. I want our new album to reflect that."

"I hope you do manage it, Ms. MacLeod. Or — what is the name now?"

"MacLeod will do."

"Didn't you just survive a wolf attack a couple weeks ago?" J asked Corwyn. "Do you think wolves should be hunted?"

Willa tensed.

"I think it's very interesting, don't you," Corwyn said with an intense gaze, "that people these days feel they need to protect predators. Have you ever wondered why that is? Perhaps, in the long run, we all sense our own destruction, and even crave it."

"Uh-huh..." the writer said, his composure rattled.

"Or perhaps, social mores have become so emasculated that the only way humans find it palatable to have power is vicariously." Corwyn's gaze didn't waver.

"What do you think has emasculated our society?" the reporter asked. Willa saw him trying to gather his wits.

"Low-fat food and diet drinks," she interjected quickly. "Why don't you try some of the canapes?" she suggested. "They're all homemade, by the way — no pre-manufactured, industrial, preservative-laced stuff here. I think the meatballs might be elk. I need to talk to some of the other guests. Please enjoy yourself." She pulled at Corwyn. "I need a drink."

"Those guys don't really care about having a discussion," she told him quietly. "They only want you to say something they can twist into a juicy headline. When we read it in print you'll sound like you advocated feeding our children to the wolves — or maybe feeding the wolves to our children."

"Our children?" he asked, tightening his arms around her. "If you are planning to repopulate the Sithé, I suppose I should cooperate in every way possible."

Control your passions for fear that they will
take vengeance on you.

Epictetus

WHAT LIES
BENEATH

They ran out of disposable cups at the bar, and Willa went to
find some more. She turned on the light in the large pantry and
went to the very back. Behind her, she heard the pantry door close.

"Gettin' married. For a wild girl, that's a little ordinary," Rincon
whispered in Willa's ear, sliding his arm around her. "How long you
been knockin' boots with that dude, sugar?"

"Rincon, why are you here?" she asked.

"I want to share your happy day, baby."

"No, you don't. You want to make someone else feel as crappy as
you do. What is it this time — coke? Heroin?"

"Hey, my new band, we're into cocktails — a little this, a little that.
It hooks us up with badass music, you know? I gotta keep the juice
goin'. You know about that juice, don't you, sugar?" He tightened his
hold and Willa realized he was erect and his pants were unzipped.

She turned around and tried to duck past him, but he caught her
as she went under his arm. He pushed her up against the shelves,

ran his hands down her breasts, past her waist and pulled her hips against his. She tried to swallow her panic.

"Get your hands off me, Rincon," she growled. His body pinned her against the shelves. He slipped the single flowered strap of her dress off her shoulder. She struggled and tried to push him back. Her resistance only excited him further, and he ground his erection against her. He was stronger than she'd expected him to be. *Must be whatever drug he's on*, she thought. His hand hurt her breast. Forcefully, he wrenched up the skirt of her gown and dragged her leg over his. In horror, she felt him against her thigh and realized he intended to force himself on her. Anger went through her like an electrical current. She began to shape the Hart, antlers first.

Startled, Rincon let go of her. Willa placed the totem in her mouth and half shifted, held it. She grabbed his shirt and shoved him against the shelves. Cans tumbled off the shelf and clattered to the floor around them. One hit her on the forehead. The pain made her anger explode. She pulled the guitarist forward and then slammed him back against the shelves so everything flew off and one shelf collapsed. He went slack and dropped to the floor. Her blazing anger was only increasing, and she could feel herself losing all control. She knew she could kill him with her bare hands now. She wanted to.

When she felt hands on her, she struck at them blindly and tried to pull away.

"It's me, Moonlight," Corwyn whispered, soothing her against him. He pulled up bodice of her dress and smoothed it into place.

"It's all right. He's not moving. You're safe. It's all right." His arms went around her. She went limp.

She let the totem slide from her mouth. Her anger dissipated.

Ronan MacLeod came to the pantry door. "What the hell happened?" he shouted at the sight of Rincon on the floor. "Honey, your face is bleeding."

Corwyn turned her around. She had a gash above her eye. He grabbed a handful of paper towels and pressed them against the cut.

"Rincon followed me in here. He wanted — he was going to rape me." The very idea stunned her. "I, uh...overreacted a little. I tried to kill him." Her heart was still clamoring harshly and her hands were shaking.

"Goddamn no-good son of a bitch," her father said. "Are you all right?"

"I don't know. I wanted to kill him." Her breathing was rapid and shallow.

"She's fine," Corwyn said, kissing her shoulder to calm her. "Come Willa." He gently led her out of the pantry. "Come sit down." He got her into a kitchen chair and leaned her head onto the counter.

Sara and Regi rushed into the kitchen, followed closely by Sticks. *Find Jeb,* Corwyn told Sticks.

Sticks hesitated in the doorway. He saw the blood on Willa's dress.

"Oh my God, sweetie," Regi said, getting a wet towel to clean up the blood.

"What happened?" Sara asked, taking ice from the freezer. Quickly, she placed a bag of it on Willa's forehead.

"I'll get Scott Lossman," Ronan said. "I saw him at the buffet table as I came in here."

"Did I kill him?" Willa asked in a shaking voice.

"I don't think so," Corwyn answered. "Maybe Regi should check."

"Kill who? Check what?" Regi asked.

"Rincon is in the pantry. He assaulted Willa. I think he may be on drugs," Corwyn said.

Regi went to check, came back, and leaned close to Corwyn. "I'll take over here," she said, taking the towel and ice from his hands and continuing the pressure on Willa's cut. "Rincon's breathing, but he isn't decent, and I'm not touching him. Maybe you should zip his pants back up, Corwyn."

Ronan came back with Dr. Lossman. Regi stepped back so he could see Willa's injury.

"How did this happen?" the doctor asked.

"A can hit me when it came off the pantry shelf," she said.

"Son-of-a-bitch guy she fired from the band assaulted her in the pantry," Ronan growled.

"Where's the guy?" Dr. Lossman asked, looking around.

"In here," Corwyn said, emerging from the pantry. "Willa knocked him out."

"I'd better check him too." The doctor took his car keys from his pocket. "My emergency bag is in my trunk. Could you get that for me?" he asked, handing the keys to Sara. He went into the pantry and Corwyn followed.

Willa felt woozy; her head hurt now, and her eye was throbbing. Her heart rate had leveled off, though. She was feeling relieved now that she hadn't killed Rincon.

Regi kept up the pressure on her head.

"You're going to have a black eye, girl," Regi said. "I knew that guy was bad news. Did he — did he, you know, hurt you?" she asked meaningfully.

"No, Reg. When I realized what his intentions were, I got angry, and I did that little half-shift thing I showed you and Sara earlier.

I really wanted to kill him. I could have done it, too." A tear tracked down the side of her face. Regi kissed it away. Willa closed her eyes.

"Too bad you didn't," Regi whispered.

Sticks came in from the mudroom with Jeb.

"What happened?" he asked.

"That bad-boy guitar player assaulted Willa," Regi said.

"No way, dude."

"He shut her in the pantry with him and attacked her. Willa knocked him out. A can fell and cut Willa's forehead."

"No way," Sticks protested. "He's a dumb shit, but he wouldn't do physical shit like that."

"Listen," Regi said. "He was in there with his pants around his knees — I saw him. He's lucky Corwyn or Willa didn't kill him. Half the shelves in the pantry got knocked down."

"Can you keep that pressure on Willa's cut for a few more minutes, Regi?" Dr. Lossman asked when he came back out of the pantry. "I'll stitch that cut in a minute. I have to start an IV drip on Mr. Young. I've called for an ambulance. He has a couple of broken ribs, and I'm pretty sure one punctured a lung."

"Well, I guess you don't need me inside right now," Jeb said to Ronan. "I'll go move some cars so the ambulance can get close. Should've broken his hands when I had the chance."

The ambulance came and went, and most of the guests left right behind it. The *Rolling Stone* crew snatched a few shots of Willa covered with blood; the story they got was that Rincon was drunk, or on something and maybe drunk as well, and when he tried to help Willa get the cups, he pulled the pantry shelves down on them both. The party was suddenly over, and the news crew was pretty much stonewalled, so after taking a few last photos of the band and the stunned wedding guests, they packed up.

"I'm sorry, Lisella," Willa said. "I know you had plans with Rincon."

"No biggie, hon. There's plenty like him back home, although I'll admit that it might have been an interesting night tonight. He's still kind of obsessed with you, you know."

"Yeah, I know," Willa grimaced as she moved. Dr. Lossman had put ten stitches over her eye. "Thank you for the beautiful dresses. They were perfect. I hope we can get the blood out of mine."

"Dresses are replaceable. Just heal up and get those tracks finished. The fans love you, and we need that new album. You were beautiful today, and that husband of yours is the one I would really like to go home with."

It was finally quiet and Willa's head had stopped throbbing. She was propped in bed with orders to stay awake for a while, so she had the last Star Wars movie playing with the sound turned way down. She could hear everyone cleaning up and putting things away. Every now and then she recognized a voice: Sara's and Regi's in the house, her dad and Jeb outside. She heard Jake Collins and Sticks talking about Rincon. She closed her eyes for a moment.

The woman who came to her resembled her mother in some ways — she was smallish and fair-skinned. But her hair was black as a raven's wing, and her black eyes were fierce. A light blazed from the talisman at her neck. She shaped the half-shift Sithé as she advanced across the snow. In one hand was a sword, and in the other she gripped a man's severed head by the hair. She threw the head at Willa's feet.

"This is what happens to those who try to take what is not theirs," the stranger said in a voice cracked with wind. Willa glanced at the head. It was Rincon's.

"Who are you?" Willa asked, realizing that she was dreaming.

"I am Morrígan. I am the power in your talisman — and in you. Why did you hesitate? A true Sithé isn't afraid of power or of death. Warriors take the heads of their enemies."

"He isn't an enemy," Willa said. "I am not a warrior."

"Are you certain?" the woman asked, her eyes on fire. "The clan of the Mac Clæúds are guardians; the Mac Nessa are seers. Do you know what Clan Mac Vyn is, Willa Mac Clæúd? Or are you Willa Mac Nessa...or are you prepared to be Willa Mac Vyn?"

"No," Willa whispered, "I don't know."

"They are warriors. Hunters. Which are you, Sithé? And what is your son going to be?"

Willa heard bells. Morrígan stretched, her shape blurred, and she shifted. Rearing, she towered over Willa, a Black Hart with smoldering black eyes, her antlers a crown of fire. Then she shifted yet again. Wings brushed Willa's face. A raven circled over Willa's head and spiraled upward until it vanished from sight. Her voice echoed down the wind like the cry of a storm.

"What face does your enemy wear, Willa Mac Nessa?"

When Willa looked down at the head lying at her feet, it was Brian Nokes who stared up with blank eyes.

"No," she cried. "No, no..."

She reached out with both hands and felt someone take her arms and shake her gently.

"Willa," Corwyn's anxious voice said. "Willa. Wake up."

"Oh god," she said, opening her eyes.

"You were shouting."

"I dreamed of a Black Hart, with a black soul," she whispered, letting him enfold her in his arms.

"The Morrígan...." he said. She heard in him the terror that echoed her own — he knew this Black Hart. "You weren't supposed to go to sleep."

"Well...where is everyone? Weren't you all supposed to be keeping an eye on me?"

"I think they were staying away on purpose."

"Why? My room is usually like Grand Central Station."

"I will take that to mean a very busy place. Yes, it is that, more often than not. It was a little hard to get used to it, coming from — ah — rather different circumstances." He chuckled. She saw his mountain chamber in her mind and wished they were there now, lying in the furs and watching the fire burn low. Corwyn touched his lips to her shoulder, taking in her familiar scent. That alone was enough to raise the hair on his arms and tighten his belly.

She leaned back against him. "So. Where is everyone?" she asked, bewildered.

"I believe they are studiously avoiding intrusion. They imagine we should be undertaking our conjugal...responsibilities." His arms tightened around her. "I think perhaps they are correct."

She turned in his arms and pushed him over backwards, rising to her knees over him. "Why didn't you say so? What the hell were you waiting for — a hand-written invitation?"

Corwyn rose quietly. It wasn't light yet.

"Where do you think you're going?" Willa mumbled sleepily. "I am not done with you yet."

"I promised your father that I would take him to see your mother. I wish to show him the ancestral places."

"Umm..." she groaned. "Right now?"

"I promised."

She sat up to watch him dress. Her hands went to her waist — she sensed the small presence and how safe and secure it felt. She basked in that contentment.

"Moonlight," Corwyn said. He paused with his shirt halfway on. He crossed the room in three strides, taking her hands away so he could kiss the smooth skin of her flat belly. "You undo me when you do that." Willa took his shirt the rest of the way off.

When he rose again to dress, she asked, "Should I come too?"

"Perhaps this time it should just be your father and me," he suggested.

"Yes. You're right. Please take your phone this time."

"I will see you this afternoon," he said, putting the phone in his pocket.

"I'll hold you to that," she laughed.

I love you, Willa Moonlight, he thought to her.

She let him read what she thought in respose.

A little later she found Sara in the kitchen alone.

"Do you ever sleep in?" she asked, getting a cup of coffee.

"They say caffeine isn't good for babies," Sara said, her eyes following Willa.

Willa's hand went to her waist, protectively. Sara smiled. Willa smiled back.

"It seems that the magic was not meant to pass from the world just yet," Sara said. "It could have, you know. We have watched for many centuries, we Story Keepers. It seemed the time was nearly over. Joseph believed he would see the last Sithé pass from the world. But he kept his sacred vow to preserve the magic. We could never be certain that you were the promised hope. We could only watch and wait."

"And so I think the new Sithé will survive a little coffee," Willa said, taking her cup to the table. "Where's everyone?"

"Sleeping off all the champagne they drank after the rest of the guests left. And all the rest of what they drank. You missed out."

"No. I didn't," Willa answered with a small smile. "Sara...I see so many couples who have been together a long time — the ones that last. Few of them seem, I don't know...intense."

"New love is intense," Sara answered slowly. "For you, maybe more so. Until now, you have always strongly resisted any emotional commitment."

"Does that mean that someday I will look at Corwyn and not feel the earth move? That this wonder I feel now will be gone? No more fire?" Sadness filled her.

"When I look at Joseph, I still feel the fire and the wonder," Sara told her. "But it is different: not so edgy and demanding, but with more and deeper contentment. People spend their lives wondering if the one they found is their true love, or if that person even exists. You will never have to wonder over that."

"Joseph wasn't descended from your ancestral people. How did you and he get together?"

"The Story Keepers had scattered; they became a secret society within the new Native American tribes that arose after the clan wars that destroyed the reign of the Sithé. The Story Keepers held on to the old magic that the Sithé had bestowed on them as a gift for their loyalty. Joseph Yellowgrass is one of the remaining handful who still understand the magic. He was drawn to this place because of it, centuries ago. We met when I was very young and he was already ancient."

"I had a dream," Willa began, "of a woman, a black Sithé. She looked a little like my mother. She shaped a raven and flew away."

Sara's mouth formed a surprised O.

"The ancient Raven Queen," she said. "She gave the Sithé their power. Or perhaps she was the ruler of the Sithé. She killed men in battle; she is death, and fate, and victory. She takes many shapes."

"Why do the Sithé shape only one thing then — a creature that is prey, not predator?"

"Perhaps it was a curse, or a punishment," Sara suggested. "No one remembers. Perhaps it was a check on the magic, to prevent the Sithé's power from becoming too overwhelming. Perhaps it was to keep the Sithé a little humble. It seems, though, that in the end it was a curse after all."

"What's to keep me from learning to shape something else?" Willa asked.

"Nothing that I know of, if you can do it. Maybe it's possible. Have you tried?"

"No. The Hart comes naturally."

"Perhaps you should try," Sara suggested.

The wise man does not expose himself needlessly to danger,
since there are few things for which he cares sufficiently;
but he is willing, in great crises, to give even his life
— knowing that under certain conditions it is not
worthwhile to live.

Aristotle

Secret of the Silverhorn

Coér Mac Vyn took Ronan MacLeod across Silverhorn Creek and up to the very top of the mountain, where they entered a chamber surrounded only by wind and sky. Winter howled around the granite like a banshee, and the catacombs were cold beyond measure. But no wind entered inside to disturb the dead.

Corwyn shaped himself back into human form and shook winter from his hair in a shower of ice and a shrill of bells. Ronan looked around in wonder as Corwyn lit the lamps. A myriad of dead lined the walls, their unmolested peace the stillness of time itself.

"Most of the Sithé are here, although not all. Some died far away, or alone; most of those we never found. Some were burned to ash, or their bodies sunk in deep water — humans fear what they don't understand." Corwyn led the way, holding a lamp high for Ronan to see.

He stopped at Megan's niche. Ronan went awkwardly to his one good knee. Corwyn placed the lamp in the niche. Ronan saw the new furs, the beading, and the silver.

"Thank you," he said softly.

"For what, Ronan MacLeod?"

"For giving her an honorable burial." He touched the beading.

"I could do no less. She made the supreme sacrifice."

Ronan had folded back the furs. He saw the cuts on her wrists.

"She took her own life?" he asked, the pain rising in him.

"No, Ronan MacLeod. She gave her life for yours." Corwyn watched him carefully.

"What do you mean? You said it was an accident — that you tried to save her. That she didn't understand the rite."

"I lied."

Ronan turned to Corwyn, surprise and betrayal warring across his face. He saw the man he trusted, the man his daughter loved, and his shoulders slumped.

"Why?"

"Because I didn't want Willa to know."

"Tell me," Ronan whispered.

"There is another magic, another use for our blood besides the rite of passage." Corwyn's voice shook. "It's an ancient payment."

"Blood for blood," Ronan said.

"Yes," Corwyn agreed. "A life for a life. Megan understood this. She understood much, actually. The day she came here was not the first day I ever saw her. It was not even the first time she came here. We met after she married you and came to the ranch. She was drawn to the Silverhorn — the gift she had could well have driven her to madness, and walking in the canyon soothed her. One day,

I couldn't bear to feel the pain in her any longer. I came out of hiding so she could see me. I shaped myself so she could know what I am. I brought her here. I told her of her heritage — of the heritage of the child she carried. She had feared that her baby would be... troubled, as she and her forebears were. When Willa was born, Megan was relieved that her child was so much like you."

"Megan knew that you were real," Ronan said in wonder.

"She understood that and a lot more, after the years of discussions we had. She loved you and Willa more than life itself. The day the army informed her that you were injured and not expected to live, she came here immediately; she knew exactly what sacrifice she was making."

Corwyn pulled the fur back up on Megan and took the lamp from its niche. He led Ronan to the stone shelf that stood like an altar in the middle of the granite chamber.

He lit more lamps.

"There are two ways to do this thing," he said. "The sacrifice can be done here, by one person, but it is rare and difficult."

"And the other way?" Ronan asked.

"By two people who are in the same place at the same time."

"How did she...?"

"Know what to do? I had told her about it, one time when I told her about some of the things that were placed here on the table of sacrifice and how they were used. There are other sacrifices — other magics than blood for blood." He picked up an ornate dagger with a jeweled handle.

"This is the Blood Knife," Corwyn said. He reached for a crystal bowl that was dark on the inside. "This is the Blood Bowl. Invoked in the right way, using the right words at the precise moment, a very powerful magic is created. The one who invokes that magic will trade their life for another's. Your wife saved you. I arrived too late to save her in the same way." Corwyn raised his sleeves. There was a faint scar on one wrist.

Ronan stared at the scar, trying to understand. Tears burned down his face.

"I started the first cut," Corwyn said, "but she grabbed the knife from me and died before I could make another. Had I let my blood fall into hers from both my wrists and recited the blood-for-blood chant, I could have died in her place. I was too late."

"Oh god," Ronan sobbed.

"She told me that her life was hers to give for yours, but mine was not," Corwyn's voice broke. "She was my friend. I had no other like her. To the end, she had the sight of the Mac Nessas — when she took the knife from my hand, she said that my life belonged to another, that one day I would know that. And then she died instantly, as soon as she had finished telling me this." Tears streaked the Sithé's face. He looked sad and ancient once more. "I'm sorry," he finished.

Ronan put his arm around Corwyn's shoulders. "Thank you," he said quietly, feeling his soul come completely to rest at long last. "I understand. She was right. I've wasted so many years tearing myself apart over something that was far bigger than me."

"I wanted to come to you," Corwyn said in a broken voice, "to tell you. But I didn't know how. I was afraid."

"Fear tears a man's soul apart, Corwyn. I understand that better than any man. I wouldn't have believed you if you had come to me. If I hadn't killed you in a rage, I would have called the cops. It wasn't meant to be. Willa said it the other day — it's far simpler than we try to make it. She would have cut her heart out on this granite if you had not been here waiting for her."

"There is far more magic in her than in me, or any of the Sithé I knew," Corwyn said. "She hasn't found it yet. I am still a little afraid to show her more than I have. I will, though, so that nothing disastrous happens as she stumbles into her magic."

"She said when she met you that you were a good man. I didn't want to believe it. She was right. She's always right."

"She has the sight of the Mac Nessas," Corwyn explained.

"I wouldn't have called it that while I was trying to raise her," Ronan chuckled, wiping the tears away.

"Come, Ronan MacLeod. This is a lonely, sad, and cold place. One should come here in the summer when it is only a little cold and not so dark. There are deadly magics hidden here that prey on the unsuspecting heart. I will show you brighter places." He took up the lamp and led Ronan to another doorway.

Ronan turned to look back. "It would be a good place to come, in the end, Coér Mac Vyn. To lie here for eternity."

"Yes, Ronan Mac Clæúd, it would be."

He showed Ronan the mountain, more than he had shown even to Willa. Lastly, he came to his own chamber. He lit a fire and made tea. Ronan sat in a chair and looked around.

"It's a lonely place to live so long," he said as Corwyn put the tea by his hand.

"Now when I am here, I can only remember the light that Willa brought into this place — and into my heart."

"She likes it here," Ronan said. "She has that look when she talks about it."

"That is the look that utterly unmans me," Corwyn admitted, "and makes me wholly a man at the same moment."

Ronan laughed. "Yeah. Women do that to you, son. Get used to it."

Corwyn's phone rang. He was so startled that Ronan laughed again. "And that, son, is the chain you now wear. Tell her we're coming home now, and I'm fine."

The band members trickled in from the bunkhouse and sat bleary-eyed at the table, drinking coffee and eating leftovers. Jake arrived too, looking only a little less haggard. He took a plate and sat down.

"I was supposed to hunt with Brian Nokes today," he said, "but apparently I didn't wake up in time and he left without me. That was some party after the others left!" he said to Willa.

"I wouldn't know. I was asleep."

Sticks laughed. "Dude, nobody sleeps on their wedding night, so don't be trying that one on us. We did have something going out here though. Man, that Crown of your dad's is good stuff." He shook his head as if to clear it. "Leaves an afterimage though, man."

Willa laughed.

"You didn't drink anything at all, hon," Chloe said. "It was your party — I'd have thought you'd have a few to celebrate."

Willa studied them. "Can't," she said.

"Why not?" Chloe asked, mystified.

Willa didn't say anything as she worked on another piece of cake. She touched the sense of the tiny life in her and felt its warmth and contentment flood her.

Sticks whistled. "A baby!" he exclaimed. "Wicked Willa is knocked up!" Willa smiled softly at him.

"Whoa, mama. I ain't never seen you look like that. You *cannot* look like that. We sat right here at this table and had this discussion about things that you can't do or say in public."

"Stop it, Sticks. How far along?" Chloe asked.

"A couple weeks — three, almost."

Jake, Neil, and Jonesy said nothing. They looked hung-over, mostly, and a little uncomfortable, and kind of interested despite it all.

"Where's the dad-to-be?" Sticks asked.

"He went somewhere with my dad. I just talked with them. They're on their way back."

"Does he know?" Sticks asked.

"Of course he knows, silly. He was there when it happened." Willa looked offended.

"Woman, I got news for you. A dude doesn't know much when he's hittin' the skin. All he knows is what his small brain is telling him — that he's on stud duty. Rarely is he 'there' when it happens, even if he's there, if you know what I mean. That would take special badass magic-man radar."

Willa blushed.

Sunny got up and went to the door. He barked twice.

Regi came in, dragging a lot of cold air with her.

She poured herself a cup of coffee. "You all look like I feel," she muttered. "Only you all didn't have to be at work at seven-thirty this morning."

"Yeah," Jonesy said. "We just got up."

"I *think* we're up," Jake commented.

"I've been up since dawn," Willa said.

"Sweetie, that's because you can't drink." Regi looked at Jake. "Where is Mister Nokes today?" she asked.

"I don't know. We were supposed to go hunting but I didn't wake up. He was gone when I rolled out of bed, so I came out here. Why?"

"Because his truck is parked on the highway near the ranch fence."

Willa felt a chill go through her. She reached for her phone and dialed Jeb.

He answered right away.

"Is the security on?" she asked him.

"No, we turned all that off yesterday, and I didn't turn it back on yet. I'll take care of it now."

Too late, she thought as she ended the call. She tried calling Corwyn's number and got no answer. She tried calling her dad's phone and got an out-of-service message. A terrible sense of inevitability wracked her. She stood up, feeling helpless. Cold fear lanced her guts.

Sara came in from the laundry room.

"What's wrong, Willa? You look like you've seen a ghost!" she asked urgently.

"Sweetie," Regi said. "What is it?"

"My dad. Corwyn — he took my dad up the mountain. He will carry him down."

"Shit," Regi said, heading for the door. Sunny began to bark.

Willa followed, pulling on her boots and her fur coat as she dashed from the porch. She wanted to shape-shift, but didn't dare take the shape of a deer: Nokes was out there. Sara ran out behind her, leaving the door open.

"What's wrong?" Jake asked, getting up painfully.

Sticks was putting on his coat. "That buddy of yours is out there, hunting on the ranch."

"So what? What does that mean?" Jake asked, bewildered.

"Nothin' good, dude," Sticks said. Everyone followed him outside.

Willa tied on her snowshoes. She ran. Her heart was pounding so loud she couldn't hear her own footsteps. She passed Regi. They reached the hilltop where Sticks loved to sit. She quickly studied the landscape. Nothing. She was out of breath. She needed to change shape to run in this snow. She took the crystal stag totem in her fingers. Regi came up beside her.

"There," Regi said, pointing to the tree line. Something moved in all that white. They saw the flash before the sound reached them — the sound of a muzzleloader firing. Regi began to run again. Willa desperately imagined wings, feathers, the feel of the wind under her. She began to run, imagined soaring, raised her arms, and felt the ground drop away.

Ronan gripped the Silver Stag's antlers firmly in both fists, thrilled to move so fast after years of hobbling. They came down the trail swiftly, snow flying.

At the edge of the meadow the Stag stopped. He watched for a moment, then he stepped cautiously from the woods.

Something hit him hard and fire went through his chest; he heard the roar of a long gun. Snow stung his face as the ground came up and slammed into him. He felt Ronan roll away. He couldn't breathe. He couldn't see. Corwyn shaped himself to human form. He couldn't move. He tried to suck in air, but couldn't.

Willa! he called in his heart.

He felt hands on him.

"Corwyn," Ronan gasped. "Corwyn! You can't leave me alone with her. You can't leave her, Corwyn!" Sobbing, Ronan rolled the Sithé onto his back.

Corwyn tried to speak, but couldn't. He heard Willa in his mind — she was shrieking, panicked. *Corwyn* — his name screamed down the wind like the cry of a hawk.

He heard footsteps.

"Get away from that deer," a voice screamed. "It's mine!"

"You fucking fool," Ronan shouted. "You've killed a man!"

"No! Get away! It's mine! Get away!!" Nokes came toward them, saw them in the snow, blood pooling around the man beneath Ronan's hands.

"What is this?" he cried. "What kind of trick is this? Where's my deer?!"

"You've shot a man, you dumb shit!" Ronan shouted.

"No," Nokes screamed. "No!!!"

Corwyn heard the sound of a hammer cocking. A mountain lion screamed. A flash of tawny fur hit the man and they rolled away in the snow.

"Corwyn," Ronan said harshly, his breath on Corwyn's face. "Stay with me!"

The light began to dim; darkness closed around him like a tunnel. Corwyn felt Ronan pull at his neck.

Ronan took the ritual knife from Corwyn's neck. A hawk landed in the snow and shape-shifted into Willa as he slashed the knife deeply across both of his wrists.

"Dad! No!" she screamed. "What are you doing?"

Ronan let the blood flow from both wrists onto the wound in Corwyn's chest. Hoarsely he cried, "Blood for blood, life for life. I,

Ronan Mac Clæúd, do give my blood and life for that of Coér Mac Vyn. Blood for blood," he repeated. "I am the guardian. I give life for life."

Willa's hands were on her father, pulling at him. He resisted her, kept his blood flowing onto Corwyn, to mix with the Sithé's own blood.

"Father, what are you doing?" she sobbed. "Oh god.... Corwyn! Don't leave me. I can't live without you."

"I love you, Willa MacLeod," her father whispered. "You gave me my life back. Now I give you yours."

Light flared between his hands and Corwyn's chest. Ronan felt the raw grit of magic surge between them, felt the irresistible claw of it tear at his soul.

Corwyn felt a cord pulling him, painfully drawing him back from the darkness that closed around him. A terrible heat burgeoned in his chest. He heard Willa sobbing.

A woman shaped herself from the blackness that edged his sight — a woman with raven hair and merciless eyes. Ronan saw her too.

"Morrígan," Corwyn choked.

"I have come for the life that is forfeit. Blood for blood," she cried.

"What have you done, Ronan MacLeod?" Corwyn shouted, resisting the pull, the heat.

"I have given you your life. For Willa's sake. As you both gave me mine. Thank you, son. Take me to the mountain. Take care of her." The raven-haired woman reached down and touched Captain Ronan MacLeod.

Regi couldn't breathe from running uphill. She sucked in great gulps of air when she reached them. Ronan MacLeod sat slumped across Corwyn, with his arms around the Sithé's chest. Willa had flung herself over them both, sobbing.

A mountain lion rose up from the snow. Brian Nokes scrambled from beneath the cat's paws. He scrabbled in the snow and pulled his gun up.

Regi unholstered her pistol and cocked it.

"Drop it, Nokes," she said very clearly, pointing her pistol at him and holding it firmly in both hands. "Drop it now or I'll shoot." She squinted down the sights.

The small man gazed at her with crazed eyes. He turned his gun toward the cougar, then shifted to point it at Willa. Regi saw his trigger finger twitch slightly, and she fired. The muzzleloader discharged as Nokes dropped in the snow; the ball passed so close to her leg that Regi felt the heat and wind of it.

"Shit. Mother of all shits!" she yelled.

Joseph Yellowgrass was kneeling beside Willa. Sara came up beside Regi and gave her arm a reassuring squeeze.

Regi walked to Nokes. He was not breathing. Fearing the worst, she crossed to Willa.

Corwyn's eyes fluttered and opened. He gasped, painfully, coughing up blood. "Moonlight," he said, taking Willa's hands.

Yellowgrass helped him to sit up, and together they laid Ronan MacLeod onto the snow. There was a hole through the middle of Ronan's chest — but that wound was bloodless. The blood flowed down his arms from the deep slashes across both wrists. Where Corwyn had lain in the snow, blood had pooled — far more blood than anyone could have lost and survived. There was a hole in

Corwyn's shirt and a new red scar above his heart, but no open wound.

Regi stared around, dazed. She had just killed a man. She saw a dead man sit up and talk, while Ronan MacLeod now lay dead in the snow. On autopilot, she cleared and holstered her pistol, fumbled for her radio, began requesting emergency crews, the sheriff.... She barely noticed when Sticks gently took the radio from her and gave the dispatcher a more coherent and conventional account of the situation. Sticks eased her onto a log and sat with his arm around her while she sobbed.

Jake Collins sat down beside them, looking almost as stunned and confused as she did.

His death is my death
I hold it in my heart and cannot let it go.
Her pain is my pain
It cuts my heart and I bleed
My heart is forever scarred.
Yet there are no tears
from the heart of the Morrigan
only a sense of eternal justice.

Coér Mac Vyn

PIECES OF
THE HEART

Corwyn thought his heart would break gazing into Willa's stunned, grieving eyes. Regi came and sat by the bed and went away again as heart-sick as Corwyn. Sticks hovered, searching for some way to make her smile again. Sara told them all to let Willa grieve, that it would be better in the long run.

Corwyn wasn't so sure. Willa refused to eat and grew alarmingly thin. When he thought she couldn't cry any more, she did, endlessly. All he could do was hold her. He felt desperately at fault, trapped among all the "if only's".

It had been two weeks since the shootings. Christmas came and went, and no one noticed. Another two feet of snow fell, covering the red sacrificial payment with pristine, flawless white. Nokes's family retrieved his body from the local mortuary; nobody at the ranch cared. The local magistrate tentatively pronounced Ronan MacLeod's shooting as manslaughter, and Nokes's as justifiable self-defense, pending investigation. Regi was unofficially commended for her quick thinking, and put on temporary leave with pay until the investigation was complete. Jake went home to Boise and came back to the ranch; then he went home again, and came back again. Everyone was drifting, directionless like snow in a shifting breeze.

Neil, Chloe, Jake, and Jonesy laid down all the tracks they could, then went home to give Willa some space and time to recover. Lisella called, wanting to help — but no one could.

Corwyn brought Willa some coffee and a piece of cinnamon coffee cake. He placed the tray by the bed and kissed her shoulder. He still didn't know the right words to say.

Finally, he said quietly, "I should not have told him the true story of your mother and the ritual. He would never have attempted such a thing. You would still have him here, and the pain would not tear you so."

She turned over and stared at him with haunted eyes.

"He already knew. It's in his journal. The journal is old — it's got stuff written by many MacLeods going a long way back. The blood-for-blood rite is mentioned a few times, although nobody wrote step-by-step instructions. I have to assume he read about it. Maybe not...but how likely is it that he wouldn't read a journal he was writing in?"

"There was so much he appeared to be ignorant of — but it seems now that much of that was just his way of keeping secrets. Still, I feel responsible."

"It's hard enough knowing my dad is gone forever. I couldn't even imagine living without you. He knew that. He made the sacrifice for me, not for you. I'm very clear on this whole stupid, senseless thing. It isn't that you shouldn't be here and he should; you should both be alive. The responsible one is that jackass Nokes; if he wasn't already dead, I would kill him. I'm so angry, I really wish Regi had only wounded him so I could. I want to kill him over and over and over again. I want to stop hurting inside. I want the hollow feeling inside me to go away. I just want to stop hurting! I want to go back to feeling safe and content and untouched by whatever new tragedy the world comes up with every day. I don't want life to be complicated — I just want to be with you and keep being amazed by the simple pleasure of being with you. I don't want to open my eyes and hurt with every breath. I want it to stop hurting. It hurts, Corwyn. Make it stop."

"I can't, Willa. I feel helpless."

"I know. You all feel that way. Because really, there's nothing you can do."

"We must take your father up the mountain. Do you wish to come, or should I do it alone?"

"I can't bear to go, not yet. Take him now, for me. I have to wait until I can stand it. He will wait for me. He understands. The memorial service here was hard enough; I can't take being in that place with all those dead Sithé right now. It's more sadness than I can deal with."

"I know. I know this more than even you can know."

She stared at him, seeing how deep the sadness was in his eyes.

Corwyn took Sticks with him to lay Ronan MacLeod to rest with his ancestors. He positioned Ronan on the granite and covered him with a new wolf-fur throw; then he placed beadwork and silver over the furs. It was so cold, they didn't linger long after that.

"We will come back in the summer," Corwyn said, "when it's only a little cold, and Willa can come with us." He kissed the man who would have been his father for a little while, if things had not gone so ill. "Sleep in peace, Ronan Mac Clæúd."

Willa was waiting when they returned. "When you're away from me, I worry every minute that something will keep you from coming back."

"That will never happen, Moonlight. Maybe we should go to my place in the mountain for a while?" he suggested.

"Not yet," she answered. "I'm not ready."

That night she turned to him and kissed him gently, everywhere she could. Corwyn felt her tears like warm raindrops, everywhere her lips touched. He drew her beneath him, loving her as gently as possible — she could only weep when she responded.

Sunny moved into Willa's room, and when he slept he curled against her for comfort.

Corwyn knew that Willa needed him, but he was still wracked with his own anger and guilt and helpless despair. He began going up the mountain every day as soon as he rose. Many days he spent just running across the boundless whiteness; other days he hunted. Occasionally Joseph Yellowgrass joined him on his hunts; the old Story Keeper no longer needed to watch over him in secret. When Corwyn returned each day long after dark, it seemed as though Willa hadn't moved. He would push Sunny aside and curl his own chilled body next to Willa's, and try to sleep.

Regi came to the ranch every day.

"Where's Corwyn?" she asked once.

"Hunting," Willa answered. "Hunting for a way to stop hurting. Even though they didn't know each other for very long, I think that my dad and Corwyn loved each other. He's hiding his pain. I wish I could hide mine."

One night, six weeks later, Corwyn didn't come back. He left his cellphone plugged into the charger in the bedroom. He didn't come back the next day, or the next. Willa got up and paced. She ate in the kitchen, for a change.

On the fourth day, she went to the kitchen at lunchtime. Sara said nothing, just gave her a bowl of soup and hot bread. Willa ate in silence. It made her feel warmer and a little better. There was an untouched huckleberry pie on the counter. Willa's eyes rested on it for a moment; then her eyes went to Sara's. Sara nodded slowly. Willa got up and left the kitchen.

When she came back she was in her fur boots and coat. She stuffed both their cellphones into the pack, along with extra batteries; then she added a bottle of apricot brandy.

"You're not supposed to drink," Sara reminded her.

"A little won't hurt him," she replied. As an afterthought, she added a thermos of sweet coffee. She made sandwiches, found some nice apples, and put the huckleberry pie in a Tupperware container. Everything went into her pack. Then she stepped out into the brilliant sunshine.

When she came to the top of the hill, Sticks was there.

She sat down next to him and he put his arm around her. He smelled of pot.

"I missed you, woman," he said quietly. He leaned his head against hers and sighed. "I miss your dad and Corwyn and you. Dude, I've lost all three of you. It's been just me and Sara and Jeb, staring at each other. At this rate, I'm runnin' through smoke in half the time I usually do."

"Don't you have a home to go to, Sticks?" she asked.

"Man, Willa, this is the only home where I ever felt at home. D'you want me to leave?"

"No. Actually, I don't. I want you to stay here. It makes me feel like I have a family. I just meant that you didn't need to feel obligated to stay."

"It ain't an obligation, it's a privilege. I'm just hopin' that badass white deer comes around to scare me shitless again one day soon. I haven't seen any magic since the shooting, and it's a bummer, man. I close my eyes and I see what happened then, not Wild White Willa. And I feel pretty bad for Jake. He's broke up bad, woman." He lit his pipe and offered it to her. She waved it away.

"Oh, right," Sticks said. "Can't hurt the kid. That baby needs you to eat more, though. You showin' yet?"

She took his hand and placed it on her abdomen. It was gently rounded.

"Can't hardly tell, you're so thin," he muttered. "God, woman. You are so incredible." He looked away and noticed the backpack.

"You goin' somewhere?"

"Yeah," she said.

"It's about time. I'll hold down the fort."

"You do that. Umm… This'll probably be badass, but I think it may come out a little more badass than you're used to."

She stood up and dusted off the snow. Her misery was a hard, cold edge beneath each breath. She didn't want to shape the Hart — her anger was still too big and hot for that. While Sticks stared in fear and amazement, she shaped a nightmare — something black and fell with angry red eyes and vast, twisted horns and a predator's fangs. The snow melted around the creature's hooves. With a terrifying snort, she turned and galloped up the mountain.

Corwyn was at his table, writing. The fire was stoked up. He had returned from hunting earlier and bathed, putting on his favorite soft lounge pants. The absence of Willa was a constant ache — but he had to get away from the ranch, where he found himself sinking into the same depression she was trapped in. Running the empty snowfields, hunting, sitting in his high chamber cleared his head and shook some of the sadness from his spirit. He only wished she were here to share the running, the hunting, his home. So he waited; he hoped that if he stayed away long enough, she would have to come look for him. He knew that she also needed to break the downward spiral — and that the wind in her face, the tang of pine, and the cracked cold of late winter would help.

Corwyn heard the sound of bells and a footfall in the tunnel, and he held his breath. A hot gust of air flipped the page he was working on. When he looked up, the nightmare that stood there gave him a frightful pause; for a moment, he wondered if it was Morrígan come for him at last. He held himself still. His rapid heartbeat was the only indication he was startled. As soon as Willa shaped back to her normal shape, he relaxed his tense body and sighed.

She dropped her pack on the floor and tossed her coat over it. She stepped on the heels and pulled each boot off with her opposite foot.

Then she advanced across the chamber, shedding more clothes as she moved. Startled all over again, Corwyn stood up and backed away.

"You didn't come home," she said, in what Corwyn imagined was the voice of the terrible creature that had entered the room.

"I needed to breathe, and run," he said.

"I know," she replied in her own voice.

"I wanted you to come here — you need what I needed."

"I am here," she whispered, her hands touching the new scar across his chest. His hands covered hers then, drew her to him.

"I smell pine," she said.

"It's the soap," he said, his voice hoarse. He brushed his lips against the spot where her neck met her shoulder. He inhaled the scent of her. That was something he knew he would never tire of, never get enough of. He pulled her down into the furs with him.

She taught him to shape a hawk. It was the only other shape he could find. She thought that someday he would be able to shape a wolf, since he had such familiarity with them — but he would have to stop hating them before he could become one of them. She found that she could shape anything, even strange, fantastic creatures that had no names. When she realized that these actually frightened Corwyn, she restricted herself to more familiar shapes. Once, she swooped through the chamber when he was writing, and her giant owl wings blew out all the lights and scattered his papers. Another time, to tease him, she shaped a mouse and ran up the leg of his pants. He laughed until he cried tears of joy.

One evening, after they returned weak-kneed from running, he sat at the table sewing something from his supply of cured furs.

Willa felt ignored, so she shaped a fat, white bear and just sat there, Buddha-like. She almost fell asleep — it was a warm, cozy shape, and a bear should be hibernating this time of year. She was, however, starting to feel hungry — but she was far too drowsy and comfortable to do anything about it. She dozed off.

Corwyn finally became aware that he hadn't heard a sound from Willa in a long time. He looked up. There was a very large white bear asleep in the chair across the table from him. For a long time he just stared at her. He knew that her sense of humor had begun to re-emerge from the darkness, along with her odd, acidic perspective on the world. He picked up a feather and reached across the table to tickle her nose. She shook her shaggy head. He tried again. She swatted sleepily at the feather with a large paw. He tickled her ear. She batted at her ear. He wondered what it would be like to be a bear.... He tickled her nose again, and she opened her blue eyes, looked right at him, and grinned, showing a lot of teeth. Surprised at a smiling bear, he sat back, and Willa growled an invitation.

He stood up, gazed at Willa, and shaped a towering silver bear. He roared at her. She roared back and came across the table at him, scattering the pelts. She hit Corwyn in his silver chest and rolled him over. But she was a very fat, comfortable, slow, sleepy bear, and he was much bigger and far more powerful — and now he was also very much an aroused bear. It was easy to overpower her.

"You make a magnificent bear," she said later, snuggling into the curve of his body. His arms went around her. She had put back on all the weight she had lost. He realized that she was even a little plump — a tall, lean version of plump, anyway. Her belly was becoming very rounded. He placed both hands over it protectively. He closed his eyes, thinking to go to sleep, or maybe even to shape the bear again — that had been very interesting. He felt a tiny flutter beneath his hands. Willa went absolutely still, even stopped breathing for a moment. He felt it again, like the tremble of wings.

"Our son moves," he said in wonder.

Breathless, they waited for each little movement. Finally, the baby quieted.

"He must be asleep," she said, marveling at these signs of life inside her.

"We should name him Ronan," Corwyn said.

Willa's eyes met his. She nodded, placed her hands over his, and fell asleep.

"We need to go home," he said, watching her dress. Her fullness seemed suddenly very evident.

"This is home," she said.

"It isn't the home you need right now. And you should probably finish your new album." He picked up the journal he had been working on. "I would like to see your father's journal, too — I want the records to be complete."

"Okay. I'm ready." She began packing things into her backpack.

They put on their furs and went down the mountain shaped as a fat white bear and a splendid, powerful silver bear.

They found Sticks sitting on his usual hill, nodding off, waiting for them; it looked like he had known they were coming. Willa was not surpised he was there; Sticks had, after all, been touched by a Sithé.

Sticks looked up when he heard the sound of bells and felt a puff of wind. When the glorious silver bear and the Buddha-like white bear sat down on either side of him, they could hear his inner sigh of relief.

"Did you know," he asked, "that the native Americans call this time of year the Month of the Snow Blind Moon?"

The white bear huffed at him and snuffled at his ear.

"Dude. Joseph Yellowgrass says it means that this time of year the days are getting a little longer and a little warmer. The snow reflects the sun big-time because of day-melting and night-freezing, and it blinds your eyes." Willa gave him a little head butt.

"Bear looks good on you, woman," he quipped. Willa rolled him over with a paw. The silver bear roared loud enough to stand the hair up on the back of Sticks' neck. He stood up and brushed off the snow.

"Yeah, dude, life just doesn't get any weirder than this." He started down the hill. The two bears gamboled along on either side of him, swatting snow at him. Sticks made a snowball and hit Corwyn in the head with it. After that, it was a gentle brawl.

Willa and Corwyn changed shape at the porch-edge. They could hear Sunny barking. The three of them brought cold air and ice into the kitchen with them; laughing, they shook snow from their hair and coats. Sara Blackhawk and Joseph Yellowgrass looked up from the big table.

The three were arm in arm. Sticks stepped back to get a look at Willa in human shape, and Willa leaned against Corwyn.

"Look at you, woman. You finally gained some weight. Look at the cub, man."

Willa took Sticks' hands and placed them on her belly. The baby was moving, probably because of all the excitement. The look of wonder on the drummer's face made them all laugh.

"Corwyn, man," Sticks said, "I would not be able to live with this sexy woman right now. I couldn't keep a decent thought in my head. If you disappear again, watch out, dude — this woman is mine."

"I will not disappear. This is home."

"Welcome home, then, Coér Mac Vyn and Willa MacLeod," Sara Blackhawk said. "We have been waiting for you. We have been waiting for a very long time."

— The End —

Acknowledgments

I want to offer my thanks to my Beta reader, Jennifer Leach, ex-LA firefighter and EMT, who lives on the hill overlooking Horseshoe Bend with her Jack Russells and her goats, and somehow takes time from her Ranch Girl chores to read every word carefully and give helpful feedback.

Thanks to Don Radlauer and Yael Shahar of Kasva Press, who saw the potential in Silverhorn. I have so much appreciation for Yael, who created the beautiful layout and cover art — her unflagging patience and professional dedication over the course of this project turned Silverhorn into the kind of Old-World-Printer-style presentation I always imagined for this mythical story.